Luke pinned Jane against the kitchen counter with his hips

"I'll prove all men aren't just sex-obsessed morons," he whispered as he lowered his mouth to hers and kissed her deeply.

"I fail to see how this will cast mankind in a more positive light," Jane said breathlessly.

He slid his thigh between her legs until he knew he was putting pressure where it mattered most. "I don't expect to change your mind in one night."

Jane let her gaze fall to his jeans. "How many nights will it take?"

"It depends on how stubborn you are about changing your mind," Luke said as he trailed his hand down her hip and over her thigh, up her skirt.

Her eyelids fluttered shut as he explored her flesh. "That's not fair."

Luke dipped his fingers along the edge of her panties, teasing her. "I never said I'd keep it above the belt...."

Blaze™

Dear Reader,

Aren't we all looking for answers? We turn to self-help books to find out how to be happier, thinner, prettier, smarter, more spiritually centered.... The list goes on. Jane Langston, the heroine of this story, thinks she has all the answers when it comes to sex and relationships, and she's written a bestselling self-help book to prove it. But then she encounters Luke Nicoletti, the one man who turns her sexual-relationship theories upside down. Suddenly the expert who has advised women across America to say no to sex finds herself unable to say anything but *yes* to her outrageously gorgeous bodyguard's advances.

I had a great time exploring how easy it is to lose self-control when presented with our greatest temptation—be it chocolate, a great pair of shoes or a hot guy. Luke and Jane are two of my favorite characters and I hope you enjoy their steamy tale as much as I have.

I love to hear from readers, so please write and tell me what you think of *What a Girl Wants.* You can reach me via my Web site, www.jamiesobrato.com, or drop me an e-mail at jamie@jamiesobrato.com.

Sincerely,

Jamie Sobrato

Books by Jamie Sobrato

HARLEQUIN BLAZE
84—PLEASURE FOR PLEASURE

HARLEQUIN TEMPTATION
911—SOME LIKE IT SIZZLING

WHAT A GIRL WANTS

Jamie Sobrato

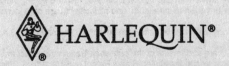

HARLEQUIN®

TORONTO • NEW YORK • LONDON
AMSTERDAM • PARIS • SYDNEY • HAMBURG
STOCKHOLM • ATHENS • TOKYO • MILAN • MADRID
PRAGUE • WARSAW • BUDAPEST • AUCKLAND

To my editor, Wanda Ottewell,
for her talent, enthusiasm and amazingly
tactful revision letters

ISBN 0-373-79120-8

WHAT A GIRL WANTS

Visit us at www.eHarlequin.com

Printed in U.S.A.

1

A girl has to put her own emotional needs above the urges of the guy trying to get in her pants.

—Jane Langston,
in the January issue of *Excess,* magazine

JANE LANGSTON WAS eight years old when she first understood the biological advantages of being skinny and blond. Neither particularly thin nor fair-headed, she saw her place in the world that day, upon observing the astounding differences between herself and her Barbie doll. She'd been enacting a romantic tryst between Barbie and Ken when the realization struck that she and her long-legged plastic companion could hardly be the same species of female, and that Jane, with her tomboy figure and wiry brown hair, was the less desirable of the two.

Even now, at the supposedly enlightened age of thirty, sitting in a room next to two outrageously proportioned blond porn stars didn't exactly soothe Jane's ego. It was only a slight comfort that both women claimed to be lesbians.

How she'd found herself here in the waiting room of *The Jax Reed Show* was a longer story than Jane cared to recall. Jax Reed was Dallas's crude, loudmouthed, lesbian-loving shock jock, and Jane was about to be interviewed to promote her book, *The Sex Factor.* Her publicist claimed she was the one woman who could put Jax Reed in his place, but Jane, sitting near four of the largest breasts she'd ever seen, had her doubts.

A producer wearing headphones appeared in the doorway, pointed to Jane, and said, "You're up in three minutes. Come on into the studio."

With her stomach clenched into a tennis ball, Jane rose and followed. Gina Lynn and Mona Rivers wished her luck as she left the waiting room.

The radio show was playing live over speakers throughout the building, and Jane listened to Jax introduce her as his next guest after the commercial break.

"She's the author of that crazy book chicks everywhere are reading, *The Sex Factor*. So listen up, guys, if you've got a bone to pick—no pun intended—with the woman who's single-handedly ruined the sex lives of men across America, here's your chance to call in."

Oh, joy. As if she hadn't taken enough criticism, now she'd get to do it on live radio.

Jane had never intended to become the guru of born-again virginity. Until a few months ago, she'd simply been a normal writer with a largely anonymous existence. Sure, some people knew her as the infamous tell-it-like-it-is advice columnist for *Excess* magazine. But her infamy had been limited mostly to readers of her column, and the occasional angry letters she received had always been good for a laugh.

The readership of *Excess*—a magazine devoted to pressing men's issues like who the hottest starlets are, which cars are the fastest and how to improve sexual performance—was made up of enough boneheads to inspire any woman to write *The Sex Factor*. She'd simply written a book that told women exactly how they were screwing up their lives through sexual relationships, and how to remedy the problem.

The Sex Factor had touched a nerve among twenty- and thirty-something women, and it had encountered dizzying success, spawning a nationwide movement of women saying no to sex with their boyfriends. That might not have been so disturbing if it weren't for the legion of angry boyfriends left alone in their beds.

Jane had heard from more than her share of them. In fact, her hate mail rarely caused her to laugh these days.

She entered the studio and sat down in a chair across from Jax Reed. Twenty pounds overweight, with long, greasy blond hair and perpetual sunglasses, he was the epitome of a guy with thwarted rock-star dreams.

He nodded a greeting while an assistant talked to him about upcoming segments, and Jane adjusted the headphones the producer had given her until they were comfortable.

"Today we're talking to Jane Langston, columnist for *Excess* magazine and author of the controversial book, *The Sex Factor*. Hey, Jane."

"Hi, Jax." Jane tucked her hands between her knees to keep from fidgeting, and reminded herself to breathe.

She could handle this guy. Although she didn't admit it often, Jane listened to *The Jax Reed Show* while she was reading her e-mail in the morning. And she'd imagined a thousand times how she'd respond to him if she were ever on the show herself. He loved to turn everything into a conversation about sex, the raunchier, the better. Jane knew the trick to handling Jax was never to let him shock her, and to play along with his game.

In his usual fashion, he skipped over the pleasantries. "Okay, given the message of your book, I gotta ask—are you a lesbian?"

"Not last time I checked."

"Hmm, too bad."

"Sorry to disappoint."

He looked her up and down. "You're pretty cute, you know. Ever thought about having sex on the radio?"

"What makes you think I haven't already?" Jane said, hoping she sounded braver than she felt.

Jax snickered. "Touché, but anyway, go ahead and give us a summary of your book, just in case there's some hermit out there listening to the show who hasn't yet developed a case of blue balls thanks to you."

"If any guy has blue balls, he has himself to thank. *The Sex Factor* is simply a realistic look at sexual roles. I think I'm just the first person in a long time to be honest about how sex can ruin a relationship."

Jax wiggled his eyebrows. "Baby, I can show you how sex will *make* a relationship."

"I'll bet you could." She laughed. "But seriously, since the sexual revolution, women have learned to believe that we should behave like men with regard to sex, that we should want no-strings-attached sex, that we shouldn't use sex to gain power in relationships, and I argue that the opposite is true.

"Given that men are led around by their penises, a woman's number-one strength in any romantic relationship is her ability to give or withhold sex, and if we give sex freely, we essentially give away our greatest power."

Jax burped into the microphone. "Okay, I'm not disagreeing with you there. Problem is, my listeners aren't getting laid. What're they supposed to do about that?"

"Um, get over it?"

"Ooh, harsh. I'd like to hear what some of my listeners have to say to that. We have a caller on line one. It's Carl from Fort Worth. What do you say, Carl?"

"Yeah, Jax. I love your show, man! And I just gotta tell this Jane chick, what're you thinking? My girl says she can't have sex with me any more until I start *meeting her emotional needs* or some garbage."

Guys like Carl were what had led Jane to decide celibacy wasn't such a bad idea.

"So find out what her emotional needs are and meet them. How hard is that?"

"Damn hard when I'm not getting any action in bed."

Jax cut in. "Carl, you're boring me. Next caller is Tom in Dallas. How's it going, Tom?"

"Yeah, Jax. I just want to say to all the guys listening today, if your woman brings home that sex factor book, burn it! Use it for toilet paper! Whatever you do, don't let her read it!"

"Okay, that was Tom, and he needs to make a trip to the convenience store for some TP," Jax said as he hung up on him.

Aside from one woman who called to thank Jane for writing *The Sex Factor*, the calls went downhill fast. By caller number eight, Jane was starting to feel a little unnerved.

"Bryan, you got anything new to say to Jane here?" Jax said by way of introduction, skipping pleasantries at that point.

"I just want to tell Ms. Jane Langston that I've read her book, and I think she's very, very wrong," a disconcertingly calm voice said.

Jane shifted in her seat, unable to formulate a response before the caller continued.

"And I'm watching you, you bitch. I know where you live—"

Jax cut off the call. "Okay, that was Bryan, escapee

from the psycho ward. I think we've heard from enough nutcases for one show.''

Jane sat silent, blinking dumbly, unable to believe what she'd just heard. She was grateful when Jax continued.

''You know, I read *The Sex Factor* last night, and I think, frankly, that you've never had good sex.''

''Why do you say that?'' Jane said evenly, careful to keep her voice light, unshaken, though the tone of the last call had left her trembling.

''Any woman who's been properly laid would never give the advice you give.''

Jane forced aside her fear, for the sake of surviving the interview. ''Hmm, interesting theory. Actually, I have experienced great sex, so I know just how distracting it can be. Women and men both tend to substitute it for other more complicated, but ultimately more important, aspects of a relationship.''

''What's more important than sex?''

Jane smiled. ''It's precisely that type of question, posed by men, that prompted me to write the book.''

''I think I owe it to my loyal listeners to do something to counteract all the damage you've done to their sex lives…''

Not again.

''I'll give you one last chance—sleep with me, and I'll show you what you've been missing out on all these years.'' Jax wiggled his eyebrows at her, and Jane tried not to gag.

''I appreciate your generosity, but I'll have to pass.''

''Come on, baby. We could do it real quick, right here in the studio during a commercial break. I'm not that gross, am I?''

This was Jax's standard shtick, an offer he made to just about every woman who appeared on the show.

"I wouldn't be much of an authority on relationships if I didn't follow my own advice."

"Babe, I guarantee if you found a guy you were really hot for, you wouldn't have a chance of following that advice of yours. In fact, I challenge you to go out and find your dream guy, and if you're able to withhold sex from him like you say in your book, come back and tell me, and I'll eat my lunch from a pair of my producer Bob's dirty, stained underwear."

Eew.

Jane made a face and shrugged. "I don't want to know how you're familiar with the state of your producer's underwear, but you've got a deal."

"You sure I'm not your dream guy?"

"Sorry, Jax."

He exhaled noisily into the microphone. "You don't sound like you're gonna budge, so I'm ready to bring in the lesbian porn stars. Thanks for coming on the show, Jane."

After he cut to a commercial segment, Jax removed his sunglasses, came out from behind the table and shook Jane's hand.

"Hey, you were a good sport. Hope I didn't embarrass you too badly."

"Not at all. This was fun. Sort of." They both smiled then.

She'd always heard Jax was secretly a nice guy off the air, but she'd never quite believed it.

He sobered and said, "Listen, that last caller sounded pretty freaky. Do you have any kind of personal security arrangement?"

"You mean like a bodyguard? No."

"As much negative attention as I know you're getting,

you ought to consider it. Trust me, I've been in your shoes.'' He flashed a look of concern.

Jane shook her head. The last thing she wanted was to travel everywhere with some brawny knucklehead looking over her shoulder, someone who probably wouldn't be very motivated to protect her anyway, given how most guys felt about her book.

''I appreciate your concern,'' she said, ''but—''

''Listen, I don't normally do this, but that last caller gave me the willies. I know a top-notch security specialist who handles security for high-profile people in Dallas. You should give him a call.''

Before Jane could refuse, he tucked a business card in her hand, and she slipped it into her pocket to be polite. Maybe Jax Reed really was a nice guy.

''You're back on in ten!'' a producer called into the studio.

''Take care,'' Jax said, and Jane waved to him and walked out into the hallway.

She passed the lesbian porn stars in a daze. How had her quiet, boring life gotten turned upside down so quickly? She wasn't the type of person who needed to hire a personal security specialist.

Jane was not going to let horny men ruin her life. She refused to become a paranoid shut-in, and she wasn't going to put bars on her windows and travel around looking over her shoulder constantly.

She just needed to get past her fear, put the crazies out of her head and get on with her life. But the words of that last caller chilled her. Had the creep been lying, or was he really watching her? She'd always used a post-office box for her mail, but she supposed it wouldn't be very difficult for someone to find out where she lived.

Jane tried to focus on more pressing worries as she

traveled down the elevator and out of the building. She was supposed to meet with her sister in fifteen minutes, a few blocks away. She'd purposely arranged the meeting today right after *The Jax Reed Show* since the bridal shop where they were meeting was downtown, close to the radio station.

Jane steeled herself for the torture to come. She could think of few things she'd rather do less than try on bridesmaid dresses in front of her sister. But Heather was getting married in two months and, in what she probably considered an act of great benevolence, she'd asked Jane to be one of the bridesmaids.

Heather was one of a set of triplets, two years younger than Jane. The triplets were her opposite in just about every conceivable way. From their Nordic blond beauty to their shared pride in never having read a book since graduating from college, there was almost nothing Jane had in common with her sisters besides blood.

Jane hurried down the busy street, dodging business people as she went, trying not to think about the psycho caller. At least by comparison to taking callers on *The Jax Reed Show*, she decided, trying on bridesmaid dresses sounded almost fun.

She stepped inside the cool silence of Here Comes The Bride, Dallas's premier retailer of tacky satin dresses, and found herself in a wonderland of pastel colors. The entire store was decorated in shades of pink, from the pink striped walls to the thickly padded pink carpet, and a saleslady in a lavender suit hovered nearby.

Jane spotted her sister and mother sitting together on a sofa, thumbing through a catalog of fabric swatches.

Her mother. Wonderful—just freaking wonderful. Perhaps the only person who understood Jane less than her triplet sisters was their mother, Olivia Langston—known to the world as Livvy—former Miss Southeastern Texas. She was endlessly puzzled about how one of her daughters could waste away her life in front of a computer writing boring old books, when she could be out trying to bag a husband.

"I'm with them," Jane said to the saleslady, who was busy sizing her up and probably already had her pegged as a bridesmaid and not a bride.

"Of course," she said through a thin smile.

"Jane, dear," her mother drawled in her carefully preserved Texas accent, "please tell your sister she absolutely can*not* have the bridesmaids wear hats."

"Heather, I'm not wearing a hat."

Livvy nodded triumphantly. "You have to remember Jane looks odd in hats, anyway. They draw attention to the size of her head."

Not the head issue again. According to Livvy, Jane's head had caused unimaginable pain during childbirth, and she hadn't forgiven her yet. As far as Jane could tell, her head was not abnormally large—her mother's hips, however, were abnormally small—yet she couldn't resist glancing in the mirror to see if her head was casting a shadow over the entire store.

Heather frowned at Jane's head. "Maybe we could just get an extralarge one for you."

"No, it's bad enough that I have to stand in front of a church in a bridesmaid dress. I'm not wearing a hat, too."

The saleslady intervened. "If you'd like, I can show you to a dressing room now."

"That would be splendid," Livvy said, eager to divert attention while she'd still won the battle.

"We've picked out a few styles we think might be flattering on you, Jane." Heather followed behind with their mother, just as Jane had feared. They were both going to be there, critiquing her as she tried on the dresses.

The dressing room was, literally, a well-appointed room, complete with two walls of adjustable mirrors, a carpeted platform to stand on for fittings and a velvet sofa. In one corner stood a rack of dresses.

Apparently Jane was the test female for the dress all the bridesmaids would wear. Since Heather's friends and the other two triplets would look fabulous in whatever she picked out, they needed only to find a dress that Jane could wear without looking like the "before" picture in a makeover article, standing next to a bunch of former and current Dallas Cowboys cheerleaders—the perfect legion of "after" photos.

The saleslady selected a pink satin sheath from the rack. "Since this is your sister's favorite, why don't you start with it? These are all size tens, so they should fit."

Jane resisted the urge to point out that she was a size eight on non-PMS days. "Could I have a little privacy?"

"Of course, but someone will need to stay in here with you to help with the zippers."

Right, because she couldn't possibly manage a zipper by her poor little self. "Heather stays."

Jane avoided her mother's gaze and began unbuttoning her blouse as the two women left the room.

"Why did you have to bring Mom along?" she whispered as soon as the door closed.

"Sorry, she insisted."

"I thought we were supposed to talk today."

Heather had been asking all week for them to find some time to get together and chat. They weren't the closest of siblings, but Jane's younger sisters did tend to view her as the fount of all knowledge when it came to their problems. They may not have liked reading books, but they did respect the fact that she'd written one.

Jane finished undressing and stepped into the pink gown, then slipped it over her shoulders. Already she hated it.

As Heather zipped up the dress, she whispered, "We do need to talk. It's about..." She hesitated. "Bradley Stone."

Bradley Stone? He was a good friend of Heather's fiancé, one of the groomsmen in the wedding, and Jane's biggest crush from college. He'd been in the same psychology program that she had, and he was so different from the average Texas male, it was hard to believe he'd even grown up in the Lone Star state. He was intelligent, insightful, enlightened, sensitive...

And he didn't own a single Stetson or pair of cowboy boots. As far as Jane knew, he didn't even possess a warped passion for college football or contact sports of any kind. He was a combination of her girlhood and adult fantasies, all rolled into one perfect guy.

What on earth could Heather have to say about Bradley?

Heather took one look at the dress and shook her head, then unzipped it again. Jane slid it back off and stepped out of it.

Had her crush on Bradley grown so obvious that even her sisters knew about it? Jane thought back to the engagement party for Heather and Michael, where she'd last seen Bradley. Okay, she had to admit, she'd probably lingered at his side too long, retrieved one too many drinks for him, laughed a little too hard at his jokes.

She'd been downright pitiful.

But she definitely wasn't ready to talk to Heather about her infatuation with Bradley, even if her sister had already figured it out. Knowing Heather, she'd probably tell everyone, including Bradley, as soon as she got confirmation from Jane that there was an attraction.

"I don't like him, and I don't have anything to say about him."

Heather studied Jane through the mirror and frowned.

Oops, maybe she'd protested too much. "I've got problems of my own, you know," Jane said to cover her tracks.

Heather looked at her as if she'd just appeared from thin air. "Of course you do, Janie. You seem really tense—what's up?"

She handed Jane the next dress, another pink one, as ugly as the last.

"Didn't you guys listen to *The Jax Reed Show* on the way here?"

"Mom wouldn't let me turn it on. She says no self-respecting person would listen to such garbage."

Right, even if her own daughter was appearing on the show.

"It was awful. All these guys were calling in, angry and talking trash. Then the last caller was downright scary. He said he'd been watching me, and Jax hung up on him."

"Janie! Are you still getting nasty letters, too?"

"I've gotten a few this week." Ever since the publication of *The Sex Factor,* Jane's mail from readers alternated between glowing praise and vicious attacks. She got a sick feeling in her stomach each time she had to open a letter now.

"Did that caller say anything else? Something you could go to the police with?"

"He said his name is Bryan—though I'm sure that was a lie—and that he knows where I live."

"You've got to take this seriously. There are a lot of crazy people out there, you know."

"I know. But I don't want to become paranoid about this whole thing."

Heather unzipped the dress, and Jane slid it off and stepped out of it. "You know, one of Mikey's cousins who's also in the wedding is some kind of security expert. He works for lots of rich and famous people in Dallas."

Jane immediately thought of the phone number Jax had given her. "His name isn't Lucas Nicoletti, is it?"

"Yes! Did you meet him at our engagement party?"

"No, I don't think so." She'd been too busy drooling all over Bradley that night to notice anyone else. "Jax Reed gave me his number and told me I should call him."

Heather's eyes turned to blue saucers. She believed in signs, horoscopes, tarot cards and fortune cookies. "Janie, that's a sign! You were meant to get Luke's help."

"What do you know about this guy?"

"I know he's really cute, and that he and Mikey were childhood playmates, but that's about it. They're not close anymore, but they were such good friends growing up that Mikey had to have him as a groomsman."

"Hmm, a cute cousin of Michael's. Guess that's all I need to know to hire him."

"Of course you should talk to him first, but I really think the universe is trying to tell you something here."

"Jane? Heather?" Their mother tapped on the door. "Aren't you going to let me see?" Instead of waiting for an answer, she opened the door and walked in, catching Jane in the middle of bending over to untangle a dress from her ankles.

"Dear, that is not your best angle," Livvy said.

Jane swung around for privacy, then remembered that

the walls were mirrored. "Do you mind? We'll call you in when we've found the right dress."

"Someone's wearing cheap perfume out there. It's upsetting my allergies." She produced a dainty little sneeze.

Her mother used the old allergy excuse whenever she got the chance. It was her way of making sure no conversation took place too far from her ears.

Jane took the next dress from Heather and stepped into it. A navy-blue princess-style gown with a subtle flare at the hips and low-cut décolletage. She hoped before it was even zipped up that it would be Heather's choice. It had the distinct advantage of complementing Jane's overly curvy hips, and dark colors were, after all, slimming.

Not that Jane thought she needed any slimming down, but next to all Heather's toothpick friends, she was bound to look like a Clydesdale among thoroughbreds no matter what she wore.

Heather zipped it up, took a step back, and clapped her hands together. "It's perfect," she said, as if on command.

"Yeah, not bad." Jane surveyed herself in the mirror. She could imagine walking down the aisle arm-in-arm with Bradley Stone in this dress.

Their mother frowned. "But I thought we'd agreed upon rose petal as the color for the dresses."

"You agreed on rose petal, and I wanted seashell. But I think I like midnight blue even better. This is the dress I want—it's settled."

Jane breathed a sigh of relief. She'd narrowly escaped wearing a pink bridesmaid dress. Maybe this day wasn't turning out so badly after all.

Livvy gave them her best put-upon look and disappeared from the room to find the saleslady.

Heather leaned in close and whispered to Jane, "What

I said about Bradley—just forget it. I'm sorry I brought him up.''

''You didn't say anything about him.''

''Right. Well, I think I know why you didn't want to talk about him, and I'm sorry I even mentioned him. Just forget I ever said anything.''

It was completely out of Heather's character to behave so sensitively, but Jane wasn't in the mood to question it. ''No problem.''

Their mother came back with the saleslady, who pinned the dress in all the right spots for the seamstress.

By the time Jane had dressed and said goodbye to her mother and sister, it was already close to ten, and that meant half of her usual writing day was over. She'd have to write in the afternoon now, which was not her most creative time—definitely not after such a stressful morning.

She was working on a proposal for a follow-up book to *The Sex Factor,* but in the midst of so much controversy, she was beginning to think she ought to give up writing and pursue a career in dental hygiene or library science.

Mostly she just longed for her old, boring life, her pre-Sex Factor life, when her biggest worry was how to avoid Sunday-night dinner at her parents' house and when she never needed bodyguard recommendations from her sister. Jane hadn't realized how comfortable she'd been in her happy little rut, writing and jogging and searching for the perfect latte, until the controversy surrounding her new book had completely knocked her out of her comfort zone.

She stood at the corner looking for a cab, and managed to wave one down after a few minutes. Having two appointments downtown that morning, she'd opted not to deal with traffic and parking hell, and had left her own car at home.

She climbed into the cab and gave him her home address, then sat back and sighed as he pulled away from the curb. On the radio was none other than Jax Reed, wrapping up his show as he did every morning at ten.

The driver glanced at her in his rearview mirror that sported a dangling Texas state flag air freshener. "You listen to *The Jax Reed Show?*"

"Sometimes."

"Hear the lady was on this morning, crazy broad that wrote that *Sex Factor* book?"

Jane sunk down in her seat. "Um, no?"

"Aw, you missed a good one! All these guys was calling in, giving her hell. Man alive, it was funny."

"Hmm." Jane kept her expression neutral, not particularly interested in implicating herself as the crazy broad in question.

"I tell you, that woman deserves what she got. Anybody write a book that claims sex is bad for you needs to be taught a lesson, if you ask me."

She couldn't help but ask, "What sort of lesson?"

The cabby laughed. "Aw, you know, nothing a good roll in the hay couldn't show her."

All the saliva evaporated from Jane's mouth. She slid her hand into the pocket of her blazer and withdrew the card Jax had given her.

Lucas Nicoletti, Personal Security Specialist. This was her future life—self-defense lessons, a high-tech home security system and some guy named Lucas to tell her how far apart the bars on her windows should be.

Jane eyed the creepy cabby, pulled out her cell phone, and dialed the number on the card.

2

Men like to think of themselves as useful and in control. Women must decide exactly how a man can be useful in her life, and exactly how much control she will let him believe he wields.

—Jane Langston,
from Chapter One of *The Sex Factor*

"I NEED YOUR HELP," a low, sultry female voice said from the other end of the phone line.

"Who is this?" Luke Nicoletti asked, but received no immediate answer.

He tried to place the woman's voice. It resonated deep in his belly and made him think of hot, slow sex on a summer night. Vaguely familiar, he couldn't think where he'd heard it before. There was barely a hint of a Texas accent, suggesting a woman who was a transplant or who had either accidentally or purposely learned to speak without it. Having spent most of his life moving back and forth between Texas and South Florida himself, Luke knew all about losing his accent.

"Hello?" he asked, growing impatient.

The honk of a car's horn in the background clued him in that she might be calling on a cell phone or a pay phone.

She finally spoke again. "M-my name is Jane, and I

need to discuss your services with you." A pause. "As soon as possible."

His services? She made it sound like something clandestine, which led him to wonder who was listening in on her conversation, and what she had to be afraid of.

"Okay, Jane." That name was obviously an alias, and not even a creative one. "Are you in any danger right now?"

"I don't think so, no."

"Are you at home?"

"I will be in fifteen minutes."

Luke looked down at the calendar on his desk. The afternoon schedule was empty, because he'd set aside the time to organize files, sort through paperwork—the sort of stuff he always put off doing. But the sound of this woman's voice instantly appealed to him, and he never could resist a damsel in distress. He knew without thinking twice that he was interested, whatever her problem might be.

"You're in luck," he said. "I can meet you in a half hour, if you want."

"That would be great," she said, breathing what sounded like a sigh of relief.

"I just have one question—how did you hear about me?"

Another pause. "My sister, Michael Bell's fiancée, referred me to you."

Michael Bell was Luke's cousin and childhood playmate. He'd met the fiancée, and if this woman was anything like her sister, she was a real dingbat. But some quality of her voice told him she was different.

Luke copied down the directions to Alias Jane's house and hung up the phone. In another ten minutes, he was out of the house and on his way to the suburban neighborhood she'd described, about a twenty-minute drive from where he lived.

When he reached her neighborhood, he consulted the directions she'd given, memorized the next three turns, and tossed the paper back onto the passenger seat.

Three stop signs later, Luke turned onto her street and started looking for house numbers. The street was lined with town houses and upscale apartments. He could tell by the assortment of luxury SUVs, Saabs and BMWs parked in the driveways that the neighborhood was probably occupied by overpaid yuppies who spent way too much money on things like balsamic vinegar and aromatic face massages.

He spotted her corner residence and turned into the driveway. Parked there was an ancient white Mercedes, probably twenty years old and in need of some TLC. He'd bet Alias Jane had inherited the car as a teenager from Daddy and never bothered to buy a new one.

Luke eyed the windows, the entry and the access to the rear of the town house. Securitywise, prefab places like this were usually in poor shape, with cheap alarm systems slapped in as a selling point. No doubt he could help, if he chose to take the case.

He rang the doorbell, and moments later he spotted the movement of curtains in the front window, and then a woman asked, "Who is it?" from the other side of the door.

"Luke Nicoletti, the security specialist you called."

A dead bolt clicked, and the door opened.

There stood a woman of average height, with a wild mop of chestnut curls draping her shoulders, and intelligent brown eyes. She was pretty in a nondescript sort of way, with even features and a nice figure as far as he could tell. The sort of woman who could be prettied up or uglied down without too much effort, but left alone she could blend into the crowd. That was definitely a plus for security.

"Mr. Nicoletti, thank you for coming on such short notice." She stepped aside and let him in.

"No problem." The inside of the apartment was dark from drawn curtains. The scent of a fruity-smelling candle burning nearby gave the place a sense of hominess, but when Luke's eyes adjusted to the dark, he could see that the walls were empty and several moving boxes littered the entryway.

"Moving somewhere?" he asked.

"Actually I've just moved in but haven't finished unpacking. Can I get you a drink?"

"Water, please."

"Have a seat in the living room and I'll be right in."

Luke stepped into the room she'd indicated and surveyed his surroundings. Plush butter-yellow leather sofas and mahogany tables so new he expected to see tags hanging from them, stacks of books everywhere, and half-filled bookshelves were more evidence of her settling-in efforts. And judging from the high quality of the furniture, he'd guess she'd also just come into some money.

Her footsteps sounded on the wood floors as she came down the hallway and entered the room. When she turned away from him to place their glasses on the coffee table, he took the opportunity to give her figure a closer inspection.

Nice. She had real curves, everything in moderation, and in all the right places. The slim-fitting faded jeans and red sweater set she wore accentuated her curves without revealing any flesh, which he found intriguing. She turned back to him, and Luke pretended to be inspecting the room.

Not that he had any reason to be ogling a potential client. He tried not to mix business and pleasure, and in his business, that usually wasn't much of a challenge.

"Please, have a seat." She motioned to the couch, and then she took a seat on a nearby armchair.

"What do you do for a living?" Luke asked.

"I write about relationship issues. Maybe you've seen my advice column in *Excess* magazine?"

Excess magazine? Relationship issues? A memory from that morning appeared then. Luke had been listening to *The Jax Reed Show* and there had been that *Sex Factor* woman catching hell from the male callers. Her name had been *Jane* something-or-other.

Wait a minute.

"You write that column...." He occasionally read it for laughs, just to see what outrageous responses the smart-aleck columnist would write to the guys who asked for her advice. "And you're the author of *The Sex Factor*, right?"

She crossed her arms over her chest. "That's me."

So she was the one.

Luke's last girlfriend had dumped him after reading that book. She'd claimed he'd been suppressing her female power and not acknowledging her emotional needs, or some crap like that. Apparently they had been substituting sex for emotional intimacy, and she wasn't going to tolerate another minute of multiple orgasms.

"You don't look like I pictured you."

"How's that?"

"More puritanical, with a permanent frown from your lousy sex life."

Jane laughed, and Luke admired the way her face blossomed. She could go from pretty to stunning in an instant.

"I heard you on *The Jax Reed Show* this morning," he

said. Which explained why her voice had sounded familiar to him when she called.

Her cheeks lost their color. "Not one of my finer moments."

"It was kind of funny, up until the end there." Luke remembered the last caller had been a whack-job, probably the kind of guy who lived with his mother and got a little too excited by the underwear models in the Sears catalog. "I can see why you need a security specialist."

"Jax Reed is the one who gave me your number. My sister only seconded his recommendation."

Luke nodded. Jax was one of his clients.

"I'm not quite clear on what it is you do, exactly."

"I protect you from the bad guys."

"What does that mean?"

"It depends. Maybe you don't need anything more in-depth than a new phone number and a varied routine, or maybe you need something as drastic as twenty-four-hour bodyguard duty and a motion-sensing home security system."

"That's exactly what I *don't* want." A black cat came peeking out from under the sofa, and Jane bent over and scratched his chin. "This is Homer," she said.

"As in *The Iliad?*" Luke asked, pegging her for a fan of the classics.

"As in *The Simpsons*," she said, grinning. "He loves doughnuts."

She'd managed to defy his expectations again, and she intrigued him. It was hard to imagine this seemingly mild-mannered writer being the same woman who doled out smart-aleck advice in *Excess* magazine, and who had the entire country in an uproar over a little sex book she'd written. Luke's reckless side wanted to peel back her layers, discover who she really was.

His business side knew better than to get emotionally involved.

And his competitive side—which hated getting dumped—wanted to prove Jane wrong about sex and relationships.

They both watched the cat saunter out of the room.

"I don't think I'm the best guy to help you out with your security issues. My last girlfriend dumped me after reading your book." He tried to look offended, but Jane's surprised laugh caught him off-guard.

"I'm afraid every guy I call is going to have a personal grudge. Do you know any female security specialists in Dallas?"

"No," Luke answered without thinking twice. Maybe there was one, but he suddenly didn't want to give this client away.

"I guess I'll just forego all this security stuff then."

"That wouldn't be wise," he said, thinking of the last caller on the radio that morning.

Out of nowhere, Jax's challenge to Jane popped into his head. He'd basically dared her to apply the faulty principles of her book to a relationship with a guy she was really hot for. Luke had the sudden urge to be that guy, and it wasn't only because he wanted to protect her from creeps like the one on the radio.

This was getting too weird. Jane Langston was a potential client, and she had a lot of dumb ideas about sex.

She was the woman who'd ruined his perfectly good relationship, who'd left him high and dry for the last few months, without a warm body in sight. The smart thing to do would be to turn down this case, refer her to another security specialist and walk out of Jane's house for good.

But Luke made the mistake of glancing down at the lush weight of her breasts straining against her red sweater, and before he could stop himself, he'd opened his mouth. "If you want me to take the case, I'm yours."

LUKE NICOLETTI, dressed all in black from his combat boots to his leather jacket, looked like the kind of guy who associated with the criminal element. Yet he was clean-cut in a roguish sort of way. His shoulder-length dark brown hair brought to mind calendar hunks and daytime soap-opera stars, especially with the way it had a tendency to fall over one eye.

And his eyes were intense, dark, brooding. Jane got the feeling that he saw through her to all her goofy insecurities.

She didn't like that one bit.

He looked to be around her age, had a dark olive complexion that suggested Mediterranean or Hispanic blood—perhaps a mix of the two—and a body that suggested he wouldn't have a moment's trouble pounding bad guys into submission. He was larger than life, outrageously handsome and completely intimidating.

Jane wasn't at all sure she wanted to spend another minute with him, let alone hire him as her glorified bodyguard. But he'd already inspected her town house, listened to the crank messages she had left on her answering machine and read a sampling of the angry letters she'd received in the past month.

"What exactly do you charge?" she asked him when he looked up from the last letter.

Jane wasn't exactly a starving artist anymore, since getting the advance and first royalty check for *The Sex Factor,* but she still had to watch her budget.

"Probably more than you can afford, but I'll adjust my fees." He put down the letter and went to the living-room window, pushed aside the curtains, and looked at the lock. He poked at the window frame, then turned back to her.

"So I'll be a charity case?"

Luke smiled. "Something like that."

"No, that's not fair to you. Do you know someone who's more in my price range?"

He studied her for several moments without speaking. When he finally spoke, his dark brown eyes flashed with a secret amusement that Jane found even more unnerving than his brooding look. "I'm sure we can work out some kind of deal."

"What do you have in mind?"

He suppressed a smile. "I was just thinking of what Jax Reed said to you at the end of the interview about rethinking your whole relationship philosophy."

"It's not going to happen." Jane tried to remember what, exactly, Jax had said. She'd been so freaked out by that point, she hadn't paid much attention to Jax's final comments.

Luke smiled in earnest. "Don't be so sure about that."

"I can understand your being annoyed that your girlfriend left you after reading my book, but if you're going to help me, you'll have to get past that."

"Honey, I'm way past it. I just think that if you're so sure of your own advice, why don't you try to follow it?"

"I do." Or at least she *did*, last time she had a boyfriend. Which hadn't been in a long while, given the way men usually reacted these days when they found out who she was.

"Oh, so you're dating someone now?"

Jane felt her cheeks burning, then reminded herself that he was probably just asking the question for security. "Not steadily, no."

"Seeing someone casually then?"

"Um, no."

The corner of Luke's mouth twitched. "Semicasually?"

"I haven't dated in months. Are you satisfied?"

"Must be hard to find dates when you're so notorious. Or do you just not want to date?"

"I've been busy with book promotion stuff, writing my next book, moving into this new place…." Besides, she'd already found her dream guy, Bradley. She just needed to make him realize she was his dream girl, too.

"Right. Maybe you should consider putting your theories to the test on a willing subject."

He went down the hallway to the back door, and Jane followed.

"I wrote my book based on years of experience with men."

Well, sort of. More like, she'd based it on years of observing other bad relationships. Jane's own dating history was limited to a steady, if monotonous, relationship in college, another one in grad school, and a few dates here and there since then.

The problem was usually that once guys got a look at her sisters, the blond bombshell triplets, they forgot all about Jane. Or they somehow got the notion that dating her instead of one of the triplets meant they were getting the short end of the stick. And a few nervy jerks had even tried to use Jane to get to one of them.

It didn't help that Jane was always comparing her boyfriends to Bradley, noting the ways they didn't measure up to her dream guy. And how *could* they measure up? He was, after all, far superior to every other male in the state of Texas.

"You've been with the wrong men, then. How about

you and I go out on a date?'' he asked as he inspected the door lock and frame.

Jane choked on the water she'd just taken a sip of. She coughed and sputtered until the water went down the right part of her throat. ''Y-you? And me?''

He was definitely, most certainly, angling for an in with one of her sisters. Guys like Luke just didn't take notice of girls like Jane, especially not in Dallas, where beautiful women came a dime a dozen.

''I'm assuming you're in your sister's wedding too, right?'' Jane nodded to his question when he looked up at her. ''We'll both need a date for all the wedding festivities.''

''If you want to date one of my sisters, why don't you just ask her out? It's always seemed bizarre to me that any guy would think dating me might get him closer to dating one of my sisters.''

Luke gave her an are-you-crazy look. ''No offense, babe, but your sisters are a bunch of dimwits.''

She couldn't put up much of an argument there. Jane had spent most of her childhood believing that being a triplet meant you only got one third of a brain. But that still didn't explain Luke's interest in her.

''If you're hoping you can get me to fall for you and then break my heart, as some kind of twisted revenge plot, forget about it.''

''Actually, I'm just hoping to prove you wrong.'' He smiled. ''Is that so bad?''

Jane laughed. ''You don't have a snowball's chance, so go ahead and give it your best shot.''

But as soon as the words left her mouth, she wished she could suck them back in. Daring a studly guy like Luke to give it his best shot at seducing her sounded more than a little ridiculous.

No, she had to put all her confidence in her own advice. She'd told countless women how to handle the men in their lives, and she firmly believed in the advice she'd given. Now wasn't the time to back down. If anything, Luke's little challenge would only strengthen her confidence.

And it would be nice to have a date for her sister's co-ed wedding shower. Even better, maybe having Luke on her arm would make Bradley finally sit up and take notice.

Luke was pushing buttons on the security system keypad next to the back door, frowning at it and shaking his head. "This is a piece of junk. I'll bring over a new system later." He glanced at his watch. "But right now I've got another meeting to go to."

"Are you going to the wedding shower tomorrow night?" she asked.

"I haven't come up with any good excuse not to, so you want to go together?"

Jane nodded, sealing the deal. She would prove her theories about sex, maybe even get enough fodder for another book. Luke Nicoletti didn't stand a chance.

LUKE COULD USUALLY give himself credit for thinking before he spoke. So there was no explanation for his idiotic proposal to Jane Langston, other than that he was letting the wrong head do the thinking.

But now he'd done it, and a perverse part of him wouldn't even consider the idea of backing out. He could still turn down her case, avoid her completely, even back out of being a groomsman in his cousin's wedding. Yet he didn't have the slightest intention of doing so. He couldn't wait to get to know what made Jane tick, what had given her such wacko ideas about sex, and what he could do to change her mind.

Oh yeah, he fully intended to prove her wrong—it was the least he could do for mankind.

Luke glanced down at the clock on his dash as he turned onto Jane's street. Ten in the morning, and he hadn't told Jane he would be stopping by. He intended to do a little reconnaissance, get a feel for the rhythm of the neighborhood, see what Jane's daily activity patterns were. Truth be told, he was hoping to catch her going out, so he could follow and see just how aware she was of potential dangers.

He parked on the street, two town houses down from hers, and killed the engine. The neighborhood was quiet, other than one guy mowing the grass half a block down. There was no activity at Jane's place. Curtains were still drawn, and her car was in the driveway.

Luke had bought Jane's book, *The Sex Factor,* last night on the way home. He picked it up from the passenger seat and turned it over to the back cover. There was a black-and-white photo of Jane, her hair a wild mane of curls spilling over her shoulders, her smile slightly ironic. He flipped the book back over to the front and turned to the page where he'd left off the night before, in the middle of the first chapter, entitled "Why Sex is Ruining Your Relationships."

He figured if he was going to prove Jane wrong, he at least needed some hard facts about her faulty philosophy. So far, he'd learned that she gave men very little credit, assumed they were all good-time Lotharios and claimed they were incapable of thinking rationally where sex was concerned.

Okay, so he hadn't exactly been a model male yesterday in her presence, but for the most part he wasn't the kind of guy she described.

Luke read the next few pages of the book, glancing up

every twenty seconds or so to see if anything had changed in the neighborhood. Other than occasional passing cars, nothing new happened until he'd been sitting for a little over a half hour. He was right in the middle of a paragraph that had his blood boiling—a load of garbage about how a man automatically considers a woman his conquest once she's slept with him—when he spotted some movement out of the corner of his eye.

Jane's front door opened, and she came out clad in jogging shorts and a T-shirt, her hair pulled back in a ponytail.

Jackpot.

She trotted down the front steps and did a few stretching exercises, giving Luke a chance to admire the shape of her legs, the little hint of her hips he could catch when she bent over, the curve of her breasts against the T. Damned if his body temperature didn't go up a few degrees. She was a delicious combination of soft and firm, with lush curves that she probably tried to tame through frequent jogging. The result was a sort of soft, feminine athletic look that gave Luke an instant hard-on.

He needed to keep his mind on the job, but something about Jane kept his thoughts wandering into the bedroom whenever he wasn't on guard.

He'd made sure to wear jogging clothes himself, since they were versatile and offered him a cover, too, in case anyone wondered why he was lurking about the neighborhood. They also allowed him to follow her on foot with no problems, and his running hat gave him a bit of a disguise. First though, he planned to follow by car, just to see if she could catch him at it.

She started down the street in the opposite direction of his car, her strides long and her ponytail bouncing.

Luke turned on the engine when she reached the end

of the block, and he began to drive slowly in her direction, taking care not to catch up.

After a couple of blocks, the neighborhood ended and Jane took a path that went through the park bordering White Rock Lake. Luke pulled up to a curb, scrambled out of the car and began jogging after her. Her pace was slow enough that he was able to get within viewing distance of her again in a couple of minutes, then he slowed to match her pace.

She seemed oblivious to the fact that she was being watched. He made a mental note to give her lessons on situational awareness. She hadn't looked over her shoulder at all since he began following her, and she barely looked from side to side. She seemed utterly focused on something straight ahead.

When she reached a fork in the path and had the choice between going through a wooded area or an open, populated one, she chose the woods. Luke made another mental note to give her a sound scolding for that idiotic move. Even if she hadn't been a target for crazies because of her book, just the fact of being a woman should have kept her out of the woods.

A car alarm sounded from somewhere in the neighborhood behind them, and Jane glanced over her shoulder. Luke ducked behind a tree, and after a few moments of no sounds except the car alarm, he heard her footsteps crunching on the path again.

He waited, then began jogging again, deciding it was time to make his presence a little more detectable. If she couldn't catch him being stealthy, maybe she could pick up on his presence if he were bumbling along like a really inept criminal.

Luke picked up his pace, purposely let his foot fall on a few twigs, and pretty soon he was within easy hearing range of her. After a few minutes, Jane veered off on another trail through an even more secluded area, and he lost sight of her. By the time he made it to that trail, he couldn't see or hear her up ahead, so he slowed to a stop and listened.

The sounds of birds in the trees overhead were all he could hear, but his senses were on alert. He had a hunch she was no longer jogging ahead of him, but had possibly ducked into the trees to hide.

Luke walked along the path, looking for any place she might have chosen to hide. He spotted a dense clump of trees and undergrowth off to the left and stopped. If Jane was in there, he'd scare the hell out of her by flushing her out, but she deserved a good scare for running alone in the woods.

He waded into the brush, found a little clearing, and bent down to see if he could spot her. Sure enough, a telltale swatch of blue fabric could be seen through a little opening in the brush. Luke grabbed a long stick that was lying on the ground next to his foot, and poked it through the undergrowth until it made contact with Jane's thigh.

She screeched, and the next thing he heard was her scrambling to get out of her hiding spot. Luke hopped out onto the trail, stopping her dead in her tracks. Jane's expression went from horrified to surprised to afraid to angry in two seconds.

"If I were a bad guy, you'd be in serious trouble right now," he said.

"You jerk! You scared the hell out of me!"

"Jogging alone in the woods? I think that qualifies you for the Too Stupid To Live Awards."

Jane narrowed her eyes at him. "I've got pepper spray on my key chain, and I would have used it on you if you'd

gotten close enough. Maybe I will anyway." She held up
the key chain and aimed it at his face.

Luke took a quick step forward and swiped her forearm
with his own, wrapped his hand around her wrist, and
squeezed until she let go of the key chain.

"Now what?"

"Is this your way of teaching me about security?
You're fired."

"Honey, if you haven't figured out from this little demonstration that you need me, then you deserve whatever
harassment you get." He let go of her wrist, and when
she bent to pick up her keys, he kicked them into the
brush.

Jane's eyes shot fire at him. She asked in a barely con-
trolled voice, "Why did you do that?"

"To show you how useless your pepper spray is with
a reasonably competent psycho."

"I'm glad we're on the same page about your mental
state," she muttered as she bent down to fish her keys out
of the weeds.

If Luke had taken a few moments to think out his next
move, he probably would have nixed it, but she *had* just
called him a psycho....

He took another step toward her and kicked her foot
out from under her, then flipped her onto her back and
pinned her to the ground.

"You are so, so fired."

Okay, maybe he'd gone a little too far. "You have
absolutely no common sense about being in the woods
alone with a man. How do you know I'm not a psycho?"

"I know you *are* a psycho! That's why you're fired.
Now let me up!"

Not just yet. Even if she was spitting mad, having Jane
pinned to the ground beneath him was a pretty nice situ-

ation to be in. He adjusted his grip on her wrists to make sure she was comfortable, then settled in to give her a good talking-to.

"You, Jane Langston, are a celebrity now. And not just any celebrity—a notorious one. You've got mentally unbalanced men writing you letters, calling you on the phone, harassing you on radio shows, but does this make you think twice about jogging alone in the woods? No, you just trot yourself right out here, completely oblivious to the fact that I followed you, until I wanted you to know it."

"Look, I try to be safe. I've jogged in this park a thousand times, and nothing has ever happened. This is where I go when I need to think about my book. If I get stuck, coming out here never fails to get my writing back on track."

Luke made a concerted effort not to enjoy the feel of her body too much, not to notice that her breasts were so close and so tempting, that her mouth looked so delicate and ripe for exploration.

A crazy, dizzying physical attraction surged in him, and he wanted her like no woman he'd ever wanted before.

"You've got to find some other way to cure writer's block. If I catch you out here again—"

"You don't have to worry about it, because you're fired. Now let me up!"

Reluctantly, Luke released Jane's wrists and started to stand up, when her left heel made contact with his chest. She kicked him backward, and he fell on his back with a thud into the dirt. In a matter of seconds she was on top of him with the pepper spray aimed at his eyes.

"Give me one good reason not to use this."

3

Your mother might have spouted some cliché about cows and free milk, but trite and unpopular as the notion may be, the wisdom holds true—giving it up too soon will only make him start shopping for a different cow.

—Jane Langston,
from her work-in-progress, *Sex and Sensibility*

JANE SHIFTED HER WEIGHT on top of Luke and tried not to think about how her legs were tangled with his, how his too-large, overly muscled body was at her mercy. And she definitely tried to ignore how delicious it felt.

"If you incapacitate me and a real psycho comes along, you won't have me around to protect you."

She took a deep breath and tried to keep her hand from shaking. She didn't really want to spray Luke's eyes, but her trigger finger was feeling itchy. And he didn't need to know that her "pepper spray" wasn't really pepper spray at all, but a makeshift imitation—a bottle of Binaca attached to her key chain with a rubber band.

He did have a point about psychos in the woods. She'd developed a false sense of security after having jogged here so many times without anything happening. And after Luke's little stunt, she wasn't sure she'd ever feel the same about coming here—or even if she ever *would* come here again.

"I'll let you up after you apologize."

"Why should I apologize if you're going to fire me anyway? I was just doing my job."

Now that she'd had a few moments to calm down, and now that she felt a little more in control, she didn't want to fire Luke. His demonstration, ill-advised as it had been, made it clear to her how vulnerable she was.

"I won't fire you if you'll swear to me you'll never, ever do anything like this again."

The truth was, a perverse little part of her wanted to drag out their power play. But she was also high on adrenaline from the terror she'd felt at being stalked in the woods, which surely was affecting her judgment.

"I'm not making any promises until you lose the pepper spray."

Jane settled in, adjusted her left leg so that it nestled more deeply between Luke's legs. Geez, how long had it been since she'd been in a position like this with a guy?

No sooner did the thought "too long" form in her head than she banished it. The guru of sexual restraint absolutely should not have been having such thoughts. Must be the adrenaline talking again.

She felt a tickle on the back of her left calf, and then a sharp sting. "Aaaah!"

The shock of the pain must have triggered her index finger, because the next thing Jane knew, she was on her back, her calf stinging, and Luke was yelling and rubbing at his eyes.

While he groaned and cursed, Jane peeked at her calf. A red bump had formed there, and a fire ant was strolling toward her ankle. She flicked it off.

"Oh my gosh, Luke, I'm so sorry. What can I do to help?" She stood up and went to him.

"You did that on purpose," he growled as he continued to rub his eyes.

"No, I swear I didn't! A fire ant bit my leg."

"What the hell is that stuff? It's not pepper spray—my eyes feel…minty."

"Um, it's Binaca."

He uncovered his eyes and glared at her. "You were out here jogging alone in the woods with a bottle of breath freshener as your only protection?"

He made it sound so stupid when he said it like that. "It worked, didn't it? I also have a deadly tube of lip balm in my pocket that I would have used as a last resort."

"If I were a real attacker, that would have incapacitated me for all of three seconds."

"I keep forgetting to buy pepper spray."

Luke lay back on the ground and covered his eyes with one arm. "I'll just stay here. You go on home before I strangle you."

"I'm not leaving you incapacitated in the woods." She knelt beside him. "Or are you even hurt? I mean, how bad could a little spray of breath freshener be?"

Luke uncovered his eyes again and glared at her. They were bloodshot and watering. She doubted a tough guy like him would produce tears just for the sake of drama.

"Okay, you're not faking. Sorry."

Jane let her gaze fall to his legs, sprinkled with dark hair, muscled like a soccer player's.

Yow.

He was one fine specimen of a male. And she was overloaded with misguided sexual urges brought on by the adrenaline rush. That was the only way to explain why she was getting hot and bothered over a guy who was not at all her type—she preferred thoughtful and sensitive, not forceful and intense.

Luke sat up and exhaled noisily. "Let's get out here before I go blind. I need to flush my eyes out with water."

He stood up and Jane took him by the elbow.

"I'm really, really sorry. Just tell me what I can do to make this up to you."

He peered down at her hand curled around his bicep and then up at her. "I'm not blind yet."

Jane jerked away, embarrassed. "I just thought you might be a little unsteady on your feet."

He started walking back the way they'd come. "Okay, here's what you can do to make it up to me. When I ask you to do something that has to do with your personal safety, do it—no questions asked."

"I can't just behave like an automaton," she said, hurrying to keep up with him.

"Then I can't work for you."

Here was her chance to get rid of Luke. Even if he was a hunk with a decent sense of humor, he'd already proven to be unnerving, unpredictable and unmanageable. If she was smart, she'd tell him to get lost. But he *was* supposed to be the best....

And she'd really been looking forward to seeing the looks on the faces of her family when she showed up at the shower tonight with Luke as her date. They'd never believe without witnessing it that she could bag such a hottie.

"Okay, I'll try to do as you ask."

Luke glared over his shoulder at her, then turned his attention back to navigating out of the woods. She took that as his acceptance of their new agreement.

They made it out of the woods, and Luke asked her to

drive his SUV back to her house. She was climbing into the driver's seat when she spotted his copy of *The Sex Factor*. She noticed Luke saw it at the same time, as he opened the passenger-side door. He looked up at her and flashed a sheepish grin.

"You have excellent taste in reading material."

"Just doing a little research."

She started the car, flattered that he would even bother. "Trying to figure out how you're going to prove me wrong?"

"Something like that."

She pulled away from the curb. "Good luck."

"It's not going to be very difficult. You don't know a thing about men."

She glanced over at Luke, who was still rubbing his left eye. "I know enough. The book is written to help *women* understand what they want from men."

"Uh-huh."

He was just trying to rile her up, so she backed off. In a matter of seconds they were in her driveway.

She took him inside and led him into the kitchen where she found a water bottle and filled it with warm water. After digging a towel out of a drawer, she took it and the water bottle to Luke, who was sitting at the table.

"You can rinse your eyes out yourself, or I can help."

Luke squinted at her and then the water bottle. "I'm probably going to regret this, but you'd better help."

He leaned his head back, and she stood behind him so that he could rest it on her torso. The intimate contact put her body on alert, and she tried not to think about the fact that her nipples were standing at attention. She aimed at the more irritated eye with the water bottle and squirted a stream of it in, then caught the runoff with the towel pressed against his temple. Once she'd rinsed out each eye several times, she stopped.

"Feel better yet?"

He closed his eyes. "Mmm-hmm."

Jane got the distinct feeling he wasn't talking about his eyes. "If you're enjoying yourself just because you're two inches from my breasts, you're not doing a very good job of proving wrong my theories about men."

A half smile played on his lips. "Don't flatter yourself."

Jane gave the water bottle a good squeeze, aimed at Luke's crotch, and emptied the contents of the bottle onto his shorts. He looked from his lap to Jane, and back again.

Okay, she'd acted rashly. She'd let her emotions control the moment, and a perfectly good pair of gym shorts was wet now. Jane covered her mouth to keep from laughing.

After several moments of each of them frozen in place, waiting for the other to react, Luke expelled a disbelieving laugh. "I'm not safe around you."

"Yeah, I'm deadly with spray liquids."

He stood up from his chair and peered down at the sizeable wet spot on the front of his shorts. "I don't suppose you have a pair of size thirty-four men's pants lying around."

"I've got some stretchy women's shorts that might fit."

He leveled a look at her that ended the conversation. "I'll just borrow your dryer," he said, and started removing his shorts right there in the middle of her kitchen.

She made a pointed effort not to look at his white Jockeys.

The shorts dropped to his ankles, and he bent down and took them off. When he stood back up, his eyes were daring her to look down.

"I'll, um, get you a towel to wear." She started to leave the room, but his next comment froze her in her tracks.

"Whoops, feels like my underwear got wet too."

Jane debated whether to turn and watch the show or run from the room. The devil on her left shoulder begged her to stay, while the annoying schoolmarm on her right shoulder reminded her that she wasn't thinking at all like the author of *The Sex Factor*.

She turned around slowly and caught him with his arms crossed over his chest, not making a move to remove the Jockeys. Then the devil won the argument.

"Better take those off then. Wouldn't want you to catch a chill." She stood rooted in place, daring him to get naked in front of her.

Apparently he didn't possess the modesty of a normal human being, because without further ado, he took off his underwear and stood bottomless in her kitchen, wearing only his T-shirt and sneakers, lacking even the decency to be embarrassed.

"So where's your clothes dryer?"

Yep, she'd just looked down at his schlong for a split second, and now she understood why he didn't have any cause to be modest.

The burning sensation on her face clued her in to the fact that she was blushing furiously, but she figured she'd come this far, no sense in backing down now. "The dryer is in the hallway closet." She stepped aside and motioned for him to go first. "Be my guest."

Her gaze involuntarily dropped to his crotch for a split second again. This time, she caught movement. Definite movement. He was actually getting an erection right there in her kitchen.

He shrugged. "You'll have to excuse him. He likes to perform for an audience."

If she'd been blushing before, she must be absolutely scarlet now.

Luke tossed her a vaguely amused look and grabbed his wet clothes off the floor, then proceeded past her into the hall.

Jane figured if she'd seen what he had to offer from the front, she might as well check out the backside too, so she watched his muscular cheeks flex as he walked down the hallway. But she hadn't bargained for the sight of male perfection having such an effect on her blood flow.

It seemed all the blood from her brain shot straight to her groin, leaving her dizzy as a Southern belle at a July picnic. She gripped the door frame to keep her balance.

Luke found the laundry closet and loaded his wet clothes into the dryer. When he'd gotten it started, Jane remembered she was supposed to be retrieving a towel.

"Enjoying the view?"

She forced herself to let her gaze linger below his waist for a few moments, just to prove a point. "Wow, you just fulfilled every woman's fantasy—cute naked guy doing the laundry. Wash my dishes and I just might have an orgasm."

WHEN JANE AND LUKE WALKED into Heather and Michael's wedding shower at her parents' house, a hush fell over the room full of family members and pretty people. Jane could think of cages at the zoo she'd rather clean than spend an evening with her sister's crowd—or listening to her mother's comments about how Jane would need to drop a few pounds for the wedding—but if she had to be here, it sure was fun to show up with a hunk on her arm. Heather stood up from her seat and walked over to them, smiling a quizzical greeting. The other two triplets,

Jennifer and Lacey, looked on from across the room, wearing similar quizzical expressions.

"Did you two just drive up at the same time?" Heather asked, while the party-goers nearby listened in.

"We came together," Luke said, placing a hand on the small of Jane's back.

"Oh good, then Jane called you about her little problem!" Heather tossed Jane a surprised look.

"Mmm-hmm."

"Wow, my own big sister, needing a bodyguard. I don't think you're gonna need one at my party though, silly." Heather shook her head and trotted away.

Jane glanced around the familiar family room, hoping Bradley would spot her with Luke before they veered off in different directions. But he was sitting across the room, deep in conversation with a guy Jane didn't recognize. Oh well, maybe Luke would have the chance to make himself useful before the night was done.

He'd caused enough trouble for her today. The way she figured it, the least he owed her was to play eager date long enough for her to close in on Bradley.

Luke had finally left Jane's house, fully clothed, at noon, leaving her fifteen minutes to make it to a hair appointment. Not that a hairstylist could do much for her, but she'd been six months overdue for a trim, and she'd had the gigantic split ends to prove it. Now her untamable curly hair was one inch shorter, glossy and stiff from a zillion hair products, and it draped her shoulders in a slightly more stylish fashion than usual.

She'd hoped to get a little writing done before coming to the wedding shower, but after being mock-attacked in the woods and having a naked guy in her kitchen, her muse was stubbornly on strike.

Instead, she'd torn through her closet for an hour, in a

desperate attempt to find an outfit that would both get Bradley's attention and not make her look like she was trying to get some guy's attention.

Luke had come back by at six to pick her up, and they'd ridden to the shower in an awkward silence that only seeing someone you barely know naked could bring on.

Jane tried not to dwell too much on the unbridled sexual feelings Luke had aroused in her. She was obviously letting certain hormones affect her thought processes to a frightening degree, and she vowed to stop it. Immediately. No more ogling Luke, no more fantasies like the one she'd indulged in while getting her hair done....

Jane's insides heated at the memory. She and Luke, alone in the woods, him chasing her down, taking her like a wild animal—

Whoa! That's exactly what she was not supposed to be doing.

Seeing Bradley tonight would surely cure her of all this misguided lust. Not even Luke could compare to her Mr. Perfect, her soul mate, the one guy she was sure understood the validity of her relationship theories. Okay, so she'd never actually gotten to discuss them with him, but she could just tell by the way he conducted himself that he would agree with what she'd written.

This was her chance to make up for lost time. She'd let quite a few chances with Bradley slip through her fingers, and the more often it happened, the more awkward she grew around him. She was determined not to let Heather's wedding pass by without finally telling Bradley how she felt about him.

It was almost too much to have him in the same room like this. They normally came in contact only occasionally through their mutual acquaintance with Jane's sisters, or through Bradley's work as manager of a restaurant Jane made a point to visit as often as she could.

Now if only she could work up the nerve to ask him out. Here she was, thirty years old, and one of her baby sisters was getting married. It was the kind of event that made a girl think about what she wanted out of life, and for Jane, she was pretty sure her want list included marriage and a family. It definitely included Bradley.

Luke had wandered over to the bar, returned with a drink and small plate of finger foods for Jane, then disappeared again. The guy who'd been sitting next to Bradley vacated his seat, and she saw her chance. She'd never forgive herself if she sat through this entire party without at least talking to him.

She took a deep breath, stood up from her chair, and prayed she could make it through a short conversation without spewing garlic dip or spilling her drink. Perhaps it would be better to leave her food behind.

"Hi, Bradley," she said as she sat down next to him. Be still her heart, he looked heavenly in plaid flannel.

"Hey, um, Jane?"

Okay, so he'd forgotten her name. They hadn't spoken in a few months, after all.

Think. Think of something witty to say. "Yep. Fun party, huh?"

"Yeah, I've never been to a co-ed wedding shower before. Always wondered what went on at these things."

"Really?"

He smiled. "No. I was just saying that."

"Oh."

Jane looked around, hoping to appear casual and not panicked like she felt. All around them people were laughing and talking and generally making merry.

"So…" she said.

"So…" Bradley repeated.

He glanced at his watch, then at his empty cup. "I'm getting a drink refill. Need anything?"

"Whiskey straight with a Valium chaser."

Brad blinked at her.

"Just kidding," Jane said, mentally kicking herself for the lame attempt at humor.

"Oh, ha ha. Nice talking to you."

Jane chewed her lip and contemplated following him. No, that would definitely appear needy. Maybe he'd come back and sit beside her. She watched as he got another drink and went to stand with a group of guys talking sports. Apparently he wasn't coming back.

She got the feeling someone was watching her, and when she looked over at another clump of guys in the foyer, she spotted Luke. When their eyes met, he made a move as if he was going to come over to her, but then one of the triplets appeared.

"Janie, hon?" It was Heather. "Do you think you could help the caterers out? They're one person short, and they need someone to bring around hors d'oeuvre trays."

Jane would have laughed if anyone else had asked. But with Heather, it was just assumed that her big sister was equivalent to the hired help.

"I've developed an allergy to finger foods."

Heather frowned without a single crease forming in her forehead. Jane suspected her little sis was paying regular visits to the plastic surgeon—for preventive measures, of course.

"But, how could that be?" None of the triplets had ever developed the ability to detect sarcasm.

"The allergist said it's from overattendance of parties, probably. One too many trays of miniature wieners, and I'm scarred for life."

"Oh, wow. I'll see if cousin Lily can do it."

Heather hurried off in search of their wallflower cousin, and Jane occupied herself with a plate of finger foods.

She tried to look as though she didn't care that she was sitting alone. After a few minutes, Bradley came back and took a seat next to her again, but he was accompanied by a friend of Heather's, some girl who'd been in the Miss Texas pageant with her, judging by her perfect proportions.

Time for a bathroom break, she decided, or maybe a speedy escape out the bathroom window. No one would know she was missing until the bartender went home and they needed someone to fill in.

Jane slipped into the bathroom and shut the door. Was she ever going to learn not to make an absolute fool of herself in front of Bradley? The answer to that question clearly seemed to be no.

She switched on the light and looked at herself in the mirror. This was not how she imagined the night going, with her huddled in the bathroom feeling sorry for herself because Bradley had forgotten her name and failed to show interest in her lackluster attempt at conversation.

Before she could even react to the sound of the doorknob turning, the bathroom door popped open and Luke stepped inside.

"Excuse me, I'm trying to get a little privacy here."

Luke shut the door behind him and locked it. "Private enough for you now?"

"As soon as you leave, it will be."

He stood disconcertingly close, peering down at her with those inscrutable eyes. "What were you doing out there?"

"I don't know what you mean." Jane tried to move

around him to get some air, but he held out his arm and pinned her against the bathroom counter.

If all her female parts hadn't come alive with a rush of blood, she would have protested, but as it was, she just stood there, stunned to silence.

"You were panting after Bradley Stone like a lovesick puppy. Is he your idea of a real man?"

Oh God. Had she really been that obvious? Jane did a mental replay of her attempt at conversation with Bradley and realized with a sinking feeling that Luke was possibly right. Still, he didn't have to point it out.

A sense of righteous indignation rose up and overshadowed her embarrassment. The jerk.

"Um, none of your business, and I am *not* a lovesick puppy."

He suppressed a smile. "Okay, if you say so."

Jane started to protest, but he edged closer, and she fell silent.

How could one human being generate so much heat? Jane felt as though she might spontaneously combust if she didn't put some space between herself and Luke fast. All her pent-up longing for Bradley must have been redirected at Luke for the moment, because she had the sudden urge to grab him and kiss him senseless.

And that was not going to happen. Was it? He was so close, and she was so, so, so…horny.

Okay, she had to admit it. She, Jane Langston, author of *The Sex Factor,* the very woman who'd penned the words, "Take charge of your sexual desires or they will take charge of you," was out of her mind with pent-up sexual urges.

That was the only way to explain what she did next.

"You'd better watch out for Bradley—" Luke was in the middle of saying, when she kissed him.

With her eyes closed, it didn't matter who she was kissing—Bradley, Luke, it could be whomever she wanted it to be.

The entire world stopped spinning, the din of the party in the background died away and Jane's pulse froze for a few moments, before she came to her senses and realized what she was doing.

But just as she was about to pull away, sputter an apology and run from the room, Luke slid his arms around her and responded with a kiss of his own, as deep and intense as his eyes. His tongue brushed past her lips and explored, took possession as she opened up to him.

She absorbed his heat as their bodies molded together. He gripped her hips and lifted her up onto the countertop, pressed himself between her legs. Jane knew in that instant that she wanted to strip her clothes off and make love to Bradley—no, Luke, no, Bradley—like a madwoman.

Luke cupped her face in his hands and tasted her more gently, then tilted her head back into his palm and kissed her neck, her collarbone and up to her earlobe. Jane heard a shallow moan escape her lips, and in an instant Bradley—Luke!—covered her mouth with his again, silencing her.

Then he pulled away.

"I think you should stay away from Brad Stone."

Jane snapped back to reality, and she wondered if he'd been reading her confused thoughts. "This—this—this kiss had nothing to do with Bradley."

"I certainly hope not." A vague smile played on his lips.

"I mean, this was purely just pent-up sexual energy getting out of control."

He cocked an eyebrow at her. "Sure it was."

"I apologize," she said, feeling ridiculous because he was still wedged between her legs, still close enough to kiss. But she had no escape route, and her insolent body wasn't even remotely interested in putting distance between them.

Instead of taking her apology as an invitation to back off, Luke settled in closer, and heat shot up from between Jane's legs, where their bodies met, straight to her face.

"No need," he whispered. "I'm comfortable right here."

Jane's every possible sarcastic response faded into thin air.

And then someone knocked at the door. "Janie? Are you in there?" Heather said.

Luke's gaze darted to the door, then back to Jane. "Your sister?" he asked, not making the slightest effort to lower his voice.

"Yes," she hissed under her breath.

And before she could stop him, he reached over, unlocked the door, and opened it.

4

Moments of sexual weakness need not mark the end of control over your sexuality. Just minimize the damage by renewing your resolve, closing your legs and telling him the free milk-fest has come to an end.
— Jane Langston,
from her work-in-progress, *Sex and Sensibility*

JANE'S SISTER TOOK IN the sight of them, clutched together like lovers, and her face lost all its color. Luke had quickly noticed the condescending way the triplets treated Jane, and he figured they needed to have their attitudes adjusted. If there was one thing he disliked most about the shallow subculture Jane's sisters, Michael and his friends were a part of, it was their belief that blond hair and big tits made a woman.

"Do you mind?" he said. "We're a little busy here."

"I…I'm sorry. Whoa, I mean, I thought—" Heather snapped her mouth shut. "I'll be going now," she said, and shut the door.

"Why did you do that?" Jane whispered.

"Why did you kiss me?"

She produced a look of innocence. "Seemed like a good idea at the time?"

"It doesn't exactly fit with your philosophy of restraint."

Her face flushed, and he knew he'd touched a nerve.

"I never said I was perfect, or that practicing restraint is easy—especially during times of stress. I'm under a lot of stress right now."

Luke slid his hands up her back searching for tense muscles. "You feel pretty relaxed to me."

She glared at him. "I store tension in my neck, okay?"

He shrugged. "Is Brad Stone the source of your stress?"

Her eyes narrowed, and she looked as if she might inflict pain on a vulnerable spot at any moment. Luke readied himself to go on the defensive.

"Are you jealous of Bradley or something?"

"No. I barely know him, but I can tell he's an asshole."

"I've known him for years, and he's a great guy."

Luke had met Brad at Michael and Heather's engagement party a few months back, and he'd pegged him right away as a womanizer and a creep. He didn't even need proof—Luke had jerk radar. Either Jane was so infatuated she couldn't see the truth, or she was a lousy judge of character.

"What makes you think he's so great?"

She studied him closely before answering. "He's intelligent, handsome, sensitive, funny and he cares about helping people."

"Which is why he works at a bar when he's not riding around on his white horse rescuing little old ladies from muggers?"

"He manages a restaurant!"

"Which one?"

"O'Malley's Pub and Grill," she said grudgingly.

"Hmm."

"And he only works there because he went into debt

paying his grad school tuition and hasn't been able to afford to return to school for his doctorate yet.''

Yeah, Miss Sexual Restraint had it bad for Brad Stone, and judging by her mile-long list of his positive attributes, she was much more attracted to some idealized version of the jerk than the actual guy. Luke decided it was his personal duty to show her what a real man could do for her.

"Let me guess—you were thinking that if he saw you here with me tonight, he might sit up and take notice."

Jane's cheeks formed red blotches, one on each side, and she focused her gaze on Luke's left shoulder. "Um, something like that."

"I feel so used," he said, struggling to keep a straight face in light of her distress.

"You're only interested in me to prove my relationship theories wrong. How admirable is that?"

"What makes you think that's the only reason I'm interested?"

Jane's gaze met his and lingered, daring him to look away. "I'm not stupid."

"No, you're not. You're intelligent and sexy as hell. An irresistible combination, in my opinion."

Jane opened her mouth as if to speak, but nothing came out. Luke took the opportunity to demonstrate physically what she wasn't quite believing verbally. He dipped his head down and covered her mouth with his again, pulled her closer, and kissed her for all he was worth.

She opened up to him, a soft moan escaping her throat and mingling with their kiss. Luke immediately hardened again. He hadn't intended for them to make love right here in the bathroom, but Jane had a strange effect on his self-control. She seemed to render it nonexistent. And if she took things further on her own, there was no way he could back off.

He slid his hands down her rib cage and dipped them under the waist of her shirt. She arched toward his touch as his fingertips explored the soft, hot skin of her torso and then the rough texture of her lace bra. Her nipples were erect, and when he squeezed them gently, Jane moaned again.

He pushed her shirt up to reveal a black lace bra encasing her heavy, perfect breasts. After he'd made quick work of the bra clasp, he broke away from their kiss and dipped his head farther down to taste her bare flesh. He took one brown nipple into his mouth and heard air gush out of her lungs. She tangled her fingers in his hair and thrust her breast farther into his mouth.

If she hadn't done that—or maybe if she hadn't wrapped her legs around him and started grinding against his erection—Luke might have had a chance to regain his senses for a moment. Maybe just long enough to put a halt to their craziness.

Or not.

He wanted Jane with a nearly uncontrollable force. He hadn't come into the bathroom intending to get down and dirty with her on the bathroom counter, but everything about her drove him wild. From her lush body to her quick wit to her crazy opinions, he'd lost all common sense where Jane was concerned.

All he knew was that their clothes were getting in the way, and he wanted to see if her panties were made of the same sexy lace as her bra. He slid the little black skirt up to her waist and expelled an appreciative groan when he saw dark hair revealed through black lace. Then he knew he had to taste more than just her breasts.

He trailed kisses down her stomach, over the smooth flesh of her thigh, and up her inner thigh to that mesmerizing triangle of black lace. Kneeling between her legs,

Luke wasn't sure he'd ever felt so dizzy with sexual desire, and just as he was about to plant a kiss on the fabric over her most sensitive spot, Jane went from panting and whimpering to dead silent.

"What are we doing?" she finally asked in a shaky voice.

"Last I heard, this was called—"

"No, I mean what are we *doing?* This is crazy!"

Luke stood up and regarded her at eye level again. She was right. This was crazy. He had an erection that could drive nails into a wall, but that didn't make this the right place or time for them to have sex, or even foreplay.

Damned if she didn't turn him into a crazy man.

"You're right. We should stop."

Jane crossed her arms over her bare breasts and let out a ragged sigh. "Yeah. My sisters are probably taking turns pressing their ears to the door."

"This isn't a chapter from your book, is it? 'How to Drive Men Insane'?"

"No, that'll be the title of my next one."

She fumbled into her bra and then tugged her shirt back on. Luke lifted her down from the counter and smoothed her skirt back over her hips, pinning her with his gaze the entire time to let her know exactly how hard it was for him to put on the brakes.

"We'd better go back—" Jane said, glancing at the door.

"We're not finished yet." He held on to her hand as she tried to escape. "I don't want my date panting over some other guy."

"I wasn't panting."

"You might as well have been."

She shrugged. "Okay, maybe you're not completely

wrong, but couldn't you just help me make him a little jealous?''

''You ask me that right after I had my face between your legs?''

Jane blushed, and Luke felt a pang of something in his gut—jealousy? Was he really jealous that a woman he'd only just met had a crush on some loser she'd mistaken for Prince Charming? Okay, so he was. But regardless of the fact that they'd just met yesterday, Luke knew there was something different about Jane.

Something maddening.

''I think we need to establish some guidelines for our…working relationship. You're my bodyguard, or personal security specialist, or whatever, but you've also asked me out on a date. So what are you expecting here?''

Yeah, what was he expecting? Luke wished like hell he knew, but he gave the obvious answer. ''I'm just looking for the chance to prove you wrong about sex.''

''If you want to know the truth, I find you attractive, but I've been interested in Bradley for a long time. He and I have a sort of connection, and I'd really like to see what might come of it.''

''A connection? Is *he* aware of it?'' An image of Brad's uninterested body language when Jane approached him earlier flashed in Luke's head, and he realized in that moment that she was completely delusional when it came to this guy.

''I don't know. I think he and I just need a chance to spend some time together, but I haven't quite worked up the nerve to ask him out.''

Luke tried to ignore the blow his ego felt at having this conversation with a woman he'd just kissed for all he was worth—a woman to whom he was wildly attracted, no less. But then he reminded himself that he was dealing with the author of *The Sex Factor,* and he assured himself his attraction was purely sexual, probably born of sexual deprivation brought on by her book.

"Just be careful, Jane, that's all. You can't afford to let your guard down around any guy right now."

"Even you?"

"Even me." He closed the space between them and brushed his fingers against her cheek. "My motives are very, very questionable," he whispered right before he dipped his head down for one last kiss.

JANE LET LUKE LEAD HER by the hand down the hallway and back out into the party. Her head was in a fog, her body in turmoil and her panties in a bunch. Having Luke around was a crazy sort of torture—hot, dizzying, insane, fantasy-inducing torture.

And what the hell had just happened in the bathroom? One minute she'd been moping about Bradley, and the next she was in a lip lock with Luke. So much for being the guru of sexual restraint. Offer up one testosterone-pumped male and she had her legs wrapped around him in record time.

Memories of his kiss, his touch, his mouth on her breasts, flooded her brain all at once, and she nearly had to go back to the bathroom and provide herself a little self-induced satisfaction.

It took her a few seconds to notice that every eye in the house was glued to herself and Luke. She scanned the room for Bradley and spotted him standing across the dining room staring at her with what she couldn't help but call new interest.

It figured. She'd answered letters in her column from what seemed like a thousand disgruntled men who were suddenly head over heels in love with their ex-girlfriends after they'd been dumped for another guy—the old "don't know what you've got until it's gone phenomenon." But Bradley hadn't even gotten her yet, so she couldn't quite be sure if the phenomenon applied here.

"Janie, you're just in time for the gifts. They're opening them in the family room," Jennifer said, appearing from behind them.

Probably, Jennifer had been the most recent eavesdropper. Jane blushed to think of anyone overhearing the conversation about Brad—making out with Luke, no problem, but the last thing she wanted her sisters knowing was that she'd been silently pining after the same guy since college. Had they been speaking loudly enough for anyone outside the door to hear? She couldn't remember. She'd been too keyed up on lust to pay attention to her volume.

They followed guests into the next room, where people were already gathered around a big pile of gifts on the coffee table. Heather and Michael were perched on a sofa, unwrapping a box that looked to be some kind of crystal serving tray. Once the gift was opened, people made appropriate oohing and aahing sounds, and Jane glanced over at Luke to find him studying her. He kept his gaze leveled on her, and after a few moments she looked away again. Fine, he'd won the staring contest, if that's what he wanted.

She immediately searched out Brad again and spotted him standing on the other side of the sofa. Their eyes met, and he smiled. Not a friendly I-barely-know-you smile, but a flirtatious, you're-kinda-cute smile, if she weren't mistaken.

Jane's insides did a weird quaky thing, something halfway between giddiness and the urge to barf, and she looked away quickly before Luke could accuse her of panting again. After a few more minutes of watching paper being torn from boxes and her sister making up charming comment after comment about the endless array of gifts, Jane felt a tap on her shoulder. Lacey was standing there.

She leaned in and whispered, "We need to talk in the kitchen."

Jane followed her sister out of the crowd, and into the kitchen where a few caterers were still scurrying around putting finger foods on trays.

"What's up?"

"*What* is going on with you and Luke Nicoletti?"

Jane shrugged, hoping she looked nonchalant. "Nothing serious."

Lacey was the most perceptive of the triplets, especially when people were hiding something from her. "You were in the bathroom with him for twenty minutes."

"You were timing it?"

"He doesn't seem like your type. You always date brainy guys, not megababes like Luke."

"I date all different types of men—and what makes you think Luke isn't gorgeous *and* intelligent?"

Lacey narrowed her eyes at Jane, clearly aware there was more to the story than what Jane had told her so far.

"Heather said he's your bodyguard—and he's sleeping with you? Who knew having a bodyguard came with such perks."

"For one thing, we're not sleeping together, and for another, why are you so interested?"

"I'm just curious, that's all. I guess I need something to distract me from my own problems."

Like what? Split ends? "What's wrong?" Jane asked, dutifully donning her big-sister hat then.

"It's Jennifer. She knows I'm interested in Mike's friend, Eli, and she's going after him herself!"

"Eli, one of the groomsmen in the wedding?"

"Yes. They've been flirting with each other all night. I'm going to kill her."

Oh boy, this was serious. The triplets almost never broke rank, and for a guy to come between them—it was unprecedented.

"You actually *told* Jennifer you were attracted to Eli?"

"Yes!"

"What, exactly, did you say?"

Lacey bit her lip and thought for a few moments. "I said, 'That one's hotter than a Texas summer.'"

That did sound like something Lacey would say. "Have you told Jennifer how you feel about her flirting with him?"

"He came over to the house last week with Mike, and she was flirting with him then, too, so I told her to back off, and she acted like she didn't know what I was talking about."

"Well, for Jennifer, flirting comes as naturally as breathing, so maybe she doesn't realize she's doing it."

"That's a load, and you know it. She's just trying to get even with me because I'm looking into getting breast implants."

Jane blinked, making a conscious effort not to look horrified. Telling Lacey not to do something was the same as daring her to do it. "Hmm. Have you researched the health risks of breast implants?"

Lacey waved one perfectly manicured hand in the air. "The doctor says they're perfectly safe, so don't start lecturing me. I need to know what to do about Jennifer."

"Why don't you just start flirting with Eli yourself and let him choose which of you he's interested in?" Lame advice, but Jane was too baffled to think of anything more helpful at the moment.

"I've tried that. He just gets me confused with Jennifer."

One of the many disadvantages of having sisters identical to oneself in appearance. Jane looked over Lacey's shoulder and saw Luke standing in the doorway, motioning her over.

"Why don't you try wearing name tags, then," she said. "I've got to go."

She hurried to the doorway, as Lacey stood there staring after her. "Jane…! Janie?"

Once she'd escaped the kitchen, she whispered her thanks to Luke.

"Sister problems?"

"You have no idea."

"What do you say we slip out of here early and find some place that serves food you have to eat with a fork and knife?"

Jane glanced around at the crowd, her gaze settling on Bradley for a split second before she looked away. That giddy-barfy feeling appeared again, and she frowned. It had to be a physical reaction to making out with one guy while the object of one's affection was sitting in the next room.

She'd feel guilty leaving her sister's wedding shower early, but she was all showered out for the night. And then she spotted her mother—whom she'd somehow managed to avoid all evening—headed straight toward her. Visions of a discussion about using the bathroom with her bodyguard popped into her head.

"Let's go, now! Hurry!" She tugged on Luke's hand and wove her way past a clump of couples to the front door.

"Shouldn't we give our regards to your sister and Michael?" Luke asked as she hurried them out the door and onto the porch.

"No time for that. They'll never notice we left, there are so many people here."

When they'd made it safely inside Luke's sport utility vehicle, he gave her a quizzical look. "Care to tell me why we just flew out of there like demons were chasing us?"

"That's not as much of an exaggeration as you might think." She glanced at the front door to make sure her mother hadn't followed them outside. "My mom was coming."

Luke started the engine and pulled away from the house, then steered the SUV out onto the neighborhood street, lit up in the night by wrought-iron roadside lamps.

"Is Italian food okay?"

"Sounds great," Jane said.

"This is quite a neighborhood," Luke murmured as they passed stately home after stately home. "I've had a few clients in this area."

"We grew up in that house. The people who live around here, they've got problems like everyone else— probably more than the average family. Money screws up most people."

"Don't I know it," he said without elaborating.

"There was a family that used to live next door to us— the parents are divorced now—whose lives would have made a good soap opera. Daddy boinking the maid *and* the pool boy, Mommy too high on drugs to notice, kids running so wild you wouldn't believe it. I think they must have forgotten they had kids until the older daughter drove her dad's Ferrari into the side of the house."

"What about your family? Are they screwed up like that?"

"No, I guess I'm pretty lucky compared to them. We're just garden variety dysfunctional."

Luke gave her a questioning look that she guessed meant he wanted details.

She wasn't quite sure what else to say. For a moment, she just studied his profile as he drove. Strong jawline, perfectly straight nose, thick, dark hair hanging loose on his shoulders.

"You've met my parents and sisters. You see what they're like."

"I want to hear it from your perspective."

"Well, my dad, you've probably seen him on the evening news doing the weather report. That handsome airhead act of his isn't totally an act. That's pretty much what he's really like. Some dads teach their kids how to play ball—he taught me suntan oil application strategies.

"My mom is the original Southern belle. She still thinks women go to college to find a husband, and she can't imagine why I'd want to focus on a writing career instead of trying to bag a wealthy man. And my sisters— they're every guy's fantasy. They've never had to do much but sit around and look pretty to get by in life."

"They're not my fantasy."

She flashed him a suspicious look, but she couldn't help asking, "What is your fantasy, then?"

"Lately, I seem to have developed a taste for sexy relationship gurus with bad attitudes."

Jane couldn't think of a witty response, so she squirmed in silence, staring out the window. Did he really expect her to believe she was his fantasy woman? Maybe a one-night kind of fantasy, but not an enduring one.

"You don't believe me? You've gotten messed up in the head being around too many superficial people."

"I just think you'll say what you need to say to get me into bed."

"You might be the most jaded woman I've ever met. But I'm still very attracted to you. Maybe because you're a lot less aware of your own beauty than the typical beautiful woman."

Jane gnawed at the inside of her cheek and tried to think of the most graceful way out of this conversation. Having a guy as gorgeous as Luke compliment her looks was sort of like Albert Einstein telling her she was a real smart gal. Was he right? Had her perspective gotten skewed by having the blond bombshell triplets to grow up with? Or was he really just trying to get in her pants?

"What about you? What kind of neighborhood did you grow up in?" she asked, hoping to take the subject far, far away from herself, though the thought of Luke getting in her pants lingered in her mind.

And the memory of what they'd almost done in her parents' bathroom sent a jolt of heat to her groin. What had gotten into her? How had she gone from a restrained, sensible woman to a lusty maniac so quickly? The answer to her questions sat only a foot away.

"I'm from Miami originally, and nobody in my neighborhood drove a Ferrari. El Camino, yeah—Ferrari, no way. Our street was mostly Puerto Rican. My mom is from Puerto Rico, and my dad was half Italian and half Heinz-57, but they were divorced by the time I was old enough to remember anything."

"Do you know your father at all?"

"Yeah, I got interested in him and started asking to go visit him in Texas where he'd moved. So I spent summers here in Texas from elementary school on. The summer visits are how I met my cousin Michael and became friends with him when we were kids.''

"You two must be close still, if he asked you to be in his wedding."

"No, not really. I guess there will always be that childhood bond, but we have almost nothing in common as adults."

Jane found herself inexplicably satisfied to hear that Luke wasn't a member of Michael and Heather's shallow party crowd.

Luke went silent as he turned into the parking lot of Vittorio's, an old-time Italian restaurant that was low on polish and high on great food. They made their way into the restaurant in silence, and a waitress led them to a dimly-lit U-shaped booth. This was exactly what Jane had always dreamed of as the perfect setting for a casual date.

They sat down and took the menus offered by the waitress, and Jane opened hers and tried not to notice how close Luke sat. Instead, she stared at the monstrosity of a candle flickering on the table, a big glob of wax in a bottle crisscrossed with what looked like a decade's worth of hardened wax drippings.

"You ever been here before?" Luke asked.

"A few times, but it was years ago."

"Everything is good, but the manicotti al forno is unbelievable."

"Okay, I'm sold." Jane slapped her menu shut and noticed that Luke had never opened his. "Is this one of your favorite haunts?"

"Yeah, I don't live too far from here. The smell of garlic lures me in every time."

A waitress came to take their orders. She knew Luke by name and flirted with him in a natural sort of way that didn't even seem offensive given the fact that his ''date'' was sitting right beside him. When she left, Jane's thoughts wandered to Luke's background again. Maybe it was just writer's curiosity, but she couldn't help wanting to know what made her sexy bodyguard tick.

And maybe knowing what made him tick would give her some insight about why he was so sexually irresistible to her. Or maybe not. But at least talking about something besides sex might keep her mind off of it.

"I'm still waiting for you to tell me more about where you grew up."

Luke glanced over at her and smirked. "There's not much more to tell. I was a street punk—drove my poor mom crazy. Our neighborhood might have been a clean working-class one when we first moved there, but by the time I was a teenager, the only way to survive was to be more intimidating than the other street punks."

"So how did you go from troublemaker to security specialist?"

"My mother would have killed me if I hadn't done well in school, and school was pretty easy for me, so I kept my grades up. And the baseball coach at school took an interest in me and talked me into joining the team freshman year. By senior year, I had a scholarship offer from the University of Texas."

"That's how you ended up living in Texas?"

"Partly. I joined the army for a few years after college, but I found out I didn't like blindly taking orders, so I got out and went back to Miami. A guy I'd worked for in the army had started a security-consulting business in South Florida, and he hired me to work with him. After a few years of that, I was ready to go it alone, and since a lot of my acquaintances from college had settled in Dallas, I figured I'd try starting a business here."

"Plus lots of people with too much money live here."

"Exactly."

"Is your dad still in Texas, too?"

He nodded. "And my mom's still in Miami, remarried and living in one of those retirement communities."

The waitress brought their drinks, a glass of red wine for Luke and a Coke for Jane.

"I never would have labeled you a wine drinker," Jane said after the waitress left.

"And I never would have labeled you a Coke drinker."

"I'm a bit of a caffeine addict. Coffee, Coca-Cola, chocolate—all my favorites." She'd always found that aspect of her personality frustrating. Try as she might, she couldn't help but find comfort in a strong dose of caffeine—or a well-timed Hostess snack cake, if she was feeling particularly stressed out.

"Let me guess. Caffeine helps you write?"

Jane nodded, suppressing a smile. "I've been wondering," she said, eager to divert attention away from herself again. "Is Michael a catch for my sister?"

"Michael's all right—he has his priorities in life kind of screwed up, but he's decent at heart."

"I'm glad. Heather needs a decent man. She's dated a lot of jerks."

"What about you? Have you dated a lot of jerks that led you to write *The Sex Factor?*" His eyes sparkled with amusement or interest—Jane couldn't tell which.

Jane shrugged. She got that question a lot. "Maybe a few, but my serious boyfriends have been nice guys."

Luke narrowed his eyes at her as if reading her thoughts. "I'll bet you go for sensitive new-age types. Guys that do yoga and talk about French philosophers."

That he'd just described her last boyfriend annoyed the hell out of Jane for reasons she didn't want to analyze. "I don't go for a certain type," she lied.

"Right, you look for a guy's inner beauty, regardless of the outer package."

Jane squirmed in her seat. Had he read that in her book somewhere? "Something like that."

"So if I were a hundred-pound geek with bad teeth and a raging acne problem, you still would have kissed me in your parents' bathroom?"

He was looking far too amused with himself. Jane's insides fluttered at another reminder of the bathroom incident. She was all too aware of the fact that Luke seemed perfectly willing to go at it for another round, if given the chance.

"Whatever happened earlier tonight—it was a mistake." Brought on by raging hormones, she resisted adding, since it would prove how bad she really was at taking her own relationship advice.

"Does that mean I won't be getting a good-night kiss?"

Jane smiled, a sudden image of her dragging Luke in her front door and stripping him naked clear in her mind. And then she blurted, "I never said I'm not prone to making the same mistake twice."

5

Your girlfriend doesn't need you to get a penis implant. If you want to impress her, try listening to her when she talks.

—Jane Langston,
in the December issue of *Excess* magazine

LUKE WATCHED the color rise from Jane's neck to her cheeks. Her entire face turned a rosy shade that suggested she was far less confident than she pretended to be. He had to admire the good front she put up though, even when her own jokes came back to bite her in the ass.

He had every intention of getting his good-night kiss. Ever since they'd left her parents' bathroom, he'd been plagued by memories of those few brief moments—the taste and scent of Jane, the feel of her skin, the heat of her body, the eagerness of her kiss. It had taken all his willpower to put the brakes on, to pretend it didn't drive him crazy that he hadn't gotten to bury his tongue inside her.

His attraction to her had a force behind it that he was helpless to control. He wanted her more than he could remember having wanted anything for a very long time. And what Luke wanted, he usually found a way to have.

"Gotta admire your honesty," he finally said, breaking the silence he'd allowed to settle between them. "Since you're being honest, how about admitting that what took place in the bathroom was all about a release of pent-up sexual desire?''

The waitress arrived with their dinners, and after offering fresh-ground pepper and parmesan, she departed.

Jane stared at her manicotti and said, ''Okay, if you want me to admit that I'm a bit weak, I will. Maybe I'm not as self-controlled as I advise women to be in my book. Maybe, in that one little area, I'm a little unforgiving and harsh in my advice. Okay? Are you satisfied?''

Luke tried not to look surprised. He'd just gotten a glimpse of what he suspected was the real Jane, the one behind the attitude. ''Not quite, but it's a start.''

She stabbed her fork into a pasta tube, and ricotta spewed out one end of it.

''Has it ever occurred to you that maybe you don't know much about women?''

''Honey, I've never left a woman unsatisfied.''

''How do you know they haven't been faking it?''

Luke repressed a smile. ''A real man can always tell the difference.''

She eyed him doubtfully. ''Can you say that about her physical *and* emotional fulfillment?''

''Definitely. Would you like references?''

Okay, so he'd probably have to leave some of his early relationships off the reference list, but the women he'd dated seriously couldn't have had much bad to say about him. He simply hadn't found Miss Right yet, and most of his more recent breakups had been mutually agreed upon.

''I'll pass for now,'' she muttered to her pasta as she prepared to take a bite.

Luke had a thing about the way women ate. He couldn't enjoy dinner himself if his date was picking at a salad and sipping water. Jane ate like a real human being, and he couldn't quite explain why he found it so charming that she hadn't hesitated to order one of the most fattening dishes on the menu at his recommendation.

He decided to let her off the hook and avoid any more controversial topics for the rest of dinner. They managed to carry on a pleasant conversation about nothing in particular, and by the time dinner was finished, Luke couldn't remember the last time he'd enjoyed himself so much on a date.

It wasn't just that Jane was attractive and intelligent— she was both—it was something more. Being with her made him feel like a gap had been filled in, as though something that had been missing from his life was suddenly present. Too bad she was also the woman who'd written what was possibly one of the dumbest self-help books ever published.

They drove back to her place in companionable silence, and Luke didn't admit to himself until he'd pulled into her driveway how badly he wanted to take her inside and make love to her all night on that brand-new leather sofa of hers.

He wanted her physically for reasons he couldn't articulate, reasons that had little to do with proving her wrong. He normally wouldn't have been ready to hop into bed with a woman he'd only just met, but something about Jane made him think of tribal drum beats, sultry nights in the jungle, finding creative uses for vines. He wanted to get in touch with his Tarzan side and claim Jane as his woman.

Yeah, he was thinking crazy, but he knew what he wanted, and it was the woman sitting in his passenger seat.

Without asking, he got out and walked her to the door, a little surprised that she didn't protest. When she'd found her keys inside her purse, she looked up at him and seemed to be searching for something to say.

She finally asked, "Do you want some coffee?"

Luke crossed his arms over his chest and smiled. "Do you really mean coffee, or is that female code for an invitation to bed?"

Not that it mattered—he'd come in either way—but he couldn't help baiting her.

"You're lucky I don't have any real pepper spray on my key chain."

"Believe me, I know."

She smiled and unlocked the door. "Just come in and stop grilling me, okay?"

"Okay, cease-fire."

The front door reminded him of his official duties as Jane's bodyguard. Luke was ashamed to admit to himself that he'd let her security slip his mind all evening. For the first time, he realized his attraction to her could possibly be a detriment to Jane's safety, but he vowed not to let his guard slip again.

"I've been meaning to ask you," he said once they'd entered the kitchen, "are you free tomorrow for me to install a decent security system in the house?"

She turned to him from the refrigerator, where she'd just removed a package of coffee beans, and gave him a strange look. "Tomorrow is Sunday. Don't you take days off?"

"Criminals don't take Sundays off."

"Um, I just planned to hang around the house and finish unpacking, hang photos, stuff like that. I guess it's a good time for you to come by."

He watched as she measured out the beans and ground them up with a little hand grinder, then poured the grounds into a high-tech coffeemaker. She wasn't kidding when she'd confessed her passion for caffeine.

"So, why did you invite me in?" he asked, and her eyes flashed anger.

"What happened to the cease-fire?"

"Oh, right. I forgot." He closed the distance between them, his body temperature rising with each step he took, then pinned her against the kitchen counter with his hips. "If you want to know the truth, I lied about the cease-fire."

She gazed up at him through half-lidded eyes, managing to look both aroused and annoyed at the same time. "Forgive me if I don't look surprised."

"I keep wondering what would have happened if we'd kept going in your parents' bathroom."

"But we didn't," she whispered, sounding a little breathless.

Beside them, the coffee began to percolate, its rich scent filling the air.

"You're a writer. Don't you like to ask what-if questions?"

"I don't write fiction."

Luke slid his hands up her rib cage and traced the lower halves of her breasts. His cock instantly went hard.

"But let's just pretend," he murmured as he rubbed his thumbs over her hardened nipples. "If you hadn't stopped me…"

"But I did," she nearly moaned.

"Would you have let me dip my tongue inside you? Taste your hot, wet center…" He lowered his mouth to hers and kissed her deeply.

She clung to him and thrust her tongue inside his mouth. Luke tasted her heat and the mints the waitress had brought them after dinner, and he breathed her in, consumed her, unable to restrain for another second the force that pulled them together. When he felt her hands slip inside the waist of his shirt and up his back, he knew by the way his body turned liquid with sensation that he wouldn't be able to put the brakes on if she didn't stop them herself.

And he hoped like hell she wouldn't. He was crazy with wanting her. Maybe a night with Jane would clear his head, make him better equipped to focus on protecting her.

But then she broke the kiss, and asked, breathlessly, "Are you doing this to prove me wrong, or because you want to?"

Luke tugged gently on her hair, until her chin tilted up, offering him easy access to her flawless neck. He sucked on the side of her neck, then moved to the spot just below her ear, and then up to her ear itself. After giving the lobe a light nip, he whispered, "Both."

If she had a problem with his dual motives, her hand sliding down the front of his pants didn't reveal it. Luke's breath caught when she found the tip of his cock and teased it with her fingertips.

Only a few inches from his mouth, her tongue flicked out to wet her lips, and she gazed into his eyes with a look of complete daring. She inched her hand down until she had a firm grip on him, and she began to massage his flesh, coaxing a low moan from his throat.

"Then tonight," she whispered, "is not your lucky night."

Her hand withdrew from his pants, and a wicked little smile danced on her lips.

Luke blinked. He'd just been played, but he wasn't quite ready to end the game.

"Can you blame me for wanting to prove that men aren't just sex-obsessed morons?"

"I never said you were, but I fail to see how hopping into bed with me will cast mankind in a more positive light."

Luke held back a smile and pressed his hips against her, then slid his thigh between her legs until he knew he was putting pressure where it mattered most. "It's all part of my long-term plan."

Ignoring the body contact, she quirked an eyebrow. "You have long-term plans for me?"

"I don't expect to change your mind in one night." Though he was pretty sure he could if he applied himself. He just didn't see any need to rush things along.

She let her gaze fall to his jeans, then slowly travel upward. "How many nights do you think it would take?"

"Depends on how stubborn you are about changing your mind."

Some part of him hoped she'd be really, really stubborn.

He found her nipple again, which he teased with the lightest of caresses.

Try as she might, she couldn't hide the way her body was reacting. Her breath had grown shallow, and when she spoke again, her question came out in a whisper. "What makes you so sure you can succeed?"

He shrugged and dipped his hand into the neckline of her shirt, inside her bra to her bare, hot flesh. "Call me confident."

"How about arrogant and presumptuous?" she said, but she didn't shy away from his touch.

"I like confident better."

Her eyelids fluttered shut as he explored her flesh. "That's not fair."

"What isn't fair?" Luke asked, as he trailed his other hand down her hip and over her thigh, up her skirt. He dipped his fingers between her legs and under her panties and found her so exquisitely hot and wet, the desire to plunge himself inside her was almost unbearable. Instead, he entered her tight opening with his fingertips, and she made an animal sound in her throat.

"That," she whispered.

"I never said I'd keep it above the belt," he said before kissing her again.

He coaxed her into submission with his tongue, and as he worked her body with his hands, he was quite sure he'd won the battle... Until she broke the kiss again and grasped his wrists.

"We've got to stop this," she said, out of breath.

Beside them, the coffee had finished percolating. A rich coffee-bean aroma permeated the air, and Luke knew that from then on, the scent would have a distinctly erotic association for him.

His body, tense with pent-up desire, suddenly felt electrified.

"You're sure?"

She expelled a ragged breath. "Hell no. But we're not doing this. Not here, not now, not so you can prove me wrong."

Luke let his hands fall to his sides, and he took a step back from her. "How about so we can have a night of great sex?"

Jane smoothed down her skirt and tossed him a wry look. "Stop trying to catch me in a contradiction."

"I'm just trying to get you into bed. No hidden motives." He smiled, and with a bit of resistance, she smiled back.

"We'd regret it in the morning."

"Speak for yourself," he answered, and Jane diverted her gaze to the coffeepot, her cheeks blushing scarlet.

Luke realized for the first time that maybe she wasn't nearly as relaxed about his advances as he'd assumed.

She busied herself with pouring coffee. "Still want a cup?"

"I think I've got plenty to keep me awake tonight without caffeine. I'd better go."

Jane shrugged, clearly pleased with his state of arousal. "Suit yourself."

"I'll be here around ten o'clock. Try not to do anything life-endangering, like jogging alone in the woods, before I get here."

She didn't make any biting comebacks as she walked him to the door, and when Luke stepped out into the cool night air, then heard the door close behind him, his body relaxed a bit. Away from Jane, he could think a little straighter. He could stop the "Me Tarzan, you Jane, let's go have wild sweaty jungle sex" thinking.

He could even think about something *besides* sex.

Maybe.

JANE SAT AT HER COMPUTER, a cup of coffee steaming nearby and a chocolate chip bagel with cream cheese in one hand. She'd eaten one halfhearted bite of her breakfast, and so far she'd written two entire sentences. In the past hour. She'd risen early in the hope of catching up on the writing time she'd lost because of Luke, but the events of the night before haunted her.

She put down the bagel and took a long drink of coffee. It was her second cup, but she still hadn't quite gotten out of the funk of a poor night's sleep. And the hormones raging through her veins didn't help, either. She couldn't remember the last time she'd felt so keyed up and horny, and yet she still couldn't explain her behavior the night before.

Jane had always been in control of her emotions and her actions, but with Luke, she never had any idea what crazy thing she might do from one moment to the next. Being in his presence was a little terrifying. The fact that he was due to arrive in a matter of minutes didn't help soothe her nerves.

She glanced at the clock in the lower right-hand corner of the computer screen. Nine forty-five. She had fifteen minutes to steel herself to his caveman charms. All she needed to do, she decided, was focus on Bradley.

Yes. That was it. If she concentrated on the things she loved about Bradley Stone, she couldn't help but notice how each of those qualities was missing from Luke Nicoletti. Okay, so focusing on Bradley hadn't helped her much last night when she'd nearly had sex in her parents' bathroom and then on her kitchen counter with Luke. But she had to believe it would work this time.

Jane turned her laptop to low-power mode and carried her uneaten breakfast to the kitchen. On her way to the boxes in the hallway, she caught herself checking her reflection in the mirror. She'd definitely done more to get herself ready this morning than she normally would on a lazy Sunday, going so far as to apply light makeup and put on her most flattering pair of jeans and a snug black top.

She scowled at herself and turned her attention to the nearest box. She tore through the wads of paper until she came to a framed photo of her parents. She'd just grabbed a hammer and nail off the top of the next closest box to hang the photo, when her doorbell rang and her entire body went on alert.

A peek through the peephole revealed Luke's outrageously handsome face on the other side of the door, so she took a deep breath and opened the locks.

Her lower belly clenched when she took in the full view of him, dressed in a faded pair of jeans, a tool belt and a black T-shirt pulled tight over his chest and shoulder muscles. His hair was secured back in a ponytail, and he gazed at her with those dark-chocolate eyes that seemed to see exactly how much he aroused her.

"I finished your book last night," he said.

"Good morning to you, too." Okay, she was dying to know what he thought of it, but she wasn't about to let him see how interested she was in his comment.

Jane stepped aside, and Luke filled the doorway, a big black toolbox in one hand. He entered the hallway and set the box down.

"Don't you want to know what I think of it?"

"You've already made that clear."

"Maybe I changed my mind. I'd only read half the book yesterday."

Right. A guy like Luke admitting that he'd changed his mind was about as likely as Jane admitting she was wrong.

"You read the most controversial chapter last night. I'm betting it didn't exactly sit well with you."

"Which one is that? The one about sexual control through deprivation, or how men want what they haven't conquered?"

"It's not deprivation, it's restraint."

"Control Your Sexuality, Control Your Life" was the central chapter of *The Sex Factor,* the one that defined in the most specific terms Jane's relationship philosophy, and the one that pissed off most men.

"Yeah, you were all about restraint last night," he said as he bent and opened his toolbox.

"I did put the brakes on." Jane felt her cheeks burn. She hadn't been nearly as restrained as she urged other women to be.

"I thought the 'men want what they haven't conquered' chapter was the most ridiculous one."

"Ridiculous? It's a scientifically proven fact."

Luke withdrew a drill from the box and gave Jane a wry look. "I hate to tell you this, babe, but you're wrong."

"You can believe that if it makes you feel better," Jane said as she picked a spot on the wall and hammered the nail into it with a little too much enthusiasm.

"You know, you should find a stud for that."

Jane resisted making any smart-ass comments about how there wasn't a stud to be found. When she glanced over at Luke, he wore a vague smile.

"I can hang a picture without your expertise, thanks."

He tucked the drill into a holder on his tool belt and stood up, then walked to the front door again. "I'm going to install your new security system."

"Okay, I'll be here if you have any questions."

"I'm not wrong, by the way. You assume all men are sex-obsessed asses who do their decision-making with their dicks."

Jane feigned a look of wide-eyed innocence. "I stand corrected, then. I'll title my next book, *Men Are Really Nice Guys*. I'm sure it'll be a bestseller."

His eyes narrowed. "That's what all your male-bashing is about, isn't it? You're ruining people's sex lives just so you can cash in."

The picture of Jane's parents slipped from her hands and landed on the hardwood floor. A crack formed a path across the glass in the frame. Jane believed absolutely in her relationship theories, but she had been a bit bothered by the way her editor had encouraged her to strengthen certain assertions—especially the ones that made men look like jerks. Jane had known in her gut that the editor was operating on the wisdom that the more extreme the opinions, the more books would sell, and she'd tried to remain true to her own vision while still pleasing the editor.

Had she gone too far? The thought that even one relationship might have been unnecessarily damaged by her book made Jane sick to her stomach.

No. Luke was just trying to rile her up. He was angry, like most men, for having his sex life dampened by the truth.

Jane looked up from the broken photo and glared at him. "Now you're accusing me of being unethical, too? You sure know the way to a woman's heart. Oh, and by the way, you certainly weren't proving me wrong about the sex-obsessed part last night."

Luke approached her, his gaze steady and penetrating. When he was mere inches away, he bent and picked up the broken picture.

"Point taken. I don't know anything about your ethics, so I'll take back that last comment for now." He studied the photo. "You don't look much like your parents."

Considering the number of nips and tucks both her father and mother had had, *they* were lucky to even look like themselves. "I take after my paternal grandmother— dark-haired, fair-skinned, black Irish."

"You're lucky."

Jane blinked, waiting for the punch line. That was the first time anyone had ever called her lucky for not inheriting her parents' blond good looks, the way her sisters had. "You haven't seen my grandmother in her old age."

"Anything is more interesting than looking like a Barbie doll.'' He nodded at the photo, and Jane realized that at a quick glance, her parents really did look like duplicates of Barbie and Ken—an oddly youthful-looking middle-aged pair of plastic dolls.

Jane looked up to find Luke studying her face. Okay, so he was getting sneaky, trying to win her over before seducing her and then rubbing it in her face that she was wrong.

"You can spare me the flattery.'' She took the picture from him and placed it on a nearby box, then started digging through the packing paper to find something else to hang.

"I'll be outside if you need me,'' he said, ignoring her hostility, and when she heard his footsteps on the way out the door, Jane couldn't resist turning and watching him walk.

Why had she hired the sexiest bodyguard on earth? Why had she hired one at all? Probably, the threats she'd been getting were nothing to worry about, just hotheaded guys talking trash. Surely she didn't need Luke storming into her life and turning it upside down.

Jane had pounded two more nails into the wall before she realized that she hadn't bothered to space them out or even select pictures to hang on them. She was losing her mind, and it was all Luke's fault. She wasn't going to endure another minute of it.

Forget that dumb idea about proving her relationship theories with Luke. Proof seemed pretty irrelevant when her sanity was at stake.

To ensure that she didn't use it in a way she'd later regret, Jane put the hammer down and went out the front door after Luke. He was leaning into the back of his sport utility vehicle, and as she neared him she had a prime view of his perfect rear end and his well-muscled back.

Suddenly, she couldn't remember what she'd just been so annoyed about.

Images of Luke's bare rear end and back filled her thoughts—how he would feel to touch, how he might react if she ran her fingertips lightly over his flesh, or if she dug her nails into his skin in the heat of an orgasm. Did he like it a little rough, or nice and gentle?

Everything else about him suggested roughness and hard edges, so Jane would have been willing to bet fingernails in the back were just his style.

He stood up and turned to face her. "What's up?"

"Um…"

In the truck behind him, she spotted the wires and little boxes that must have comprised her new security system, and she remembered. She'd come out here to fire him. Right. Because he wanted to seduce her just to prove her wrong. Anger rose up in Jane's chest again.

"This isn't going to work."

Luke looked at her as if she'd asked him to dance naked in the street. "Trust me, it's the best security system around."

"I mean *this*—as in, our arrangement. You working as my security specialist is a really bad idea."

His forehead formed an annoyed crease down the middle. "Didn't we already have this conversation?"

"And you talked me into ignoring common sense."

"Common sense should tell you that when you have angry men everywhere threatening you, security should be a priority."

"I haven't had anyone actually try to harm me. They've all been empty threats."

"Why don't you let me determine that. Show me *all* the letters and e-mail you've gotten, let me hear the phone messages, tell me everything that's happened since the book came out, and I'll decide how much extra protection you need."

Jane thought of the radio caller, the way the hairs on her neck had stood up at his words.

Okay, Luke was already here. What would it hurt to let him take a look at all the evidence and then decide how much protection she needed. Maybe he'd just install the security system and then leave for good. Maybe he'd decide all she had to do was change her phone number and vary her routine, or whatever it was personal security specialists advised people to do.

"Fine."

She led him to her office and sat down at her desk. Across from her, Luke sank into the old red sofa that had been with her since her college days and looked around at her mess of an office. Normally, she didn't invite people into this room, but when she did, she usually took some time beforehand to shove papers and books into boxes and closets.

Jane flipped through her file cabinet, found the unlabeled file near the back, and withdrew the letters she hadn't turned over to the police yet, plus copies she'd made of the letters she had given to them. She handed them to Luke and watched as he leaned back on the sofa and began reading.

His expression turned from neutral to disgusted as he slowly made his way through the pile, and Jane caught herself tapping her fingers on the desk, nervous to hear him say that the letters were nothing but the work of novices, pranksters and harmless idiots.

She studied her desk calendar and began making mindless notes on it about things she needed to do in the next week—tasks she couldn't help but remember to complete, like going grocery shopping and taking out the garbage.

Anything was better than contemplating what Luke's scowl might mean. Just as she'd run out of space on her calendar for the week and noticed that she had an oil change coming up, Luke put the papers on the corner of her desk and sighed.

She looked up at him, but he didn't speak.

"Well?"

"Taking a more thorough look at these, I noticed something. Did the police tell you most of these look like they're written by the same guy?"

"Um, they mentioned the possibility."

"A single angry stalker is more of a threat for you than a bunch of letters from random jerk-offs."

"So you really think one person is behind all the threats?"

"Not all of them, but most. This creep should be taken seriously."

Jane narrowed her eyes, opting for sarcasm to hide the chills that nearly overtook her. "Which means you think I absolutely need you, right?"

Luke's gaze remained fixed on hers. "You need me more than you know."

6

For men, sex is only slightly more complicated than shaking hands. They aren't plagued by the emotional intricacies of it the way we are.

—Jane Langston,
from Chapter Fifteen of *The Sex Factor*

LUKE FOUGHT TO KEEP his thoughts focused on the matter at hand. No more thinking about what he wished he and Jane had done last night. No more imagining what he'd do with her if she gave him half a chance today. Sitting here in her office wishing he could take her on that paper-strewn desk wasn't going to help. Jane needed him to focus on keeping her safe.

She needed him to do his *job*.

If he did a little extracredit work in the bedroom, she could only benefit, but right now he had to keep his mind off sex and *on* how to keep Jane safe. She may not have been fully ready to accept how her life had changed in the face of sudden celebrity status, but it was Luke's job to make her understand.

He went back outside to get the rest of the equipment to install the security system, and Jane followed him out the door. He turned and gave her a questioning look.

"I just noticed on my calendar that it's time for an oil

change," she said. "I need to check the manual to re-member which kind of oil to buy."

He went to his SUV and opened up the back, then grabbed the spool of wire and a few stray tools. He was just closing the hatchback when he heard Jane emit a high-pitched screech.

"Luke!"

He peered around his Toyota to see Jane backing away from her car, the passenger door still open.

"What's the matter?" he said, already dropping the tools and wire as he started up the driveway.

"C-come here!" She was staring at something inside the car, and when he approached, Luke saw a book—or the remains of one—lying mangled on the passenger seat.

"Is that how you treat library books?" he joked, then realized by her frightened expression that she wasn't in the mood for humor.

"The car was locked. I had to unlock it."

Hmm. He decided not to blurt any more stupid com-ments. Okay, so the car was locked, and she apparently hadn't been the one who'd mutilated that book...

It was a copy of *The Sex Factor* that looked as if it had been attacked by a toddler with a black marker, then fed to a starving pit bull.

"You're absolutely sure the car was locked?"

"Yes, I remember specifically hearing the sound of the lock clicking when I turned the key... And since all of this craziness started happening, I've been obsessive about checking and double checking all my door locks, includ-ing the car."

A quick glance confirmed that the driver's side was locked too. Okay, so the creep who'd done this knew how to pick car-door locks. Not a huge feat, especially on an older-model car like this one. The fact that he—or she—

had chosen to lock the car again was meant as a message to Jane, to make sure she felt violated, to let her know she wasn't even safe behind locked doors.

"Don't touch anything else until the police come. Why don't you go inside and call them while I look around and make sure nothing else is out of place?"

Jane tossed him a suspicious glare. "This isn't your psycho way of proving your necessity, is it?"

"I don't dislike your book *that* much," Luke said as he peered into the back seat of the Mercedes, which was empty.

He let the insult to his professionalism slide. After all, Jane had reason to be suspicious of everyone, and it was smart of her to question even him. A hell of a lot smarter than jogging alone in the woods, so maybe there was hope for her after all.

While Luke inspected the rest of the car, the yard and the outside of the house, Jane disappeared into the house. Twenty minutes later, a police officer arrived and took their statements, gathered up the evidence and promised to let them know if they found any leads from it.

After the officer left, Luke followed Jane into the house. "Are you okay?" he asked as he watched her carefully lock the door.

She turned to him, hugged herself and shrugged. "I don't know. I feel like throwing up."

"You have every reason to be freaked out. Just don't let this creep ruin your life."

"It's not exactly reassuring to know I have such devoted enemies out there."

"That's why you've got me. We just need to talk about how this changes your security needs."

She eyed him warily. Luke guessed she was even more freaked out by the mangled book than she was willing to admit, and he couldn't blame her. Having one's private property invaded and one's work trashed in such a blatant way was a tactic meant to frighten and unnerve—a very effective tactic.

He made a mental note to get the names of everyone Jane came in contact with on a regular basis and run background checks to see if anything significant came up. He'd also have to do some surveillance, keep an eye on Jane's place to see if he could catch anything suspicious going on. The thought of sitting in a car for hours on end never appealed to him, but it was infuriating to have someone break into her car right under his nose.

He had another client's case to wrap up in the next few days before he could devote all of his attention to Jane, but he was beginning to suspect that the danger to her was real and immediate, that whoever was stalking her had a long-range plan, and that he would be patient in carrying it through. The book was just a taste of things to come.

But instead of viewing the threat with the clinical detachment he usually felt, he had to admit that Jane was a different kind of client, who evoked totally different emotions in him. He wanted to go to her and comfort her, wrap his arms around her and kiss away all her tension. He wanted to protect her in an altogether male way, by first comforting her with his body, and then defending her with every resource he had.

For now, he needed to get his head focused on the task at hand—installing her security system, but all his male instincts were pulling him in a different direction...toward Jane.

JANE LEANED against the wall and stared at the boxes in the hallway, the boxes she'd intended to unpack today.

Instead, she felt like curling up in bed, or jogging ten miles, or maybe eating an entire box of Twinkies. If she'd had a boyfriend—if she'd gotten up the nerve by now to let Brad know how she felt about him—then she could have called him. She could have curled up in his protective arms and let him chase her fears away with hot, slow kisses and other, even hotter, even slower, pursuits.

Instead, she had a security consultant with an attitude—one who hated her book, no less. Jane caught herself chewing on her left thumbnail, suddenly engaging in a bad habit she'd broken years ago. Not a good sign. She expelled a ragged sigh and headed for the kitchen.

After searching the pantry, she confirmed her fear that there wasn't a Twinkie to be found. So that left what—curling up in bed? She refused to let Luke see how scared she really was.

Being alone right now felt lousy anyway, so she opted against an emergency trip to the grocery store and instead went to see if Luke could use any help. Following the sounds of hammering in the living room, she found him lying on the floor with his head inside a heating duct, wires scattered around him. She couldn't help but admire his hard chest, his lean waistline and hips, his well-muscled thighs, sprawled out for her perusal.

"Need any help?"

"Not really. I'm just running some wire."

"Oh."

She was absolutely not going to let her gaze linger on the sliver of skin exposed where Luke's T-shirt had come out of his pants. And she definitely wasn't going to look any lower, to the bulge of flesh that she'd already seen, that she'd already gripped, hot and pulsing, in her bare palm.

No, she was just going to turn around and walk right

back out of the room. Ignore the heat that throbbed between her legs. Ignore any stupid notion of what might
happen if she let Luke try to prove her wrong about sex.

But then he pushed himself out of the heating duct and
looked up at her with those inscrutable brown eyes. He
smiled a half smile as he reclined back on his elbows.

"You were just checking me out, weren't you?"

Jane's first instinct was to protest mightily, but that's
exactly what he expected her to do. If she knew anything
about men, she knew that the best way to keep them on
their toes was to do the unexpected.

She fought her embarrassment to present him a neutral,
even blasé, expression. "You *are* the hired help, right?"

"So you don't deny it?"

"Don't feel too flattered. I also stop to appreciate the
guy who mows the lawn."

"But you've never invited him to bed."

"I've never invited you to bed, either."

"Because you're afraid." He pushed himself up off the
floor and began rummaging through his toolbox.

"Afraid? Right." Why did it feel like he was reading
her mind? "I'm afraid of being horribly disappointed.
Most guys with a tool like yours are so impressed with
themselves they never bother learning what to do with it."

He peered over his shoulder at her, one eyebrow
quirked. "A tool like mine?"

"Don't act like you don't know what I'm talking about.
You never would have stood in my kitchen buck naked
from the waist down if you didn't think you were well-
hung."

A smile played on his lips, and if she weren't mistaken,
she'd swear he was fighting back laughter. "Nice act, but
I'm not fooled."

"What?"

"You're just afraid of being wrong."

Jane felt all the blood that had been pulsing between her legs race straight to her temples. She wasn't afraid of being wrong, was she? Didn't she care most about the truth, about understanding it and helping other people understand? Was she battling her sexual feelings just to support her relationship theories, or because she really believed they were true?

Suddenly, nothing made sense.

She'd written a book that made people angry enough to deface it and break into her car to give it back to her. Was that because it told the unpopular truth or because it was flawed? Or just because she happened to have one seriously unbalanced reader? She felt her knees wobbling, and she unlocked them to keep from passing out. For the first time, she wondered if maybe it was possible...maybe she really was wrong.

"What do you think would happen if we slept together?" she heard herself ask, unsure how the question had even formed in her mind, let alone on her lips.

He turned to face her and gave her an odd look. "Babe, if you don't know that, you're not much of a relationship expert."

"No, I mean, the aftereffects. Do you think it would somehow leave us happier, healthier people? Do you think our relationship would be improved somehow—what?"

Luke slid his gaze down the length of her, heating her body from top to bottom. "All of the above."

"How can you be so sure?"

Jane felt her conscience tugging at her. She knew she was being led down a slippery slope, but she somehow couldn't resist following at the moment. She wanted to feel herself sliding, falling, tumbling head over heels... But into what?

"I'm not, but I'm willing to take a chance. The only way I've ever gotten anything worth having in life is by taking risks."

"Taking risks in your sex life is never a good idea."

"You drive a car, right? And I'll bet you wear a seat belt?"

Jane nodded, trying not to roll her eyes at the surely strained metaphor to come.

"Every time you get into a car, you take a risk, but you put on the seat belt to minimize the risk. Sex is no different. You could walk everywhere you go to avoid risks, but you'd never get very far, and you'd miss out on a lot of great trips."

She opened her mouth to argue, but nothing came out. Had she really been missing out on lots of great trips all these years? Had her avoidance of risks kept her walking around the same boring neighborhood over and over? Would having sex with Luke take her somewhere she'd never gone before?

Suddenly all her wiseass comebacks disappeared from her head. She probably could have argued with his logic, but...

She didn't want to.

Instead, she wanted to forget about being Jane Langston, author of *The Sex Factor,* the book that had made half the men in America hate her. She wanted to do something crazy, something that would make her forget for a little while why Luke was installing a new security system in her house. She wanted to take a wild ride in a fast car without knowing the destination.

She blinked slowly as her mind grasped exactly what she was about to do, and out of her mouth came a statement she could barely recognize as her own. "Let's do it."

"Do *it?*" He gave her a look that let her know he wasn't interested in playing games.

"You've convinced me, okay? I'm willing to take a risk, see what happens."

"You sure you mean that? Maybe you're just talking crazy because of the incident earlier."

"I'm totally serious—maybe crazy, too, but totally serious."

He took a step closer to Jane, and her panties got wet. He took another step and their bodies were nearly touching. "I don't think that's such a good idea. Maybe you should wait until you're not feeling so emotional before you decide to sleep with me."

They were so close Jane had to tilt her head back to meet his gaze. But he was staring at her mouth as though he meant to kiss her any second now. His actions were contradicting his words, so she decided what he needed was a little more encouragement in the right direction.

So what if she was acting rashly? Emotionally. Like a woman who desperately needed a little distraction, a little companionship. That's exactly what she was. To hell with the repercussions. Right now she just wanted to forget everything.

Jane slid her hand around Luke's neck and pressed her lips to his, pressed her body against him. She coaxed him into a hot, frenzied kiss that did indeed wipe away her every last worry. What, exactly, had she been worried about, anyway?

He danced his tongue around hers, slid his hands over her backside and gripped her, pressed her pelvis into his erection. Jane clung to him, tasted him, let her mind and body pretend that he was someone who cared for her, someone like Bradley, with whom she could spend a lifetime and not just a night.

When he lifted her up and carried her into the bedroom, then tossed her onto the bed and climbed on top of her like a wild predator, Jane forgot even the name that had been living on her lips for years... *Bradley who?*

Sunlight poured in the window, creating a warm haze in the room that seemed perfect for Sunday-morning sex. She closed her eyes and reveled in her own uncontrollable desire as Luke stripped her of her jeans, pushed her sweater up above her breasts and over her head, then rid her of her underwear and bra.

She heard herself emitting little gasps of pleasure when he found her breasts with his mouth and sucked first gently, then hungrily. He pushed them together and teased each nipple with his tongue, massaging her flesh with his hands, making her feel full, ripe, completely, utterly female.

Then one of his hands was between her legs, coaxing her from damp to dripping wet in a few expert strokes. He slipped one finger inside her, then two, then three, and Jane cried out at the sweet burning of her flesh stretching to accommodate him. He found some insanely sensitive spot inside her and coaxed her into a wave of pleasure so sudden and strong that she couldn't begin to slow its approach.

Kneeling between her legs, he found her clit with his other hand while his fingers still worked their magic inside her, and he watched her melt in his hands. His eyes heavily lidded, his gaze remained fixed on Jane's until the freight train of her orgasm came roaring through. She squeezed her eyes shut tight and arched her back as waves and waves of pleasure rocked her.

She heard herself crying out like a wild woman and wondered if the voice was really hers. Jane, who had quiet, respectable sex with sensitive, respectable guys, didn't scream and buck when she made love. She purred, she murmured, she sighed, but she didn't do what she was helpless to stop at that moment.

The waves passed finally, and Jane slumped into a mass of quivering flesh on the bed. She was barely aware of Luke's fingers slipping out of her, of his damp fingertips gliding up her belly, over her rib cage, around her torso. He lay on top of her and pressed his body against her, then nuzzled his face into her neck.

"You liked that?"

"I want you inside me," was all she could think to say. "Now."

He raised up on his elbows and pinned her with his dark gaze. "No games, right? You really want this?"

"Yes," she breathed as she pushed his shirt up and explored the hot, smooth landscape of his chest.

Forgetting her every inhibition, she was up and undressing him. She was taking the condom he withdrew from his wallet and ripping it open with her teeth. She was climbing on top of him, enjoying the view of him uninterrupted by clothing. She was sliding the condom on as if she'd done it a thousand times, not just observed the practice from across the bed.

Then, without ceremony, she mounted him and cried a wild animal cry at the feel of his erection as she took the full length of it into her body. Not even his three large fingers had prepared her for the feel of his size, stretching her and showing her body its sexual limits. Now she understood, in a flash of coherence—size did matter, after all. There were things a hammer could do far more effectively than a Q-tip.

She began to move, and little aftershocks of her earlier orgasm shook her, sent her into a fast rocking rhythm that felt more right than anything else she could imagine.

Luke gripped her hips and stilled her. "Let's take it slow, babe. I want this to last longer than a minute." He wore a private smile that make Jane feel like they'd been lovers for years.

And then he raised her hips, positioning her so that he could do all the moving while she hovered above him. He began to work himself inside her so slowly, so exquisitely different than the pace she wanted, that Jane had no choice but to cry out at the sweet torture of it. She gasped and writhed and tried to free her hips from his grasp, but he held firm, and continued his slow pace.

When Jane stopped fighting it, she let her head fall back as she learned to appreciate the pleasures of denial. This, she decided, was a million times better than chocolate. Like no pleasure she could have imagined.

Luke traced her nipples with his fingertips, explored her flesh, then, as he increased the pace, he tugged at her nipples ever so gently, applying just enough pressure to drive her wild again.

She began to rock her hips in time with his, urging them closer to the edge, but then he pulled back again. He toppled her in one swift movement and pinned her hands at her sides, pinned her body to the bed with his.

"No, no," he whispered. "No more fast finishes. Today we take it nice and slow."

Today. Implying that there would be other days, possibly nights. Possibly many. A giddy sensation rose up in her chest.

She squirmed against his restraint and he freed her hands.

"Does it turn you on to be restrained?" he asked.

"Yes," she answered without thinking twice. Who was this wild sex fiend she'd suddenly become? The old Jane

Langston would never have admitted an interest in bondage. She'd have labeled it demeaning or jaded or warped.

Whatever. All she knew right now was that Luke could ask her to do just about anything, maybe dress up as a French maid and pretend to dust his house, and she'd consider it a turn-on.

"I'll remember that for later," he said, as he nudged himself between her legs.

She spread herself wide for him, wrapped her legs around his hips, arched her back as he penetrated her again and this time began to move inside her at just the pace she longed for. Fast and hard.

He began to gasp and cry out along with her as they neared the edge, and then he stopped.

Jane opened her eyes to find him studying her with a wicked look. He had no intention of letting her come again so soon. No, he was going to make her work for it this time, she suspected, and she decided two could play at that game.

Focusing all her energy between her legs, she contracted her inner muscles around him, as tight as she could, then released. She did it again, and again. Beads of sweat broke out on Luke's forehead. He closed his eyes and his entire body stilled as she worked her muscles.

And then he began to thrust into her again. This time though, he moved with less control, with more of the frenzied wild animal lust that Jane herself felt. She clung to him, and they muffled their moans with deep, exploring kisses, until somehow they worked themselves off the bed and onto the floor.

Luke managed to break the fall so that she felt only the slightest discomfort as they landed on the thickly padded white carpet of her bedroom floor. She gave the briefest thought to rug burns until she realized that they'd taken half the covers on the bed with them.

He continued their lovemaking nearly uninterrupted until Jane felt herself quaking, coming so close... He stopped again, his own gasps and perspiration making it clear that he was just as close to release as she was. But he possessed a superhuman sense of self-control that Jane, in her wild-animal mode, couldn't hope to replicate. She clawed at his back, writhed and moaned, locking him against her with her legs.

After he planted the softest of kisses on her lips, he whispered, "I want to taste you now."

Pleasant as that sounded, Jane couldn't imagine him withdrawing, taking away that heavenly sensation of being filled by him.

"Not now—"

But he'd already escaped, and then he lifted her back onto the bed and positioned her bottom just at the edge of it. If she hadn't been quaking and senseless, she might have mustered more of a fight. In her present state though, Jane could only utter the slightest protest as he propped her feet on his shoulders and plunged his tongue into her.

"Oh," she cried. And then she forgot whatever protest she'd considered making.

He coaxed, he tasted, he teased her clit with his tongue as he explored her again with his fingers. He worked a magic so exquisite that Jane cried out with even greater abandon than before. Surely the neighbors would hear her and decide she was either in serious trouble or had the best sex life in the neighborhood.

And then he did it. He let her fall over the edge as he massaged her with his tongue and fingers. She felt herself bucking and heard herself moaning, all the while her body at the mercy of his, under the control of an orgasm more intense than she'd imagined possible.

Several minutes later, she lay tucked in his arms, not sure if she'd actually blacked out or had just been rendered so senseless that she couldn't remember how they'd gotten in that position. Luke kissed her gently on the forehead, on the nose, on the cheek. He traced her belly button with his free hand and pressed his thigh against her still-throbbing clitoris.

If she'd been hoping to impress him, she'd surely blown it. Here she was basking in the afterglow of her second orgasm and he hadn't even come once yet. And if she didn't feel so absolutely weak at the moment, she'd hop right up and do something about it.

But he continued with the butterfly kisses and touches, and she could do nothing but enjoy it. In her sexual stupor, she had one recurrent thought—Luke Nicoletti was the most amazing man on earth.

7

The intensity of any sexual encounter is most influenced by the emotional intimacy of the participants. In other words, if you're screwing her but you don't love her, you're never going to find fulfillment.

—Jane Langston,
in the October issue of *Excess* magazine

WHEN SHE SUGGESTED A BATH, Luke considered pointing out that he wouldn't be able to walk to the bathroom without collapsing midway into a quivering heap. But something about the tone of her voice and the look in her eyes told him she'd make the excruciating walk across the room worth his effort.

"You stay here, and I'll get the water ready," she said.

It would have been pointless to argue. After all, he feared he'd come like a schoolboy as soon as he slid inside her again, if he didn't have a few minutes to compose himself. He watched her walk across the bedroom to the adjoining bath, all the while admiring the delicious curves of her ass, the smooth length of her thighs that were strong and athletic from all those jogs in the park.

He'd played this teasing game more times than he could count, but never with these results. Luke prided himself on his control, but with Jane, he'd had to summon reserves of it so deep he hadn't been sure they'd existed.

He'd nearly lost it several times, then somehow miraculously pulled out in time to make the pleasure last a while longer.

Jane, with her soft, welcoming body and her wild animal enthusiasm, was far more than he'd bargained for. He had only intended to show her how great sex could be with the right man—and he'd ended up finding himself blown away by her unrestrained sexuality. She wasn't at all what he'd expected.

Luke rolled onto his stomach and pressed his face into the lavender pillowcase, inhaled Jane's scent that lingered on it, willed his pulse to slow down and his body to relax. He listened to the water running in the bathroom and tried not to think too much about the combination of Jungle Jane and a hot bath.

A few minutes later, the water stopped running and she peeked around the corner. "It's ready," she said as she crooked a finger at him.

He tried to appear casual as he climbed off the bed to go to her and not as though his first instinct had been to come running.

The windowless bathroom was illuminated by a few candles, and the air was warm already from the hot water. She motioned for him to step into the king-size tub, and when he'd eased himself down into it, she climbed in too and straddled his hips.

His erection edged toward her, his entire body anticipating that at any second, she would lower herself onto him and ease his sweet suffering.

But she didn't.

Instead, she trailed her wet hands over his chest and through his hair, freeing it from its ponytail. She gave him a look that let him know he was in for unimaginable pleasures. Perhaps at a price, though. Wild Jungle Jane seemed to have been replaced by another version of her, one intent on using all her sexual powers to tease and seduce.

"I love a hot bath," she whispered as she reached for a cup on the edge of the tub.

She dipped it into the water and brought it up, then poured it over her chest. Luke watched breathless as the water glistened on her full breasts. He reached out to touch them but she skirted his touch and shook her head.

"Ah-ah," she chided. "No touching. It's my turn to play."

Oh, yeah. He was in trouble.

Big, big trouble.

She brought up another full cup of water and this time tilted her head back and poured it over her hair. Luke watched entranced as the water drenched her, and his erection strained between her legs, so exquisitely close he could almost feel her around him.

But not quite.

She reached for a bar of soap and began to lather it on her body. Over her belly, her arms, her breasts. She lathered slowly, clearly aware of its effect on him, lingering on one breast, then the other, until the soap covered her skin. And then she slid her soapy fingers between her legs and began to massage oh-so-slowly, letting the back of her hand brush the tip of his cock, but nothing more.

Instead, she gave herself pleasure, stroking until her breath quickened and Luke was ready to plunge himself into her without waiting another second.

Then she found his cock with her hand and began to massage him with a feather touch—much less than he wanted, and she knew it, reveled in it with wicked pleasure.

"I want you now," he gasped, his head straining back against the edge of the tub.

She stopped stroking and smiled a private little smile. "But I'm not finished washing up."

After she'd poured the water over herself again to rinse off, Jane began rubbing the soap over his chest, then down his belly to his cock. When she reached it, she gave him a few cursory strokes, then put the soap aside. And she dipped her head into the water.

He watched as she found him with her mouth in the hot bath, took him in, teased him to the edge of insanity with her tongue. Luke gripped the sides of the tub, struggling not to release, holding out against the too-sweet pleasure of her mouth.

But that's not where he wanted to release. He grasped her shoulders and pulled her out from under the water, and tugged her up against him as she gasped for breath.

"No more playing around," he whispered, his voice forced.

She reached for a new condom on the edge of the tub, and he took it from her and put it on in record time. With their bodies pressed together again, he plunged himself into her hot depths before she could protest. And then he began to move in her.

Lightning flashed behind Luke's eyelids. His insides quaked. His soul awoke to the rush of feeling that flooded him, and he had the vaguest notion that making love to Jane was going to change him in ways he couldn't yet imagine.

Gripping the soft flesh of her hips and rear, letting his fingertips brush the sensitive cleft of her bottom, Luke went deeper and deeper until she took in all of him, until her body, tight around him, stretched to accommodate his, and she felt like the most perfect spot on earth.

Jane lifted her breast to his mouth, offering it to him, and he took in her tight brown nipple. The friction of his teeth and tongue must have been just what she needed, because she threw her head back, gasping, and he knew she was close to climaxing again. This time, he would go with her.

Water splashed out of the tub as he began to thrust harder and faster. And just as his body began to tense for release, he slid his thumb between her legs, rubbing her most sensitive spot.

Luke couldn't hold back another second. He heard his own breath coming out fast and ragged, and he knew he could no more control his body than he could stop a tornado. Instead, he let himself go. As Jane's soft moans turned into lusty cries of passion, as her muscles contracted around the length of him, Luke exploded.

His release came hard and strong, jolt after jolt of white-hot pleasure, drawn out by Jane's own aftershocks, until he wondered if he would just let himself drown there in the tub if they could remain locked in that embrace forever.

What must have been minutes later, he became aware of a few tendrils of her wet hair clinging to his face as she lay draped over him. The water, still hot, had grown calm again after the storm of their lovemaking. His cock, still inside Jane, stirred, but he only wanted to stay like this, perfectly still, holding the most amazing woman he'd ever had the privilege of pleasuring.

After they'd each regained their senses, they got out of the tub, toweled off, and climbed into bed, where they lay for what felt like half the afternoon, dozing off, then waking up and exploring each other all over again, making love one more time, slowly and easily, like old lovers.

By the time Luke noticed his hunger, it was two in the

afternoon, and he remembered that he hadn't even gotten halfway through installing the new security system. That thought brought reality crashing back in on his little foray into fantasy. He hoped they could still maintain a professional relationship after what had just happened, but he realized their lovemaking was far more explosive than he'd anticipated.

Instead of convincing Jane that sex in itself could be a good thing, he was afraid he might have just convinced himself that Jane was a woman he wanted for his own. In spite of her crazy ideas. In spite of everything. He wanted her.

JANE STRETCHED, feeling absolutely sinful lying in bed naked on a weekend afternoon, having just had wild, lusty sex with her glorified bodyguard. That was something Jane Langston, author of *The Sex Factor,* would never have done. But Jane, the woman, couldn't muster an ounce of regret for abandoning her principles just this once.

If that's what it took to give her this one incredible afternoon of mind-blowing sex, then so be it. She deserved a little pleasure in her otherwise dull and proper life.

Luke had only minutes ago given her a sweet, lingering kiss before explaining that he needed to finish installing the security system. He'd refused her second offer of help and tugged his jeans on, then disappeared into the living room. She'd realized as he left that they hadn't even eaten lunch that day, and she decided that as soon as she'd had a few more minutes to savor the moment, she'd get up and make something for them. Jane rolled over onto her belly and stared out the window, smiling at nothing, when the phone rang.

She reached for the receiver on the nightstand, annoyed to have her perfect afternoon interrupted.

"Hello?"

"Spill it, Jane. What's the story on you and Luke Nicoletti?"

It was Jennifer or Lacey—their voices were nearly identical…. Definitely Jennifer. Lacey had already cornered Jane at the party with that very same question.

"What makes you think there *is* a scoop?"

"You disappear into the bathroom with him, then Heather walks in on you about to get it on?"

Oh right, Jane had somehow managed to forget about that. She briefly imagined what her sisters' reactions might be if they knew what she'd just spent the day doing with Luke, and a smile spread across her lips.

"It's just a little fling, that's all. Nothing serious."

"But isn't he, like, your *bodyguard?*"

"Personal security specialist."

"Oh. Well, I guess that's okay. I mean, um, I just didn't think a guy like him and a girl like you would be interested in each other."

"You mean, you didn't think *he'd* be interested in *me.*"

"No! I mean, you did write that Sex Factor book, telling everyone to stop having sex. I just thought you didn't like sex."

Jane grimaced as she sank back into her pillows and tugged the sheet up against her chest. She'd always thought of herself as a voice of reason in a sex-obsessed culture, but did people really think of her as someone who didn't like sex?

"Of course I like sex! I know I'm not exactly behaving like a model of self-control, but… Let's just say that Luke has a strange effect on me."

She heard a loud, dramatic sigh over the phone. "I

know exactly what you mean. That, actually, is why I'm calling."

"Because you're hot and bothered?"

"Because I need advice."

Jane rolled her eyes. Of course. Why would any of her sisters call her if not to get advice from the "expert?" Not that Jane was much of an expert on fawning men and too many dates for one weekend, but the triplets all deferred to her on relationship issues. Having a career based on giving advice could get tedious, to say the least.

"What this time?"

"Remember Eli Caldwell, one of Michael's groomsmen?"

"Yes. What about him?" Jane asked, though she already knew. She was about to get Jennifer's version of the love-triangle drama Lacey had told her about at the wedding shower.

"It's not so much him as it is Lacey. She knows I want Eli, and she's going after him anyway. How do I tell her to bug off without looking like a jerk?"

"I thought you all had a strict policy about not dating guys who were interested in more than one of you?"

Yet another reason Jane was happy not to be one of the triplets—men and their weird identical sibling fantasies.

"We did, until this. Eli's been sort of flirting with both of us, but I think he's just getting us confused. I told Lacey a few months ago that I thought he was hot and that he'd asked me out."

"So you've gone out with him?"

"A couple of times, and things were moving along just fine, but then he started flirting with Lacey, and she flirted back!"

"Then he's a jerk, and you should run the other way. Lacey deserves what she gets for behaving this way."

Assuming Jennifer was even telling the correct version of
the story—likely neither of them were being honest. Jane
had learned long ago that her sisters had a way of making
themselves out to be the heroine of every story.

"But I swear, I think he's just getting us confused. I
thought there might be something special between us."

"If he were having trouble telling you apart, wouldn't
he be flirting with Heather, too?"

"I guess, but she's always hanging on Michael's arm,
so it's easier to pick her out."

"Okay, but still, if a guy was really interested in you
alone, don't you think he'd take the trouble to memorize
your slight physical differences every time he saw you
with your sister?"

There was silence on the line for a moment. And then,
"I guess so."

"You should lose this guy. He obviously doesn't care
which of you he scores with—and probably he's hoping
for a two-for-one deal."

Another dramatic sigh. "You're right, as always."

Luke appeared in the doorway. "Hey babe, there's a
guy at the front door, claims he's your landscaper." He
quirked an eyebrow, probably remembering her earlier
comment about ogling the guy who mowed her lawn.

"Who was that?" Jennifer asked. "Do you have Luke
there *right now?*"

"Um, I've gotta go. Talk to you soon." And she hung
up the phone.

She mentally vowed to herself that she was going to
stop playing the role of All-Knowing Big Sister immediately. She had a feeling the advice she'd given to
Lacey and now Jennifer wasn't going to help either of
them much.

"Oh, sorry. I didn't realize you were still on the phone."

"My sisters and their complicated love lives," Jane offered for an explanation as she climbed out of bed, dragging the sheet with her and using it as an impromptu robe.

"An hour ago I saw you totally naked, up close and personal, and now you're feeling modest?"

Jane shrugged and let the sheet fall to the ground as she bent over to grab her jeans and top. "What can I say—I'm a modest girl."

She felt Luke's gaze on her as she tugged on her clothes without bothering to find her panties and bra. "I like that in a woman," he said with a hint of teasing.

"I'll bet."

She grabbed her purse and followed him to the front door, where he stood ominously at her side as she paid the lawn guy for last month's service.

When she'd closed the door, Luke said, "So you think that guy's hot?"

Jane turned to face him and found him wearing a little smirk.

"I think he wears his jeans well, and he walks around topless a lot. It's hard not to notice."

"Hard not to notice when you're a sex-starved relationship guru."

"I'm *not* sex-starved. And I never set out to be a guru of anything." She tried to look annoyed, but her annoyance dissolved as soon as she looked at Luke and remembered the pleasures he'd given her.

"But you are. Women take your word as gospel." He closed the distance between them and pinned her against the wall with his body. When he spoke again, his voice was soft, his breath tickling her ear. "And what just happened between us? I'm willing to bet that was all about your trying too hard, for too long, to follow your own bad advice.''

Jane ignored the traitorous stirring in her lower belly. She opened her mouth and told the biggest lie she'd produced in a long, long time. ''What just happened between us was nothing special. Just plain old garden-variety meaningless sex.''

He slid his hand up her shirt and found her bare breast, her erect nipple. His fingers lingered there to coax and tease. ''I never would have pegged you for such a wild one.''

Jane felt her cheeks burn. ''Yeah, well…''

She was speechless, unwilling to lie any further, unable to think of any witty reply.

''And it wasn't meaningless. Trust me on that.''

''We've known each other for all of what—forty-eight hours? Do you always spend meaningful, sex-filled afternoons with your new female clients?''

Luke withdrew his hand from her breast and took a step back. Jane suddenly felt cold and braless. His expression went from playful to dark in an instant. ''I've never even flirted with a client, let alone slept with one. I took a big risk with you today.''

''The biggest risks are the ones we take with our pants off,'' she said, repeating a line from *The Sex Factor*.

''Don't start quoting to me from your book unless you want me to do the same.''

Jane was impressed that he recognized the line, even more impressed that he might be able to remember anything else she'd written. In spite of herself, she felt flattered. ''I know better than anyone all the ways I've contradicted my own advice today.''

''Do you regret it?''

Did she? She supposed she should, but memories of a

few hours ago made regret impossible at the moment. "Do I have to answer that?"

"You're afraid to admit it was something special."

"Why would I be afraid to admit if it were?"

"Because it would mean admitting your whole book premise is flawed."

Oh, yeah. Good reason.

"I can admit when I'm wrong." Occasionally.

He smiled. "I'm waiting."

"Why did you do it?"

"Do what?"

"Take such a big risk with me, like you said? Just to prove me wrong?"

"Because you're a worthy cause. Don't make me regret it, okay?"

His words should have annoyed the hell out of her, but instead, Jane had the odd feeling Luke had just left himself vulnerable and exposed, wide open for her. She had to be losing her mind.

"There won't be any regrets so long as we set boundaries up front." She was definitely losing her mind.

"What kind of boundaries?" he asked.

"We both need to remember that our sexual relationship is just that—a sex thing. Nothing more, right?"

An insane, out-of-control, completely inexcusable sex thing.

"Not yet."

Not *yet?* All Jane's beliefs about men and their ridiculous fears of commitment were contradicted in that one little sentence. He had to be putting on a show for her, trying his best to make her feel as though she didn't know what she was talking about. Fine, if he wanted to play games, she'd play along.

"Since you're probably much more familiar with

meaningless sexual relationships than I am, why don't *you* tell *me* what the rules are?'' she asked, then savored the look of annoyance that crossed his face.

"I don't have meaningless sex, and if you think that's all this is, then you're crazy."

Jane blinked at his strong reaction. She'd expected a little more weakness in his protests.

"So you don't have any ground rules?"

"If we're going to be sleeping together, I expect it to be a mutually exclusive arrangement. No outside sex."

Jane's insides heated up at the thought of today's encounter being a regular occurrence. She wasn't sure she'd ever be able to concentrate on any task more complex than mopping the floor if she constantly had sex with Luke to look forward to.

"Of course not," she heard herself say. Since when had she agreed to their having a regular-sex thing? How had one little slip of her self-control snowballed into...*this?* And why wasn't she feeling even a tiny bit guilty about it?

"I'm finished installing the security system. I just need to do a few tests on it now," Luke said, changing the subject as casually as if they'd just been discussing the weather.

He turned his attention to the new keypad near the front door, and a few seconds later an alarm blared loud enough for half the neighborhood to hear.

"This will be set up to automatically notify the best security service in the city if it's set off, and armed guards will arrive within fifteen minutes of the alarm sounding."

"I don't think I can afford that."

"Don't worry, I'm giving you a steep discount. And if at some point you can't afford the monthly security service charges, you can cancel it, but for right now, this is a good precaution. Probably within a year, you can relax your guard a bit and let the service lapse if you want.''

"Within a *year?*" Jane's heart fell to her stomach. "You really think it will take that long for all this harassment to die down?"

"I hope it doesn't, but we have to be realistic. Your book is still on the bestseller lists, and as long as it's selling strong you're going to keep picking up new enemies.''

She wandered into the living room in a daze and sank onto the sofa. How had she gotten herself into this mess? If she'd ever doubted the power of words, she'd never again need convincing. All she'd wanted to do was write a book that might help people have better love lives, and instead she'd managed to outrage half the men in America.

Jane gnawed at her lip, wondering what would happen when the book was printed internationally. Would she get hate mail from England and Australia, too? Would men with exotic accents leave angry messages on her answering machine?

Her editor, agent and publicist had all assured her that so much attention was a good thing, even the negative attention, but they weren't the ones finding mangled, vandalized books in their cars.

And speaking of books… Jane had a vague recollection of a book signing she'd committed to doing some time this month, but she suddenly had the sick feeling she'd forgotten to mark it on her desk calendar. She jumped up and went to her desk. There was no such event written for any Monday in the near future. Chewing her lower lip, she stared at tomorrow's date: May 2.

And then she remembered clearly a conversation with

her publicist in which she'd agreed to do a signing at a
nearby chain bookstore. *On May 2.*

"Luke?" she called into the hallway, and he appeared
from outside a few seconds later.

"What's up?"

"It appears I might need some extra security tomorrow.
Please tell me you'll be free."

8

Giving in to temptation can only lead to trouble.

—Jane Langston,
from her work-in-progress, *Sex and Sensibility*

LUKE STOOD next to an aisle of books with titles like *Reclaim the Romance* and *The Savvy Woman's Guide to Sex.* He eyed their spines, marveling at the amazing number of titles all about essentially the same subject. The popularity of self-help books only confirmed to him that a lot of people were looking for a way to buy themselves happiness for twenty-four dollars and ninety-nine cents. People had been having relationships and sex and everything else for countless generations, and now all of a sudden everybody needed a book to tell them how to get it on?

Jane was sitting a few feet away at a table stacked with copies of *The Sex Factor,* chatting with readers who lingered around the table. Luke could hardly take his eyes off of her to scan the store for potential threats. She nearly glowed with the sort of relaxed beauty that came from being well-pleasured. And it made him stand a little taller to realize he'd done that. He was the source of her glow.

He'd avoided pointing out to her, ever since their lovemaking the day before, that she'd been thoroughly proven wrong. That could wait until she was ready to admit it on her own. Besides, he wasn't sure he much cared anymore about who was right or wrong between them.

No, he knew already that what he cared about was Jane. He wanted to protect her, and he wanted to be more to her than a lover. He'd thought about it all night.

After he'd shown her how to set the security system, she'd seemed okay with his going home. And he hadn't wanted to push his luck by suggesting they have dinner together. Instead, he'd eaten carry-out alone in his apartment, images of making love to Jane playing over and over in his head.

He knew better than to think that it was possible to have such amazing sex with just anyone. The current that had passed between them suggested a connection much deeper, a connection they'd be fools not to explore. But he'd have to wait for Jane to realize that herself. He certainly wasn't averse to providing her with little hints here and there, in bed, out of bed, wherever the opportunity arose.

Only his feelings for Jane kept him from feeling like the ultimate jackass for sleeping with one of his clients. The unprofessional aspect of it nagged at him, but he knew it was worth it if it gave them the chance to explore the possibilities of their relationship.

Luke's gaze traveled around the gigantic bookstore. It was evening, and the store was dotted with business professionals still in their work clothes, families having just come from soccer practice, the usual bookstore types, and a disproportionate number of twenty- and thirty-something women. They were the ones gravitating toward Jane's table.

He hadn't spotted anyone yet who looked like a threat. An occasional man wandered up, curious, but as soon as he figured out what the book was, he hightailed it away as fast as possible. Most people were more than willing to be rude, obnoxious, even threatening in a letter or on the phone, but face-to-face—that was a different matter.

Luke listened in on Jane's conversations, but nothing really caught his interest until he heard a woman ask her how she could extricate herself from an intense love affair with a guy she'd been having great sex with.

He couldn't wait to hear Jane's response. His view of her, in profile, suggested she was mighty uncomfortable having to answer it in front of him.

"Why do you want out of the relationship?"

"Well, it's not so much that I want out," the woman said, noticing Luke then and lowering her voice. "I just read your book, and it's made me realize how obsessed I've been with, well…sex. With this guy."

"I see. So you want to backtrack a bit in the relationship, or break it off completely?"

The woman shrugged. "There's no way I could be with him without wanting to have sex, so I guess I'll just have to end the relationship completely."

Jane nodded, frowning.

Go ahead, babe, answer that one.

"Do you love him?"

"I think so. Maybe. I guess that's the problem—I'm afraid that maybe we've been substituting sex for deep emotional intimacy, and I don't want to go any further with that kind of shallow relationship. I have no idea if I love him or just love having sex with him."

"Have you expressed these concerns to him?"

"I've tried, but we just end up in bed."

"If you really love him, and if he really loves you, then the two of you should be able to agree to stop having sex long enough to sort out the intimacy issues in your relationship. If he can't deal with that, then he's not the guy for you."

The woman nodded, looking doubtful, then wandered away toward the romance section. Probably she was going to need some good reading material to endure all those nights of sexual restraint to come.

Luke could put up a damn good argument against Jane's advice, but he kept his mouth shut. Sexual intimacy could enhance emotional intimacy—it didn't have to hinder it. And if he got the chance, he'd demonstrate that very fact to her.

He was just about to settle in and imagine all sorts of things he'd like to demonstrate to Jane, when he spotted a guy who set off his internal alarm. Dishwater-brown hair, five-o'clock shadow, denim jacket in need of a wash, the guy wore an eerie look of calm as he made his way from the magazine section over to Jane's table. He hung back at first, surveying the scene, taking note of Luke's presence, then approached slowly.

Luke decided not to take any immediate action. His instincts pegged the guy as a potential harasser, or maybe just a curious onlooker, probably not a serious threat. Just to be safe though, he kept his gaze focused on the man, made sure he knew that he was being watched.

Jane greeted the man with a wary smile, aware as she was that her book generally wasn't received well by the male half of the public.

"Hello," she said, when he reached the table.

He picked up a copy of *The Sex Factor* and thumbed through it. "I heard you on the radio the other day—on *The Jax Reed Show*."

Jane's smiled became a little more strained. "Not one of my finer moments, I assure you."

"You really believe this stuff you write?"

"No, I think it's all garbage. That's why I write it and put my name on it."

"I think Jax was right—you need to get laid."

"Excuse me?"

Luke took a step forward, and the man glanced nervously between him and Jane.

"Who's that? Your hired goon?"

Jane looked up at Luke. She was doing a pretty good job of disguising her panic behind a calm facade.

"He's my personal security specialist. If you'd like me to sign a book, you're welcome to stick around, but if you're just going to make speculations about my sex life, you might want to make your way over to the reference section and find yourself a book on conversational etiquette."

The guy leered at Jane, and Luke's entire body tensed for action. "You're hotter-looking than I thought you'd be. I wouldn't mind showing you a good time in bed."

Luke rounded the table and took a firm hold of the loser's elbow. "I'm going to give you one chance to walk out of here on your own," he said, keeping his voice low to avoid a scene. "Get lost."

"Back off, man." The guy smiled and held his hands up in a gesture of peace. "I was just having a little fun."

The jerk was trying to play it cool, but he didn't waste any time leaving the store. Luke was pretty sure he would have run if it wouldn't have made him look like an even bigger ass.

Luke turned back to the table after he'd watched the guy get into a late-model Ford truck and drive away. A few customers who witnessed the incident eyed him with curiosity. Jane's interested crowd had wandered away.

"What a creep," she said, shaking her head. Her face had paled noticeably.

"He's gone, so just put him out of your head."

"Thank you. I don't know what I would have done if I'd had to endure any more of the witty repartee."

Luke smiled. "I bet you could have handled him yourself. But you shouldn't have to." He sat down next to Jane in an empty chair. "He probably wasn't a serious threat—just your typical disgruntled loser—but you never know when a loser will cross the line and become something worse."

Something worse—a stalker, a rapist, a murderer. He didn't want to give Jane those details now. She needed to keep a clear head to finish the book signing, but when they got the chance, he did want to make sure she understood all the potential threats to her safety. Now that he'd had a chance to observe her in public—and witnessed the harassment she could receive at something as benign as a suburban bookstore event—he wanted to make sure she never forgot all the dangers that lurked in her seemingly safe world. She'd gotten a big taste of danger yesterday with the book in her car, but she'd also spent the rest of the day acting as if it hadn't bothered her. He needed to be sure she understood.

Another fan had approached and was thanking Jane for her wonderful advice, so Luke stood up and took over his post watching the store again. When they were alone, Jane turned to him.

"This ends in another ten or fifteen minutes. Want to grab something to eat after?"

He nodded. "I know a great Chicago-style pizza place around the block."

She closed her eyes and moaned deep in her throat. "Mmm, pizza. We're there."

Luke wished she hadn't done that. Now he had to stand

in the middle of the sex and intimacy section with a growing hard-on and no relief in sight.

THE CUMULATIVE EFFECT of all the craziness in her life
was slowly driving Jane batty. When she couldn't even
enjoy a double pepperoni thick-crust pizza, she knew she
was in serious trouble.

Luke watched her poking at her slice of pizza with a
fork.

"You don't like it?"

"I love it. I'm just a little sick to my stomach after
dealing with that guy at the bookstore."

"Forget about him."

Luke had brought her to yet another heavenly dive, a
place that knew how to make great food with a minimum
of pretension. There were settled in a dimly lit booth,
across from each other, and nearby a jukebox played an
old Commodores hit. At any other time in her life, Jane
would have considered this the perfect date. Hot guy,
great pizza, perfect atmosphere. She had her dream career—was even enjoying great success at it—and she was
in the prime of her life. Not only that, but she'd just had
the most incredible sex imaginable yesterday.

So why did everything feel out of control? The answers
were many and obvious, and she wasn't going to replay
them in her head again.

It was bad enough having to endure all those conversations at the bookstore earlier, exposing herself as a blatant hypocrite in front of Luke. He'd been polite enough
so far not to point out that she'd just done with him the
exact opposite of what she'd been advising other women
to do. Jane swallowed her guilt and decided she'd allow
herself a night not to think about it. Tomorrow was an-

other day—and tomorrow she'd pick up where she left off obsessing about the validity of her sex philosophy.

Tonight, she feared she had more immediate worries. Like the creeps who thought she needed to be taught a lesson in bed.

Luke polished off his third slice of pizza and leaned toward her.

"Hey, zombie woman? Care to share your thoughts?"

"Oh, you know—the usual. Stalkers, deviants, my general lack of safety in the world right now."

"I'm glad you're taking the threats seriously, but don't let it ruin your life. That's why you've got me—to show you how to deal with it all."

"You mean I can't just snap my fingers and make them go away?" Jane forced herself to take a bite of pizza, and for a brief moment the taste allowed her to relax.

And then the moment passed.

"You need to be on guard all the time. Are you familiar with the concept of situational awareness?"

"Um, I think so?"

"You displayed an amazing lack of it while jogging the other day."

"That was a special circumstance—I was brainstorming."

"But anyone who wants to harm you will look for times like that when you're vulnerable, and that's when they'll strike."

Yep, there went her momentary sense of relaxation.

"So should I attach rearview mirrors to my head to make sure no more crazy men follow me on my jogs?"

His expression told her he wasn't finding her jokes all that amusing. "Situational awareness is a state of mind you can develop. It means keeping a low-level sense of guardedness at all times, looking for potential threats wherever you go, keeping in mind how you might get out of any bad situation that could occur at a given place.''

''I'm a writer, not a CIA operative.'' Though at times like this, CIA operative didn't sound like such a bad job.

Luke gave her a look of forced patience. ''When you go to the grocery store, how do you decide where to park?''

''I find the closest spot.''

''How about when it's dark?''

''I find the darkest, most out-of-the-way spot available, preferably situated between a spooky van and a Dumpster.''

''Very funny. Do you actually think about safety when you're in a dark parking lot?''

''Of course I do. What woman doesn't?'' Jane asked before she took another bite of pizza. It was getting better, the more she allowed Luke to distract her. In a few minutes she might even have a real appetite worked up again—maybe even for something besides Luke.

''We'll need to work on some basic self-defense techniques this week. Just to make sure we've got all the bases covered. And I'd like to practice some more sophisticated techniques with you, too, things we hope you won't ever have to use.''

Jane was liking his ideas better and better. Her memories of two days ago in the park, their bodies pressed together, dominated her thoughts on self-defense lessons.

''So this will involve lots of, um, close contact?''

His expression remained neutral. ''Yeah, lots of it.''

''Hmm. That could be interesting.''

He cracked a smile. ''We'll have to keep ourselves focused on the task at hand, of course. This is serious business.''

Jane finished her pizza with visions of Luke wrestling

her to the ground and showing her all the techniques he knew dancing through her head.

"How about we get started tonight? With the lessons, I mean," she said without thinking.

Stress again. It had to be stress that took her from worrying about crazed stalkers to having self-defense lesson fantasies in a matter of minutes.

Luke glanced at his watch, an expensive Swiss brand that suggested exactly the sort of clients he normally worked with—probably not people who attacked him with breath spray and gave him oral sex in the bathtub. Jane smiled to herself.

"Not tonight. I need to meet with another client at eight tomorrow morning, and I've still got some work to do before the meeting."

Jane quirked an eyebrow, not sure whether to feel disappointed or relieved. "You wouldn't be brushing me off, would you?"

He smiled slowly. "I can't think of anything I'd rather do than go back to your place, but after what happened yesterday, I know we wouldn't get much sleep."

She blinked, amazed at the sudden rush of emotion in her chest. Was she actually *offended* that her bodyguard had just turned down an opportunity to get intimate with her? Had that really been her only motive in asking him back to her place? She swallowed a dry lump in her throat.

Maybe it had.

And she'd become the sort of woman she scolded soundly in *The Sex Factor* for letting sex control her life. How had this happened? But the question no sooner formed in her head than she knew the answer.

She needed only to close her eyes and imagine the most amazing Sunday afternoon of her life to know.

"Jane? Are you okay?" Luke was peering at her as if she'd just fallen asleep on her plate.

"Yes, I'm fine," she said, shifting in her seat.

"How about we meet up tomorrow for the self-defense lessons? I should be free after lunch."

She frowned, pretending to go over her schedule in her head. It was true she had writing to catch up on, and in spite of the way her body responded at the thought of seeing Luke tomorrow, she decided it was best to finally start following a bit of her own advice and make him wait.

"I really need to catch up on work all day tomorrow. How about later in the week?"

"We need to get an overall security plan for you in place as soon as possible. I don't want to wait too long until our next meeting."

Uh-huh. Jane resisted a smile. "How about Thursday?"

But then she caught a glimpse of his hand resting on the table, so large and perfect. Smooth café-au-lait skin sprinkled with dark hairs, long capable fingers that had worked with such skill—had made her cry out and writhe around shamelessly. She squeezed her thighs together and frowned. So much for her newfound self-control.

"Are you sure you can't make time on Wednesday? I just don't want to put this off any longer than necessary."

"Wednesday is perfect," she blurted with a little too much enthusiasm.

Luke tossed her an odd look but said nothing.

By the time they paid for dinner—arguing over the bill and finally settling on Luke getting the tab and Jane leaving the tip—and made it out to the parking lot, Jane was nearly humming with pent-up desire. She wanted to grab him, tug him into the back seat of her car, and demand a quickie to get her through the next two days.

Two entire days. How would she survive? How would

she focus on writing when an onslaught of erotic images filled her head and threatened to drive her mad?

Jane drove home with her teeth clenched together, tried to listen to National Public Radio for all of two minutes before a discussion of some obscure poet became too much, and eventually gave up trying to resist thinking about Luke. She wanted him desperately. Wanted to feel the heat and firmness of his body against her again, wanted to feel him pumping inside her again, wanted to try out all the techniques and positions and scenarios she'd read about with a clinical detachment in magazines like *Excess* over the years, but had never had the urge to try before.

By the time she reached her town house, which was blazing with lights thanks to the automatic random light settings Luke had installed with the security system, she feared she'd be awake all night.

Jane found it oddly soothing to enter a house with the lights already on. Homer the cat greeted her at the door with a yowl. She'd forgotten to feed him that morning, she realized then. Great—all the craziness with Luke had even turned her into a bad-cat mom.

She fed the cat, wandered around the house switching off unnecessary lights, and then slumped on the sofa, completely frazzled. The night stretched before her like an endless jail sentence. So she did what any writer would do—she went to her computer.

A minute later her office was aglow in the light of her laptop. She logged on to her e-mail account and downloaded seventeen messages. Most looked like letters from readers, another few were junk mail, one was a forwarded joke from her great-uncle Millard, and two were from Heather about the bridesmaid dresses. Jane couldn't bring herself to open any of them. Instead, she found herself wondering what Luke's e-mail address was, and whether he'd check it tonight.

She had to stop thinking about him. She opened the document that contained her work-in-progress, *Sex and Sensibility,* and realized she was the least qualified person on earth to write that book. Its subtitle, *How to Be a Twenty-first-Century Girl with Nineteenth-Century Values* glared at her from the screen.

She was not that girl.

Panic seized her chest. Would she have to abandon the entire project, break her contract with the publisher and ruin her writing career? She certainly couldn't keep writing about issues like abstinence and self-control while she was in a lust-induced frenzy over her bodyguard.

Her life was spiraling out of control, and all she could think about at that moment was her weekend spent with Luke. What she needed was to regain a bit of her former mind-set. Prior to the day she met Luke Nicoletti, she'd been a different woman. She'd had sensible desires.

Of course! All she needed to do was to get her mind back on Bradley, and she'd forget all about Luke. She closed her eyes and tried to summon up a picture of Bradley. Blond hair cut meticulously short—none of that rebellious long, silken hair... Hair that tickled her face when he kissed her, when he made love to her—

Stop it!

Okay, back to Brad. Skip the hair. There was always his face. His face that, that...that she couldn't picture right now if her life depended on it. Well then, she just needed to go back and imagine how they'd first met, in college Psych 203. The course had been titled Social Psychology, and... She couldn't remember a damn thing about it—or Bradley—right now.

Jane propped her elbows on the desk, buried her face

in her hands, and sighed. She was so incredibly horny, so in need of release, there was only one way to get past it and get herself thinking clearly again.

Her hand slipped down between her legs, giving the slightest bit of pressure to her throbbing core. No, she couldn't do this, not with that damn manuscript title glaring at her. She closed *Sex and Sensibility,* then stared at her e-mail again. Then she remembered Luke's business card, sitting on her desk only inches away, and it suddenly became very important that she touch that one little possession of his.

She found it in her business card file and pulled it out, let her fingers glide over the black raised lettering on the white card—Lucas Nicoletti, Personal Security Specialist. And that was when she saw it—his e-mail address, printed there clear as day.

She could e-mail him. Maybe give him a little taste of the torture he'd inflicted on her by not coming home with her. Yes, that was what she would do.

She opened a new message, typed in his address, then tabbed to the subject header. She typed in ''A Bedtime Story,'' then tabbed down to the message field.

Once upon a time there was a woman who was wide awake on a lonely Monday night. She couldn't banish from her mind thoughts of a certain man, a man who'd brought her unimaginable pleasure only the day before. But tonight, he'd gone home alone too, and she wondered if his body ached for her the same way hers ached for him.

She lay awake, haunted by images of what they might have been doing if only they'd been together. She would take him to her bed, explore his flesh with her hands and mouth, find all the places that made him cry out with pleasure. She already knew a few of those places. She knew the feel of him, hard and throbbing inside her mouth, or buried deep inside her.

She longed for that feeling again, had a burning need for it, and when she finally fell asleep, she feverishly dreamed about it, about him, about the magic their bodies worked together.

Jane stopped and reread what she'd written. Not the most inspired prose she'd ever penned. And not in a million years could she ever actually send such a message. She wasn't sure what she'd intended to write to Luke, but this wasn't it. No, she'd just delete the whole thing.

She moved the mouse arrow over to the appropriate spot and clicked one time. A little message popped up on her screen: "Your message has been sent."

Sent? Jane blinked, and her stomach clenched into a golf ball.

Yes, sent.

Oh. Dear. God.

She'd accidentally gone on autopilot and hit the same button she always hit when she finished composing a message—the send button.

She heard a strangled sound escape her throat, and she gripped the sides of the computer screen. "No! No, no, no, no, no!"

This couldn't be happening. She absolutely could not have just sent an erotic e-mail message to her new bodyguard. Her breathing grew shallow and she had to force herself to take slow steady breaths.

Count to ten. Don't panic. One, two, three...

Just to be sure she hadn't gone insane, she opened the sent folder in her e-mail program and saw it—the message entitled "A Bedtime Story" had been sent to Luke's e-mail address at 9:49 p.m. on May 2.

Damn. She double-checked the recipient address against the one printed on Luke's business card, hoping she'd somehow gotten it wrong, but no, it matched exactly.

Jane reopened the message and read it with fresh eyes, imagining how Luke might actually interpret it when he read it. By the time she finished, her face was burning and she had the sort of light-headed, giddy sensation that came from blood rushing to the wrong parts of her body.

Damn.

There was only one way to interpret her message. Blatantly sexual. She hopped out of her seat and paced around the office.

Did this make her a pervert? A hopeless weirdo? Would Luke want to stop working with her after this?

No, she had to calm down. He was, after all, a more-than-willing party in their haymaking yesterday. Maybe he'd even be flattered. Or turned on.

Jane froze in her tracks. She was right back where she'd started, trying to act with restraint and ending up sending an erotic message to her bodyguard. Her professional career was going to be ruined.

She'd be labeled a hypocrite, a crackpot and a harlot.

And still, tonight, the only thing she wanted to think about was making love to Luke.

All the labels were true.

She wandered around the house, feeling jittery and feverish, until she found herself in the bathroom, staring at the tub where they had shared the most amazing sexual experience of her life.

Without thinking, she turned on the water and stripped off her clothes. She poured a bit of peppermint bath oil into the water, lit a candle, flicked off the lights, then stepped into the bath. It was nearly hot enough to scald, just the way she liked it. Jane settled inch by inch lower into the water until she was reclined back in the very spot Luke had been only a day ago. After a few minutes, she turned off the water with her foot and sighed into the silence.

With her eyes closed and her body immersed in the hot water, she could let go of the panic and let desire take control.

She slid her hands over her aching breasts, down her belly, and she paused. She didn't want her release to happen without him. But she did want to clear her head. He wasn't here tonight, and if she didn't do something about her half-crazed state of arousal, she'd never get a word written, nor would she sleep at all that night.

So, she'd be doing it for her career. Better to have a little solo pleasure than to give in to one's inappropriate desires for a man she shouldn't have been sleeping with.

That was it!

Yes.

She'd just add a chapter to *Sex and Sensibility* about the occasional need for masturbation, and she'd be demonstrating to herself how life experience only improved her outlook on relationships. It didn't have to be a contradiction.

Not a contradiction at all.

Jane slid her hands down farther, exploring, then stopped again.

This wasn't what she wanted. Feeling herself up in the tub didn't even compare to the exquisite pleasure she'd found with Luke. She expelled a ragged breath and opened her eyes. The bathroom clock read 10:42 p.m. She glared at the flickering candle, feeling a strong urge to inflict damage on something.

That was when she heard the doorbell ring.

9

The trouble with casual sex is that there is nothing casual about spreading your legs and inviting someone else in to play.

—Jane Langston,
in Chapter Five of *The Sex Factor*

LUKE STOOD at the front door he'd sworn he wouldn't enter tonight. He'd thought he might gain a little perspective on the intense emotions bombarding him where Jane was concerned if he had a little time to think. But then he'd gone home, intent on getting a full night's rest after the night before of barely sleeping at all. He'd been so keyed up about Jane, sleep seemed almost unnecessary, but missing it was catching up with him.

He'd been beat, until he sat down at his computer to do a quick e-mail check before heading off to bed. It had given him a jolt to see Jane's name and e-mail address in his inbox, and he hadn't hesitated a moment in opening the message entitled, "A Bedtime Story."

What he'd gone on to read had sealed his fate. He knew he wouldn't sleep until he'd had her, so he'd simply gotten back in his Land Cruiser and driven as fast as he could all the way to Jane's house.

He rang the doorbell a second time, and a few moments later he saw the curtain in the living-room window move.

Then he heard the click of the locks and Jane was standing before him.

She had a towel wrapped around her damp body, and her hair clung to her shoulders in wet ringlets. He caught the scent of mint emanating from her, and an instant erection strained against his jeans.

"Damn it, Jane."

She assumed a look of wide-eyed innocence. "What's wrong?"

"I got your e-mail," he said, his voice becoming strained by his arousal.

He'd imagined maybe finding her still in her street clothes, up late working or drinking coffee or whatever it was writers did. He hadn't imagined finding her like this, freshly showered and ready to be ravished.

Her lips parted, as if she meant to speak, but he caught the look of arousal in her eyes and knew. She hadn't been toying with him or joking when she'd sent that message. She'd meant every word of it.

He stepped inside the door, closing the distance between them, and when she closed and locked it, he reached out for her towel and gave it a good tug. The lavender terry cloth fell to the floor, along with Luke's stomach.

Damned if she didn't make the most tempting visual offer he'd ever seen. She didn't even flinch at her sudden nakedness. Instead, she just watched him, her chest rising and falling with each breath, her silence an invitation.

Luke pinned her against the door with his body while his hands snaked around her soft, damp waist and his mouth covered hers. In their kiss he unleashed all the desire that had built up in the last day—especially in the half hour or so since he'd read her message. His tongue brushed past her lips and found hers, and as they gasped and searched and probed, he savored the already-familiar feel of her.

He broke the kiss and looked into her eyes, tracing her jaw line with his thumb. "Do you always take a bath this late, or were you expecting me?"

"I actually didn't mean to send that message. I was going to delete it, but..." She flashed an embarrassed smile. "I accidentally hit the send button."

Luke caught a glimpse in her eyes of the panic she must have felt upon hitting the wrong button, and he grinned. "Interesting. So you needed a bath to unwind after that?"

"Um, yeah. I guess so."

An image of her, naked in that king-size tub, flashed in his mind, and the sense of urgency that centered in his groin grew.

"Did you touch yourself?" he whispered.

Jane slid her hands inside his shirt and ran her fingers up his back. "I...tried, but it wasn't the same."

When he spoke again, Luke could hear the strain in his voice. "What wasn't the same?"

"Touching myself—it didn't compare to you touching me. I tried picturing you, but it wasn't right, wasn't what I wanted."

She found the front of his pants and unfastened them. Then he felt her hands tugging his boxers down, taking him out, gripping him. He closed his eyes and let his head sag, his forehead resting on hers.

"What do you want?" he asked, just to hear the answer from her lips.

"I want you, right here, right now. Inside me."

Luke slipped one hand between her legs and found her nearly dripping wet—and not from her bath. She hadn't been kidding about wanting him.

He lifted her up and braced her against the door. And

when she wrapped her legs around him, he held her there with his hips and his erection found its home, straining at the entrance. She was so ready he slid right in, and she clung to him as he began to move inside her, going a little deeper each time.

With each thrust, she seemed to melt into him more. Her breath came out in shallow pants, and he watched a look of sheer ecstasy transform her face into one he recognized from the day before. She'd lost all her inhibitions again, changed from Jane the author into wild Jungle Jane, his perfect lover.

Something about their union felt different this time, more intense, more real. His mind nearly numb to all thought, he could only drive himself into her again and again in a frenzy brought on by the sweet sensations of her hot wet flesh encasing him.

If perfection existed, he'd found it.

Luke felt himself getting too close to the edge, buried so deep within her. He knew he wouldn't be able to stop and take his time if he didn't slow down now. But then he felt her urging him on, bucking against him. And as he increased the pace, blind to everything but the goal, she cried out. Her muscles contracted in waves, and he lost all control then. His release was blinding and hard, in time with hers. They went over the edge and into free fall in perfect unison.

Luke held on to Jane, buried his face in her hair, wishing he could somehow consume her. He wanted her all for his own, no more playing around. So what if they'd only just met—when it was right, it was right.

And this was right.

Only after he'd recovered from the spasms of pleasure and regained his ability to think clearly did he realize that all those hyperintense sensations were the result of his not wearing a condom.

Damn it, he'd never screwed up this badly before. Not even with women he'd been with long-term. He'd always prided himself on his meticulous use of protection. And now this. His gut clenched as the possible repercussions flashed in his mind.

Jane had come to her senses too and was placing butterfly kisses on his shoulder and neck.

"I forgot to wear a condom," he said.

She froze, and he felt her holding her breath. She finally released the air in a curse.

"I'm sorry. This has never happened to me before." He withdrew himself from her and let her back down on her feet.

"It's just as much my fault as yours." She looked him in the eye but seemed almost embarrassed having to discuss such a clinical issue on the heels of their lovemaking. "I take birth control pills, and I was clean on my last checkup. I haven't had sex since then, except with you."

"I'm clean too." He took her into his arms and held her against him.

Inhaling her peppermint scent, savoring the feel of her warm and naked against him, he almost forgot about the huge mistake they'd just made. Remembering, he picked her up and carried her into the bedroom, where he lay her down on the bed and then stretched out beside her. Raising up on his elbow, he realized for the first time that he was still completely dressed. He hadn't even taken off his boots.

"Whoops," he muttered as he swung his feet back off the bed, then unlaced and tugged off the boots. When he was back in place beside her, he rested one hand on her bare belly and propped his head on his other hand.

"I'm sorry about that. I guess I should have—or we should have…" She sighed.

"Slowed down?"

"Yes."

"That's the best hello I've ever gotten."

Jane giggled, then expelled a weary sigh. "It's a little scary to lose control like that."

No kidding. The pull between them was almost too strong, too intense for people who'd only just met. Luke wanted to explore the possibilities between them, but if it meant making another stupid mistake like the one they'd just made, he knew something had to give. They needed to slow down, gain a little control over their desires… Easier said than done.

His hand, resting on her belly, got an itch to move downward. His fingertips barely brushed her pubic hair, and if he just moved a few more inches south, he'd be right where he wanted to be.

Damn it. He jerked his hand away from her and rested it on his own hip, his fist clenched in frustration.

"Is something wrong?" Jane asked.

"I was just about to lose control again, that's all."

She closed her eyes and sighed. "I was hoping you'd touch me. Guess I ought to get dressed, hmm?"

Yes, she should get dressed. That would take away some of the temptation, at least. But he couldn't say it. Instead, when she began to sit up, he grabbed her by the waist and held her there beside him. His cock went from half-mast to full in an instant.

"Stay here," he heard himself say against his better judgment.

A slow smile spread across Jane's mouth as she rolled toward him and spooned against his side. "If I'm going to be naked, it's no fair that you get to keep your clothes on.''

She had a point there, dangerous as it was, but before he could make a decision, she began unbuttoning his shirt. He watched her, growing more aroused with each unfastened button. In the dim lamplight from the nightstand, he could see that her hair was beginning to dry in thick ringlets, and her creamy skin had the sort of glow in the soft light that the Old Masters had tried to capture in their subjects.

In fact, she did look like a painting, lying there beside him. A very erotic, riveting painting. Then the painting began to kiss his chest, and he decided she was right— clothes were only going to get in the way.

JANE AWOKE to the sound of Luke getting dressed. She rolled over and watched him in the moonlight for a moment before glancing at the clock. It was nearly five in the morning. He'd slept over, and she couldn't quite say why that thought gave her such a thrill—or why the thought of his leaving left her feeling vaguely panicky.

He must have heard the change in her breathing from sleeping to wakeful, and he turned to find her watching him.

''I need to go home and get ready for my meeting.''

''Can I make you some coffee?''

''No, don't get up. I'll grab something at my place.'' He sat down on the edge of the bed and leaned over, then placed a soft kiss on her lips.

She found herself actually sort of glad she'd accidentally sent that e-mail earlier. It meant she'd gotten to spend the night burning off all the sexual energy that had built up inside her, and now she felt mentally prepared to resist Luke's charms for as long as it took. She'd be able to focus completely on writing again, let him do his job of protecting her, and all would be well. Maybe she could even stop feeling like such a hypocrite all the time.

"Lock the door behind me, okay?" Luke said as he stopped in the bedroom doorway.

Jane crawled out of bed and grabbed her robe from the back of the bathroom door, then followed Luke out to the foyer. He gave her another lingering kiss before he left, one that left her imagining they were a real couple.

Jane went back to the bedroom, flopped down on the bed and sighed. She could smell Luke's sage-and-leather scent on her pillow, which wasn't going to help her put him out of her mind. Instead, she hugged the pillow to her and made a mental note to wash the sheets later, after she'd gotten another few hours of sleep.

But her brain wasn't ready to sleep. Instead, Luke's challenge to her the day they'd met popped into her head. He'd told her he wanted a chance to prove her wrong. And she'd been confident enough in her relationship theories to think he didn't stand a chance.

So now what? Had she really been so horribly wrong all these years? Had her advice to countless women been misguided and prudish? The sad truth was, she had no idea.

How *had* having sex with Luke influenced her life in the past two days? It had been incredibly pleasurable, that was for sure, but she couldn't say the impact on her had been altogether positive. For one thing, sex was suddenly all she could think about. For another, the long-term repercussions had yet to be determined, and they were bound to be negative, weren't they?

She tried to imagine what kind of future she and Luke could have—her, a woman who firmly believed in restraint and moderation in all matters sexual, and him, a guy who unleashed passions in her she didn't even know existed until two days ago. She'd never seen a relationship that started out based on sex, like theirs had, grow into a lasting love.

Maybe, subconsciously, she'd been setting them up to fail and prove her relationship theories right by hopping into bed with him right away. Maybe under other circumstances, they might have a more promising future...or not. She honestly couldn't imagine being in the same room with Luke without lusting after him. No, theirs was a relationship doomed from the start, born of sexual urges gone unchecked.

Jane tugged the covers up tight against her chest and wondered if she could continue following her desire for Luke for a short time—all in the name of field research, of course. The idea sounded unethical, at best. What she should do was just cut the sexual relationship off before it snowballed into an obsession. She'd gotten it out of her system as of last night, she hoped, at least enough to move on and let Luke be her bodyguard and nothing more. Feeling at peace with the decision, she forced all thought from her mind.

As soon as she closed her eyes, the phone rang. Jane's heart pounded double-time at the unwelcome sound, and she immediately thought of the threatening calls that had stopped since she got her number changed. No, this couldn't be. It was likely just Luke, calling from his cell phone for some reason, since he was the only person who knew she was awake.

Smiling, she picked up the phone on the nightstand. "Did you forget your underwear?"

On the line, she could hear breathing. "I know your bodyguard just left," an unnaturally low voice said.

Jane's stomach did a flip-flop, and she felt a cold chill

run through her. Her first instinct was to slam the phone down, but she sat frozen with fear. Whoever this creep was, he was watching her, and he knew she was alone.

"Where are you?" she asked, surprised at the steadiness of her own voice.

"I'm close."

Jane glanced around the room, staring at shadows. She realized as she did it that her behavior was irrational, but she couldn't control the impulse.

"Who are you?"

"I'm a concerned reader, Jane. I'm worried that all your lousy advice is going to get someone hurt. Someone like you, or your sisters."

Jane gripped the phone, fear ripping through her. "How do you know my sisters?"

"I can't tell you that, Jane, but I know who's getting it on with who, and I'm disappointed that you've started humping your bodyguard. That makes you a hypocrite and a whore."

The line went dead, and Jane sat on her bed, suddenly shivering. She tugged the covers up to her chin but felt too vulnerable just lying in bed like a frightened child. A weapon—she needed a weapon. She immediately regretted not owning a gun, but at least she had the kitchen knife she'd started keeping in her nightstand a few months ago. After she'd dug it out of her nightstand drawer and gripped it in her hand, testing the feel and weight of it, she felt a tiny bit more secure.

But suddenly, every window, every doorway, felt like a danger zone. Was he watching her now? Was he lurking somewhere close by? Why would he watch her house and call her when he knew Luke had gone, if not just to toy with her and leave her feeling vulnerable?

Jane hurriedly dressed, taking care to avoid the bedroom window. She could only hope the phone call meant he had no intention of attacking her now, because it wouldn't help him to have given her a warning.

But why had he mentioned her sisters? Why now, after all this time, and how did they fit into the picture? Another knot of fear formed in her belly as she thought of them being in danger. She may not have liked her sisters all the time, but she loved them fiercely.

Her hands shaking still, she picked up the phone and called the police. The operator promised to send an officer out right away to make sure no one was watching the house now. And then she called Luke, only to get his voice mail. As she listened to his recorded message, she decided there was no point in leaving a message when he couldn't do anything at the moment, anyway, so she hung up.

And she waited. Creeping from room to room, she peeked through the curtains, looking for any sign of her stalker, but she saw nothing.

Fifteen minutes later, a squad car pulled up and she watched a police officer get out and come to her door. Once she'd assured him she was okay and that she hadn't seen anyone around, he left to check the neighborhood and promised he'd let her know if he found anything.

Knowing the police were nearby gave Jane a slight sense of peace, until she thought of her sisters again. And then she realized she should have called them all immediately to warn them.

Jane hurried to the phone and dialed Lacey and Jennifer's apartment. They lived the closest to Jane. Once she'd called them and warned them to be on alert for anything strange, she called Heather's house.

After six rings, the answering machine picked up, and Jane left a message about the call she'd gotten. When she hung up the phone, she sat down on the edge of a chair. She was overflowing with nervous energy.

Heather probably hadn't answered the phone because it was so early in the morning. Maybe she'd heard the message and would call Jane back. Or maybe Jane should try calling again....

She hit the redial button and listened again as the phone rang six times and the answering machine picked up. This time, she left no message. She dialed again, and got the machine again. Dialed a fourth time and hung up in frustration when the answering machine clicked on yet again.

Jane put the phone down on the table and picked her knife back up, clutching it between her knees as they bounced nervously and her mind raced. She had to do something besides sit there, or she was going to go crazy.

She couldn't think of a single reason why Heather wouldn't answer the phone after so many rings, unless she was spending the night at Michael's house. But Heather had told her only last week that she and Michael were sleeping separately for the month leading up to the wedding.

A thud against the front door gave Jane a jolt of terror. The knife clattered to the floor and she scrambled to pick it up. When she peered out the front window to see what had made the noise though, all she saw was the morning paper lying on her doorstep—and the delivery lady driving on to the next house.

Her heart beating wildly, she collapsed on the couch for a moment. The sight of something as normal as the newspaper delivery lady, with the sun rising over the rooftops outside, made it feel as though the phone call hadn't really happened, as though it had just been a bad dream.

But it had been real. She had to go to Heather's house, she realized then. She wouldn't be able to relax until she knew all her sisters were safe, and maybe she could even spend the day hanging out with Heather to distract herself from her own knife-clutching, jittery nervousness.

Jane shoved her feet into some jogging shoes, brushed her teeth, and gathered her mess of curls into a ponytail. By the time she stepped outside, the morning was drenched in sunshine, and her neighbors were getting in their cars, driving off to work. No psychotic weirdos in sight, but that didn't make those first few steps toward the car any less terrifying.

On her way to her sister's house, she turned on the radio and tuned in to Jax Reed. He was busy ranting about something his producer had done to piss him off, so Jane half listened as she drove and watched her rear-view mirror obsessively.

The house Heather had recently bought with Michael, to be their home after they got married, was only a fifteen-minute drive, and when Jane pulled into the driveway, she got a sick feeling in the pit of her stomach to see Heather's Miata parked in the driveway. If her sister was home, why wasn't she answering the phone?

Jane rang the doorbell and waited a minute, then rang it again and knocked loudly just to be sure she was heard. A few moments later, she heard footsteps in the hallway, and then Heather opened the door and stood there, safe and sound, obviously having just woken from a dead sleep. She tugged a red satin robe tighter around her waist and blinked into the morning light. Her hair was standing out in odd directions, and her red lipstick from the night before was smeared on her chin. Strange. Heather always removed her makeup before bed.

"Jane? What are you doing here?"

"Why aren't you answering your phone? I've been trying to call."

"Oh. I turned the ringer off last night."

Jane heard footsteps in the hallway and decided not to ask why. Obviously Heather and Michael's little one-month stab at restraint had failed miserably.

"So nothing strange has happened here?"

"No, why?"

"Can I come in? It's a long story."

Heather's expression went from confused to panicked. "Um... Um, sure. You can come in, but... It's just that Michael's friend Bradley is staying here right now. He's using the guest room while his place is being fumigated."

Bradley?

She couldn't possibly have meant *her* Bradley... Could she?

"Where's Michael?"

"Oh, um, he does an early-morning workout at the gym on weekdays before work."

"So much for your vow of abstinence, huh?"

Heather blinked, looking first confused and then chagrined. "Yeah, so much for that," she said and stepped aside to let Jane in.

Heather's living room was a tribute to herself. A giant portrait of her hung over the sofa, and her modeling portfolio shots, from her short-lived stint as a wannabe model, occupied much of the other space on the walls. Barring that, the room was comfortable and homey, so long as you could be comfortable lounging on a white couch and resting your feet on a white rug.

Jane nervously glanced around for what she hoped was Michael's heretofore unknown *other* friend named Bradley, and she was about to sit down on the couch when *her* Bradley exited the hallway bathroom and stood shirtless, staring at her.

"Oh," she said, "hi!" But the greeting came out a bit

too enthusiastically, making her sound like a used-car salesman.

Heather's gaze darted back and forth between Bradley and Jane, until she finally said, "I was just telling Jane how Michael invited you to stay here while your apartment gets fumigated."

He flashed a huge grin. "Oh, right. I've got an…ant problem. Damn ants."

He came into the living room and sank into an over-stuffed white chair, seemingly oblivious to the fact that he was topless. Jane took the opportunity to look at his chest and found herself oddly unmoved by it. Not even the hard bulges of his pecs stirred her inner slut.

Heather mumbled something about getting dressed and making some coffee and disappeared down the hallway. Meanwhile, Jane realized exactly how much preparation she'd done to her appearance before coming over—next to none. She pictured her frizzy ponytail hair, her puffy sleep-deprived eyes and her fashion-challenged outfit and decided that if Bradley really was her dream guy, he could overlook her lackluster appearance.

After all, she'd come here to check on Heather, not flirt with a guy. But then she realized—this was her big chance!

She could simultaneously make her move with Brad, clear her thoughts of Luke and set her romantic life back on the right track in one fell swoop. It would just require a bit of bravery, a good dose of faith and an ounce of luck, and she'd have Bradley right where she wanted him.

Fate had dropped this opportunity in her lap, and she would not waste it this time. Before she left Heather's house today, she'd ask Bradley out. Maybe invite him to that new exhibit at the Dallas Museum of Art.

"So, ant problems, huh?" Jane winced at her own lousy opener. She'd have to do better than that.

"Yeah." Bradley yawned and picked up the remote control, then stared at it, obviously searching for a Power button. "Ants everywhere."

"I'd like to talk to you about something, if you don't mind." Jane's mouth went dry, but she would not back off this time.

"Okay, sure," he said, setting aside the remote. "What's up?"

"I was wondering if, sometime, maybe, um…"

Heather came down the hallway, dressed now, her bed-hair tamed and her face washed clean of makeup. "Would you both like coffee?" she asked.

"Yes," she and Bradley answered in unison.

Suddenly Jane got a weird vibe about Heather and Bradley. Heather's unwashed face when she'd answered the door, the slinky robe she'd been wearing, the absence of her fiancé in the house… Could it be that her sister and Bradley were…

No, it couldn't. No way. Heather was about to get married, and she wasn't Bradley's type at all. In college, he'd dated cool Bohemian chicks who wore black, read Sartre and smoked a lot. But still, she couldn't shake the feeling that something fishy was afoot.

When Heather was gone again, Jane turned her attention back to Bradley, back to her big opportunity to ask him out. But an image of Luke appeared in her head. Dark, dangerous, outrageously handsome Luke, making love to her against her front door, then again in her bed. *Luke, the man she'd just slept with last night.*

She felt like a major sleaze. How could she sleep with a man one night and wake up the next morning to ask another one out? Of course, she believed that with Bradley, there would be no premature sexual activity, no frantic lovemaking in the foyer. There would be a long courting process first, then love, then sex. Just as it was supposed to be.

But still. There was Luke. Looming in her mind. Confusing her emotions.

"Were you saying something?" Bradley asked.

"Oh, right. I was just wondering if you could maybe, sometime…give me the name of your exterminator. I've got an ant problem, too."

10

When in doubt, don't!

—Jane Langston,
from Chapter Fourteen of *The Sex Factor*

JANE HAD PROMISED HERSELF she wouldn't do it again. She'd made a solemn vow not to obsessively check her bestseller list status this week as each of the lists came out. Doing so only made her crazy, and a dip on any one list was enough to send her into a chocolate-eating binge.

She logged on to the Internet and checked her e-mail, all the while her Web browser beckoned. The temptation to hop on the Internet and see how her book was faring—especially on the *New York Times* list, where it had managed to hover at number nine for the past four weeks—was huge.

Instead, she opened a message from her sister wanting to know if she was okay. Ever since her early-morning visit a week ago, when she'd explained to Heather why she had stopped by, her sister had been completely freaked out. She called at least twice a day now to check on Jane, and she sent her an e-mail every night that Jane was expected to dutifully answer, reporting her well-being. It should have been annoying, but she actually found it endearing to have Heather fussing over her.

The other two triplets had joined in to a lesser extent,

and yesterday Jane's mother had even called to check up on her and ask if she'd considered getting a full-time bodyguard.

A full-time bodyguard. Just the thought of having Luke around twenty-four-seven gave Jane the willies.

But, Luke himself had suggested it when she'd told him about the call and the fact that her stalker had been watching and knew when Luke left her house. Jane had refused to have him move in and completely disrupt her life. Yet, late at night, she couldn't help but second-guess her decision. When the house was dark and Jane had nothing but her new security system to keep her feeling safe, a familiar man in the house started sounding like a pretty damn good idea.

Since she'd refused that option, Luke had insisted on increasing surveillance outside her house and checking possible connections between the stalker and her sisters. She never knew when he'd be lurking about and when he wouldn't, and at times the thought that Luke was so near drove her crazy.

Ever since the night they'd spent together a week ago, she'd made it clear to Luke that they needed to cool it, that she couldn't go on having meaningless sex with him, because it was only distracting her and creating havoc in her life. He'd been surprisingly laid back about the whole thing too, not even flirting when he stopped by to touch base with her, and keeping their self-defense lessons strictly business. She couldn't help thinking he was only continuing to prove her relationship theories correct— he'd gotten the free milk, and now he was ready to move on to the next cow.

She typed a quick reply to Heather, then deleted junk mail and closed her Internet connection, proud of herself for resisting the urge to check the bestseller lists. Now if she could just get herself to write a few pages of *Sex and Sensibility* or maybe finish her *Excess* column that was due next week, she'd really have reason to be proud.

She opened up the document and scrolled to the end, where she'd last been working. But the damn title was glaring at her again. *Sex and Sensibility.* Maybe she needed to change it, since sensibility wasn't a quality she seemed to possess and therefore wasn't exactly qualified to be writing about.

She winced at the memory of her awkward encounter with Bradley, a prime example of her lack of sensibility. A woman with any kind of sense would simply be straightforward, ask him out, and see what happened. Jane, on the other hand, had silently pined after him since college, squandering each and every opportunity she had to express her interest. Why hadn't she seen her own weakness before now? And what was the matter with her, that she couldn't move beyond a casual acquaintance to something deeper, something real?

Glancing at the clock, she noticed it was past time when the mail was usually delivered, so she hopped up and went to the front door to check the mailbox, happy for the opportunity to be distracted from her train of thought. A box sat on her doormat—a box that strangely didn't have an address, yet it was taped up with her name printed across the top. No other information and no postage. Just her name.

Jane stood frozen in the doorway, her stomach revolting at the package. Whatever it was, she knew it was from *him*. She slammed the door and locked it, then went to the phone and called Luke.

He said he'd come right over and made her promise not to touch the package, so while she waited for him to arrive, Jane paced around the house, her knife in one hand and her heart thudding wildly in her chest.

When Luke arrived, she opened the door for him. He eyed the package on her doormat, then pulled out a pair of plastic gloves from his pocket.

"You didn't see anyone unusual around today?" he said by way of greeting.

"Besides that creepy guy wearing a black ski mask and wielding an ax? No."

Luke gave her his half-lidded look of forced patience. "Do you always make jokes when you're scared?"

Jane shrugged. "Pretty much."

After slipping the gloves over his hands, he knelt beside the box and cut the tape with a pocket knife. Once open, the contents of the box became immediately apparent—it was stacked full of magazines. And judging by the covers on top, they were all graphic, hard-core porn. Jane caught a glimpse of the covers and her stomach revolted again. She turned her attention to the white envelope Luke had just pulled out of the box.

"Looks like he left you a note, too." He slid open the envelope and removed a piece of paper with what looked like more of the same childish handwriting that was on the outside of the box. "I think he's writing with his other hand—the one he doesn't normally write with."

"Either that or I'm being stalked by a first-grader."

Luke didn't seem to hear her. He frowned as he read the letter, and Jane's queasy stomach took a turn for the worse.

"What now?"

He turned the paper around and held it up for her to read.

Dear Bitch,
I thought you could use a little help jump-starting

your sex life. Maybe reading these will give you some ideas for your next book.

Jane tore her gaze away from the letter before she could read any more. She didn't want to see it, or the magazines, or her front steps. She just wanted to go hide in the house and never come out again.

"I'll call the police," Luke said, his expression grim.

Jane watched as he placed the letter on top of the magazines and closed the box. Her stomach churned, so she wandered into the living room and slumped on the couch. She could hear Luke on the kitchen phone, explaining the situation to someone, and a minute later he hung up and came into the room.

"Are you okay?" he asked.

"Oh, I'm great now that I'm all stocked up on summer reading material."

Luke frowned. "I'm going to do more frequent surveillance, just so you'll know. I won't be telling you when it's happening, but if you need to get hold of me, my cell phone or pager will be best."

Jane closed her eyes, trying to decide if having Luke lurking about outside her house made her feel safer or not.

Or not. What it made her feel was off balance, out of control, at any moment likely to lose the last scrap of her sanity from wanting him. Completely insensible was what she felt.

JANE, PERCHED ON the velvet dressing-room couch, took in the sight of her sister in the fitted wedding dress. She looked perfect, and inexplicably tears welled up in Jane's eyes. Suddenly, they were little girls and playing "wed-

ding day" with white towels over their heads as veils,
pretending to walk down the aisle by doing a herky-jerky
march down the hallway.

Her little sister was getting married. The truth of it
struck her deeper than it ever had before, and she blinked
back the sentimental tears.

"What do you think?" Heather asked.

"It's beautiful."

Heather admired herself in the mirror for another moment, then turned to the saleslady. "Could you please
leave for a few minutes? I need to talk to my sister privately."

The same saleslady they'd encountered on Jane's first
visit to Here Comes the Bride flashed a thin smile and
said something about calling if any more of her assistance
was needed. When she was gone, Heather's cheery expression disappeared.

"Janie, I've got big problems—"

Jane resisted the urge to scream. No more passing out
bad advice to unsuspecting women, and no more playing
All-Knowing Big Sister. She had to put her foot down
now, before she did any more damage or drove herself
crazy. "Stop right there. Whatever the big problem is, I
don't want to hear it."

"But—"

"You think I'm such an expert, but the truth is, I don't
know what the hell I'm talking about. You're better off
solving the issue yourself, without my advice, whatever it
is."

Heather stared at her, her mouth gaping open, her brow
in a state of near creasing. "But, I'm thinking about not
getting married."

Jane tried not to roll her eyes at the news. Heather loved
drama, and what could be more dramatic for a bride than

prewedding jitters? She wasn't buying it. Heather was clearly head over heels for Michael, and she'd been planning her own wedding ever since their childhood towel-wearing days.

"Everybody gets scared before their wedding. But like I said, I'm not handing out any more advice. If you've got issues, you need to talk to Michael about them, not me."

Okay, so she was being a little coldhearted, but Heather would be better off for it. Jane didn't have an ounce of proof that any of her advice had ever brought anyone lasting happiness.

Her sister gave her one last doubtful glance, but then shrugged her shoulders in defeat. "I guess you're right."

"How do the shoes look with the dress?" Jane asked, eager to distract Heather with her favorite subject.

She picked up the skirt of her dress to reveal a pair of strappy white satin heels. "Aren't these the best? It's a shame to hide them under a dress. I might wear them to the rehearsal dinner, too."

Jane nodded her approval, but Heather was too busy admiring her feet in the mirror to notice.

After Jane tried on her altered bridesmaid dress to make sure it fit, they said their goodbyes, and she found herself driving home alone and wanting to be anything but. She'd driven the route from downtown to her house often enough that she went on autopilot and found herself thinking of Luke, until she took the highway exit closest to her neighborhood.

After a few blocks, she got a creepy feeling. Jane peered into the rearview mirror and frowned at the headlights that had been following her since the highway. Maybe she was being overly paranoid, but it sure did seem like she was being followed. She tried to make out the car, but it was too dark. All she could see were head-lights.

She traveled through her neighborhood with a growing sense of dread, and when she came to the turn onto her street, she hesitated. The car was still behind her.

No, she was just freaking out over nothing. She'd pull into her driveway and the car would keep going. It was probably just one of her neighbors wishing she'd quit driving so damn slow. She switched on her left turn signal at the last second and made the turn. The car behind her followed without signaling. That, Jane decided, was her cue to call Luke.

Her heart raced as she kept driving past her house and weaved back through the neighborhood toward the main road. She fumbled in her purse until she found her cell phone, then punched in Luke's number with one hand while she steered with the other.

The car that had been following her made a right turn onto a side street, and she could see as it turned that it was actually a blue minivan. Probably a soccer mom on her way home from a late trip to the grocery store. Jane suddenly felt like a monumental idiot.

Luke answered after three rings, sounding like he'd been asleep.

"It's Jane. I'm sorry, I thought I was being followed, but the car just disappeared. Temporary insanity, I guess."

"Where are you?" His voice had gone from groggy to dangerously clear in an instant.

"I'm in my neighborhood right now, but the car is gone."

"How long did it follow you?"

"A few miles, maybe." Jane pulled over to the curb and let her car idle. She exhaled all her pent-up tension. "I'm not sure, though—at least since my exit on the highway."

"It's good that you called, whether the car was following you or not. You might have scared him off by picking up your cell phone."

Jane imagined herself going home alone, still wondering. She hated the constant feeling of vulnerability that hung over her these days, a feeling that someone else was in control, and that she was constantly waiting for something bad to happen.

"Should I go to the police station, just to be safe?"

"Do you know how to get there?"

"Um, no."

"How about a fire station?"

"No."

"I'm not sure where the closest one is to you. Drive to my house."

Jane blinked. Had she been waiting for him to invite her over? It suddenly felt as if she had. She bit her lip and wondered if she could really resist temptation once she was in his lair, in that private space of his she'd never entered before.

"I...could go to my parents' house, or my sister's."

He was silent for a moment. "No, come here. I'd feel better if I knew you were safe."

"But—"

"No buts. If you need anything from home, I'll go back with you later to get it."

She couldn't say no. What she wanted most right now was to feel safe. "How do I get there?"

As Luke gave her directions, she scribbled them down on a notepad, then repeated them to him.

"Call me if you have the slightest problem, okay?"

Jane assured him she would and hung up the phone. It felt good to have a big, burly guy looking out for her, even if he was getting paid to do it.

She made her way back toward the highway, peering at Luke's directions in the dim glow of the streetlights. It wasn't until she was about to exit the highway again that she got the feeling she was still being followed. Jane took the exit and looked around for a busy store to duck into and make another call to Luke. There was a brightly lit diner half a block down, so she headed toward it, and the car followed.

Jane kept her eyes on it and saw that it was painted blue—the same shade as the minivan she'd spotted earlier. It also had the large windshield and short nose of a minivan. She couldn't make out a driver.

Her palms grew damp on the steering wheel, and at the next stoplight, she picked up the cell phone and dialed Luke again.

"It's me. Do you know the All-night Diner a few blocks from your house?"

"Yeah, what's wrong?"

"I think I'm being followed by the same person again. I'll meet you at the diner, okay?"

"Jane, there's a police station three more stoplights down from there on the right side. Go there right now. That's where I'll meet you."

He sounded dead serious, like this was an even worse situation than she'd feared. Jane listened to the line go dead as she pulled through the green light and glanced back again at the car behind her.

Her mouth went dry, and she decided to focus on counting stoplights instead of staring in her rearview mirror. So it wasn't until she heard the sickening scrape of metal and felt her car being pushed from the side that she realized she was being run off the road.

Jane fought to control the steering wheel as she caught sight of the blue minivan veering a second time into the side of her car. She steered right, hit a curb, and bounced up onto a grassy area, where she sat and watched the minivan speed through a red light and send several cars screeching to a halt. In her shock, she managed to notice that the vehicle had no license plates.

With shaking hands, she reached for her cell phone a third time and dialed 9-1-1. As she explained to the operator what had happened, a man pulled up in a pickup truck, got out, and peered into her window.

"Are you okay?" he called out, and she nodded, trying hard not to cry.

She called Luke next, told him where she was, and then sank her head onto the steering wheel and practiced taking deep, cleansing breaths. She couldn't let fear control her.

Easier said than done.

No matter how brave she pretended to be on the surface, she couldn't shake the feeling that her life had slipped from her grasp. It was in the control of a lunatic and a hunky bodyguard.

Five minutes later, a police car arrived and took a statement from her, and when she'd just finished talking to the officer, Luke pulled up.

He spent several minutes discussing her case with the police officer before coming to Jane's car, where she'd sunk into the driver's seat, and leaning down to peer at her with his signature intensity.

"You're really not hurt?"

"No, just my car," she said, nodding toward the sizeable dent stretching along the left rear side of her dear old Mercedes.

"That, we can fix." He took her hand and pulled her up from the seat. "Until we catch this guy, we need to consider more serious protection measures for you."

Jane squeezed her eyes shut. More serious protection

measures meant more loss of control. All she wanted was her old, comfortable routine back. She wanted to be able to write again, and she wanted to be able to go shopping without having to fear for her life.

"Do we have to discuss this right here, right now?"

He enclosed her in his arms and pulled her against his chest. "No, you're right. Let's go back to my place. Will you be okay following me?"

Jane inhaled the scent of his leather jacket and nodded.

A few minutes later, she was following his sport utility vehicle through a respectable old neighborhood of single family homes. It looked as if most of them had been built around the turn of the century and restored in recent years. After a couple of blocks, she followed Luke into the driveway of an old Georgian-style house that wasn't at all what she would have expected him to live in.

Luke, with his black boots and leather jackets, hadn't struck her as an upscale historic-home kind of guy. But it probably fit with his income. He couldn't have been earning a modest living providing security for the moneyed folks of Dallas. Now she recalled little details about him—the expensive Swiss watch, his perfectly manicured hands—that were much more congruent with this upscale community than his rebel image.

Jane parked in an empty spot next to him and got out of the car, then scanned the area, unable to stop looking for stalkers or renegade minivans. She locked her car and then checked each door to make sure they were really locked, all the while aware of Luke watching her.

"You're safe now, Jane. You can relax."

"Easy for you to say."

He closed the distance between them. "No, it's not. I would never forgive myself if anything happened to you.

Tonight was a failure on my part. I should have been more vigilant about your schedule.''

"How could you have known some lunatic was going to run me off the road tonight?"

"It's my job to keep that from happening."

Jane considered arguing, but it seemed pointless. He took her hand and led her up a short flight of stairs to his front door. Once inside, she couldn't stop marveling at her surroundings.

This was where Luke lived. It was hardly what she had imagined. She'd pictured a spare bachelor pad, complete with empty pizza boxes and dirty socks on the floor. Maybe a recliner in front of the big-screen TV.

But there wasn't a big-screen TV in sight, nor a recliner, nor an empty pizza box or a single dirty sock. Instead, the place exuded a warm, masculine elegance that Jane had seen only in decorating magazines. It was clearly a guy's place—but a guy who cared about his surroundings, who paid attention to details and who was as meticulous as he was tasteful.

She thought of her own messy office and hallway littered with unopened boxes and felt a wave of chagrin. She'd had no idea she was revealing her messy side to a neat freak when she invited Luke in.

She surveyed the shiny oak floors, the pale beige rugs, the earth-toned furniture, the spare but stylish framed prints carefully placed in just the right spots on the walls. Black accent pieces broke up all the earth tones and balanced out the whole look.

Jane turned to Luke and smiled as she shrugged off her jacket. "I had no idea you were into interior decorating."

He hung his jacket on a coat rack by the door, then took hers and did the same. "I'm not."

"You have a gorgeous home."

"I just buy stuff I like and put it in here. Pretty simple."

She shook her head. "You're being modest."

"Okay, well, I also hired a decorator to come here and put all the stuff in the right places for me, and she added a few things to pull the whole place together."

Jane blinked. Luke Nicoletti was full of surprises—definitely the first guy she'd ever met to hire an interior decorator for his bachelor pad.

"You have lots of women to impress, I'm sure."

"Clients, actually. I have my office here at home, so if a client stops by, the place needs to look presentable."

"Aha." That, at least, made sense. "I didn't know you worked from home."

He shrugged. "It's convenient. I get my clients almost exclusively by referrals, and I come to them—they don't usually come to me."

"Except when they're being run off the road by minivans."

"Exactly." He smiled and pulled her to him, wrapping her in his arms. She felt him place a kiss on her head, and she wanted to melt.

But she couldn't. There was still the little matter of her needing to resist his charms at all costs to retain her sanity.

"Would you like something to drink?"

"You have coffee?"

"I'll have some made in a few minutes. Have a seat and relax."

Jane sank into the impossibly comfortable sofa. When Luke disappeared into the kitchen, she took the opportunity to peer under the couch for dust bunnies. There were none. She tried to picture him dust-mopping the floors and couldn't. Okay, so he must have hired a cleaning service, too. That, she could picture.

She kicked off her shoes and stretched out on the sofa, suddenly so weary she couldn't keep her eyes open. Finally, she was someplace that felt safe.

LUKE PLACED the two coffee cups on the table and was about to ask Jane if she wanted a sandwich, when he noticed her asleep on his couch. He sat down in a chair across from her and studied the way the worry lines had disappeared from her face in sleep. She was beautiful in a whole different way when she looked so peaceful. Peacefulness—not a quality she possessed when awake. Alive, passionate and vibrant, yes. But Jane was about as peaceful as a thunderstorm, and he suspected that a large part of her keyed-up manner had to do with being harassed and stalked. Now he could see a certain innocence in her face, something that was disguised behind attitude and sarcasm when she was awake, and he found himself falling for her for a whole new set of reasons.

Falling for her. He was getting used to the idea, but he had no way of presenting it to Jane. She'd run away as fast as she could, and he couldn't have that. He needed her nearby to keep her safe, and so to keep her safe, he had to keep his feelings to himself.

Luke went to the closet to get a blanket, then returned and spread it over Jane as gently as he could. But when the blanket touched her, she was startled awake, and she sat bolt upright, blinking into the lamplight.

"What happened?"

"You dozed off for a few minutes—that's all."

"Where…" She frowned, surveying her surroundings, and after a moment she seemed to remember she was at his house. The tension drained from her brow, and she sat back.

"You're welcome to use my bed, if you want to go to sleep."

The offer sounded loaded with implications, even to his ear. He hadn't meant anything by it, but when it came to Jane, there was no such thing as an innocent invitation to his bed.

She eyed him warily. "Will you be sleeping there, too?"

"I'm not sleeping on the floor." He would have happily slept on the couch, but the opportunity to bait her was irresistible.

"I'll just sleep on the couch then, if you don't mind."

Luke stood up from his chair and went to the couch, where he sat down beside her. He was tired of the sexual tug-of-war, and they were going to settle this matter once and for all. She tried to scoot away, but he wrapped one arm around her waist and held her beside him.

"You want to sleep with me, and you know we're great together, so why do you keep fighting it?"

"I'm not fighting anything. I just came to my senses."

"And realized you hate having great sex?"

She fought to keep a straight face. "That's not it at all. I was doing exactly what I advise other women not to do—letting my sexual urges control me, sacrificing emotional intimacy for sexual intimacy, generally behaving like an idiot."

"Basically, it pissed you off that I proved you wrong."

"No!" Jane expelled an exasperated breath. "I mean, no, you didn't prove me wrong, so I had nothing to be upset about. On the contrary—you proved my theories correct."

"How do you figure?"

"Our relationship was based totally on sex. There was no emotional development."

"Speak for yourself. You didn't give us a chance."

"No, *we* didn't give us a chance, by hopping into bed nearly the moment we met."

Luke wasn't sure whether he wanted to shake her or kiss her senseless. If they kept going like this, they'd just argue in circles all night. He turned her face toward him and dipped his head down, covering her mouth with his. It didn't take a relationship expert to figure out that this was the most pleasant way to stop an argument.

He'd expected her to resist, and she did. For all of two seconds. Until the automatic electricity between them turned on, and she tilted her head to deepen the kiss. Luke felt her tongue slip past his, felt the urgency of her embrace, and knew that she was just as desperate for him as he was for her.

But after a few moments she stiffened and pulled back.

"See, we're doing it again. This proves my point exactly. Every time there's a chance for emotional growth between us, we get physical instead."

"Maybe I was just kissing you to remind you of the way it feels."

"Just because something feels good isn't a reason to do it."

"True, but we're not talking about sniffing coke or torturing puppy dogs."

Jane stood up and crossed her arms over her chest as she walked to the window. She stood there, looking out at the view of the front yard lit up by lights in the bushes and on the front porch, and Luke imagined she was probably trying to decide how best to prove herself right.

Finally she turned and looked at him again. "I'd be

lying if I said the intensity of the sexual attraction between us didn't scare me a little.''

"Don't you get it? It's not just sexual. Two people aren't drawn together as strongly as we are unless there's something more to it than hormones.''

"I have to disagree with you there. If it were more than a sexual attraction, we'd be able to control ourselves and let the relationship develop naturally—but of course we can't, because there's nothing natural about the way our relationship began in the first place, with you wanting to prove me wrong.''

Luke felt pressure building between his eyes. He closed them and took a deep breath. "Jane, I never would have made that comment seriously. I propositioned you because I was attracted to you, plain and simple.''

She frowned. "You swear this wasn't just about proving my book wrong?''

"I swear.''

"I still think we've allowed our sexual attraction to stunt the growth of any emotional intimacy we might have had.''

"You're talking like a relationship guru now. It's a load of crap when applied to real life.''

Okay, so maybe he should have kept the "crap" comment to himself. Jane's cheeks took on an angry red glow.

"Maybe I should go. We're just going to argue all night.''

She started toward the door, but Luke stood up and blocked her way. "Wouldn't you rather argue with me than get run off the road by a crazed lunatic?''

"You've got a point there.'' She turned and stalked over to an armchair, which she flopped herself onto.

He sat on the coffee table in front of her, forcing her to look at him. "I'm sorry about that last comment. It was rude and inappropriate. What I should have said is that you can theorize all you want, but theories don't always apply to real-life relationships."

"Apology accepted," she said, looking like she'd still enjoy giving him a good kick in the shin.

"Sometimes you've just got to stop looking for expert advice—even if it's your own—and take a few risks. Live your life according to how you feel in your gut."

"Sounds like something you read in a book." She flashed a grin.

"Didn't I tell you I'm writing one? It's going to be all about how to get your woman to stop reading relationship books and start sleeping with you again."

She rolled her eyes. "Okay, okay. Let's call a truce for tonight."

Luke extended his hand to her, and she slipped her own hand into his. He drew it to his lips and kissed it, then turned it palm up and let his fingers trace the lines there. When he'd placed a lingering kiss on her palm, he looked up at Jane to find her watching him with a dreamy look in her eyes.

It made him sick to have to wipe that look away with the subject he had to broach next. "We need to talk about what happened tonight, and the implications of it."

Jane tugged her hand away and tucked it between her knees. "Can't we just talk about that tomorrow?"

"Would you feel comfortable going home alone tonight?"

She frowned and gave the question some thought. "No."

"Then yes, we need to talk about it now."

"I don't really expect you to let me stay here. I thought maybe you could go with me to my place to pick up some things, and then I'd go to my sister's apartment for the night.''

"There was the box of porn last week, and now the incident tonight—this is getting more serious.''

"What are you saying? That I need twenty-four-hour bodyguard service?'' She flashed a weary half smile, but Luke kept his expression neutral. He didn't consider Jane's safety a matter to be taken lightly.

"I think we need to consider it.''

Her smile faded instantly. "So what? You follow me everywhere, go with me to the bathroom, escort me to the post office?''

"You get to use the bathroom by yourself, but for a while, until this guy is caught,'' Luke paused, trying to decide if a straightforward approach was best right now. Was she prepared for what he had to suggest? He could only hope so. "I think it would be wise to let me move in with you.''

11

Women are not sexual receptacles that exist solely for your pleasure, and if you can't figure that out, you should probably be looking for your dates in a barnyard.

—Jane Langston,
in the August issue of *Excess* magazine

TWENTY-FOUR-HOUR *bodyguard duty.*

Jane flung a pair of red bikini underwear into the laundry basket and scanned the bedroom for other carelessly discarded garments on the floor. How on earth could she survive one night alone with Luke, without sleeping with him—let alone an indefinite number of nights? The whole idea was preposterous, and yet, what other choice did she have? The other option was to live in constant fear, afraid even to go grocery shopping or to the gym, her writing ability crippled by the worry that outside her house lurked a lunatic.

And then there was the Luke-in-her-house option. Living here with her, sleeping on her fold-out couch, sitting at her breakfast table in the morning, lurking about when she needed to work. At least she might be able to work, with some sense of protection.

At least she could feel safe.

She hadn't given him an answer immediately. In the

end, she'd fallen asleep on his couch the night before, and he'd driven her back home this morning. He'd told her he would be back by noon, and he'd expect a decision.

Jane carried a basket load of laundry to the washer and dumped it in, then started the machine before she realized she hadn't added soap. Her annoyance grew as she dug all the wet clothes back out and added the powder soap, then flung everything back in.

Her choices were to live in constant fear, or to live with the greatest sexual temptation of her life, right here inside her house, twenty-four hours a day. She'd been so tough for the past week, so doggedly resistant to Luke's charms, she had actually been gaining her professional confidence back. But she knew that most of her resistance was aided by her avoidance of him whenever possible, and if he lived here, even for a short while, there would be no avoiding Luke.

She'd be stuck with him, stuck with her overwhelming sexual feelings—and if she slept with him again, stuck with the proof that she was a fraud as a relationship expert.

When Jane heard the doorbell ring, the sound sent a jolt of fear through her. She remembered the disgusting box of magazines from the week before, the feeling of utter violation she'd been overcome with upon seeing the contents of the box. Then her thoughts turned to last night, getting run off the road by someone who clearly meant it as a warning, and she knew. She had to let Luke move in.

She peered through the living-room window and saw him standing on her doorstep, so she opened the door and let him in.

"You look a little frazzled," he said as a greeting.

"I've been cleaning."

He grinned, glancing around. "I can tell. Something you don't do often, huh?"

"I tried to talk the lawn guy into coming in and cleaning naked, but he said he doesn't do windows, so I was planning to ask you next."

Luke let his gaze travel the length of her and back up. "I've got no problem with getting naked for you, but I'm not going to clean your windows, either. Not unless you ask me real nicely."

"How about twenty-four-hour bodyguard duty. Will you do that naked?"

He laughed. "Does that mean you're willing to let me move in?"

"I'm willing to try it. Temporarily. For a few days."

"I want you to commit to this until your stalker is caught."

Jane sighed. "And what if he isn't?"

"He will be. Soon."

"I say we reevaluate the situation on at least a week-by-week basis. Maybe he'll find some other hobby besides harassing me, and you won't need to be around me all the time."

Luke took a step toward her and reached out, slipping his hands around her waist. He tugged her against him, and Jane couldn't muster the will to resist. Her body melted into his.

"Maybe I want to be around you all the time," he said.

Jane got a queasy feeling in her stomach. Her heart felt divided in two—one part of it hanging on to the security blanket of all her hopes about the possibilities with Bradley, the other part wondering what could become of her and Luke, if she gave them a chance. But she was so close to asking Bradley out, after all these years, and she couldn't possibly ignore the opportunity to finally date her dream guy.

Could she? Why did she have so much trouble mustering up the energy to pine after him these days? And why was it so hard to produce a picture of him in her head?

Jane swallowed the sudden dryness in her mouth. "You just want to be around here all the time so you can keep me from writing another book that might ruin your sex life again."

He smiled. "There's that, too."

Jane squirmed out of his grasp and tried to laugh off the situation, but she couldn't shake the sick feeling in her gut. She didn't want Luke to get emotionally involved, if she wasn't willing to do the same. And yet she felt a tug deep inside herself to go wherever their attraction took them.

It was just the sexual attraction muddling her thoughts. That was all.

"So, I guess you'll need to go home and get some of your belongings or something? How does this twenty-four-hour bodyguard thing work, anyway?"

Luke shrugged. "However we want it to work. I've already got the bags out in the car."

"You didn't know if I was going to say yes."

"I figured I'd do whatever it took to convince you." He loomed over her, and then he reached out to slide one hand along her jawline. "I have my methods of persuasion."

Oh, yes, he did. Her body came alive with liquid sensation at the look in his eyes. She forgot everything except the fact of his body, and hers, so close together.

Luke slid his hand lower and cupped her breast, let his thumb tease her erect nipple. Jane felt herself instinctively arching her back, and she did a mental headshake.

This was all wrong.

It took every ounce of her willpower to place her hand over his and move it away from her breast.

"Believe me, I know all about your methods of persuasion," she said, her voice strained.

"But you've become immune?"

If only. Jane slipped out of Luke's grasp and put some distance between them.

"Maybe."

"I guess I'll grab my suitcase then."

Once he was out the front door, tension drained from Jane's shoulders. She'd barely survived five minutes trying to resist Luke. How could she possibly resist him for days or weeks? She paced across the living room, chewing her thumbnail. She had to think of something fast. Something that would get to him, that would appeal to his sense of…duty. Yes, above all else, she sensed, Luke really did want to keep her safe.

And that thought made her insides melt all over again. Having a guy like Luke feel so strongly about her safety gave her a ridiculously giddy feeling. But he was simply doing his duty, she reminded herself. Doing what he was being paid to do, what it was every good bodyguard's job to do.

And if Luke thought it would distract him from his job to pursue their sexual attraction any further, then she was pretty sure he'd be willing to put the brakes on. That, she suspected, was the key.

Luke reappeared in her doorway carrying a black suitcase and a black leather overnight bag. And the question suddenly arose in her head—where to put his stuff?

"Um, I guess you can put your things…in my bedroom."

"I could store them in your office, if that would make you more comfortable."

"No! I mean, I use that space to work, and if it's disrupted in any way, I tend to get a little cranky."

He raised an eyebrow. "A suitcase would make you cranky?"

"Don't ask. It's a creativity thing."

"Okay, so I'll use the bedroom." And he took off down the hallway, headed for her private space.

Jane wondered if she should offer to clear out a few drawers. An image of his Jockeys mingling with her intimates popped into her head, and she banished it before her traitorous thoughts could turn erotic. She should, at the very least, clear out some room in the closet, so she hurried down the hallway after him.

"I'll make some space for you in the closet," she said.

He was unzipping his suitcase on the bed. "You don't have to."

Jane went to the closet and began pushing aside clothes. "I forgot to clear out a drawer, but I can—" She didn't get to finish the sentence, because when she turned back to Luke, she found the solid wall of his chest.

He grasped her by the waist. "Are you going to let me move into your bed, too?"

Jane took a deep breath—through her mouth, to avoid inhaling his intoxicating scent.

Now. She had to lay down the ground rules pronto.

"Luke, if you're going to be living here, we have to stop this."

"Stop what?"

"This sexual *thing* between us. It's going to get out of control if we don't stop it now—and how will you do your job properly if you're constantly distracted by some sexual attraction?"

His expression went blank, but she could tell she'd touched a nerve. "Maybe you've got a point," he finally said.

"Just helping you do your job." She flashed a cheesy smile.

Luke shook his head. "You're just trying to make me feel guilty with this distraction excuse."

Damn it, he was sharp. "No, I'm afraid for my life. You're the only person standing between me and some whack-job who sends me threatening letters and pornography and tries to run me off the road with his minivan. I just want to make sure you have your mind on the job."

Luke backed away and turned to the window. He gripped the wrought-iron bedpost and leaned against it, appearing deep in thought.

"Do you really think I've been distracted?"

"I think you've done a fine job so far, but if the threat is greater now, and if we need to be more careful, I think that includes not going at it hot and heavy every time we get the chance."

She refrained from pointing out that that's exactly what she would have advised in her books or her column, that she was only following her own good advice for once where Luke was concerned.

Luke smiled. "How about just every other time we get the chance, then?"

"Stop it!" She tried to keep serious, but she couldn't help grinning.

"You're right. We can't afford distractions right now." He turned back to his suitcase and began removing clothes.

That was easy—far too easy. Something was up, but she couldn't guess what it might be. Luke was probably trying to use a reverse psychology tactic on her, and if so, he was way out of his league.

Jane watched as he took shirts and pants to the closet and placed them on empty hangers. When nothing remained in the suitcase except underwear and socks, he slid the case into an empty space on the closet floor and shut the door. Just glancing around, it was impossible to tell that her bodyguard had just taken up residence in her house.

"My couch pulls out into a bed, so you can sleep there at night."

He tossed her a wry look. "How convenient."

"I bought it thinking someday I'd have visitors and would need a place to put them."

She definitely hadn't been thinking her visitor would be a live-in personal protection expert with a sexual agenda.

Luke opened his overnight bag and pulled out a shaving kit, toothbrush and toothpaste. "Will I be using the hallway bathroom?"

"Um…yes." She hadn't quite imagined how dizzy it would make her feel to think of Luke showering, shaving, brushing his teeth…every morning, right here in her own private space. It would become his private space too, for whatever short time he was here. The sight of his toothbrush felt oddly intimate in a way that nothing else he'd unpacked so far had.

And intimacy, Jane realized in a sudden, cruel burst of understanding, was what she feared most.

She'd become a pro at keeping people at arm's length, making sure she didn't get hurt, even substituting her career for real relationships. She'd been working so hard to prove to herself and everyone else that she deserved recognition, she'd managed to convince herself that having a successful career was the same as having a successful personal life.

The question now was, did she want her personal life to include Luke?

"THE NUMBER ONE THING to remember, when it comes to self-defense, is that you can always fight back."

Jane stood a few feet in front of Luke, arms at her sides, looking as enthusiastic about their lesson as a beached jellyfish. He'd been after her to continue their lessons where they'd left off with the last one, but she had produced excuse after excuse about why she couldn't do it. Today, when he'd caught her surfing an online auction site instead of working on her next book like she'd claimed to have been doing, he insisted they have a lesson immediately, pointing out that her safety was infinitely more important than her finding bargains on junk.

Living with Jane was proving even more difficult than Luke had suspected. Not only had he failed to make any progress in the case, but he'd also managed to go damn near insane with wanting her. He'd been living in her house for nearly two weeks, and they'd been two of the longest weeks of his life.

He would have been happy to just have her company at mealtimes, but she went out of her way to avoid him, and whenever they were together and he was starting to think she'd relax and enjoy his presence, she'd make some excuse about having work to do and slip away to her office. The only positive thing that had come from his moving in was that there hadn't been a single instance of harassment in the two weeks that he'd been there.

Luke couldn't decide if the lull was due to the harasser deciding Jane was too difficult a target now or because that's what he wanted them to believe—probably the latter, which was why he insisted on the self-defense lessons.

"Tell me what you do if your attacker has a gun."

"I duck behind the nearest armored vehicle?"

"You run! So long as he doesn't have you under his control, you run, because the chances are slim that he can hit a running target. Even if he does hit you, it probably won't be in a vital spot."

"Probably?"

"If you get to choose between being raped and murdered and being shot in the shoulder, I'm betting you'll take the shoulder wound."

Jane paled noticeably. "If those are my only two choices…"

Luke continued to quiz her on lessons they'd gone over during their first session. "Where are the most vulnerable spots on your attacker?"

"His groin, of course."

"And?"

She shrugged, clearly still not into the lesson. "His stock portfolio?"

"His eyes and throat. You go for them with whatever you have available—fingers, keys, a pen, a stick from the ground, whatever."

"Okay, I remember all this from the first lesson. Are you happy?"

"Why are you acting like you'd rather have teeth removed than review this stuff with me?"

But he knew the answer as soon as he posed the question. She was afraid of getting physically close to him, afraid of the inevitable sparks. He resisted a smile. This, he knew, meant his strategy had been successful. She might have thought giving him that crock of a line about their needing to focus on her safety without being distracted by their sexual attraction had worked on him, but he'd seen right through it.

He'd simply had a strategy of his own to counter with. He figured, what would it hurt to let her believe he wasn't going to try seducing her anymore? It would only give him more time to make her see that what they had was different, that it was far deeper than just sexual.

Jane was afraid of something he couldn't quite put his finger on. Something about having him in her house, sharing her closet, brushing his teeth in her guest bathroom—he knew it scared her. If he had to guess, he'd say she was afraid of the intimacy those issues symbolized. And he was determined to break down that wall. A little self-defense training could get things rolling, and it was something she desperately needed anyway.

"Okay, I'll try to be an eager student, I promise."

Luke had hauled a large blue vinyl-coated training mat out of the back of his SUV, and it was spread on the floor beneath them, with the coffee table pushed out of the way to make room for it.

"Let's get started with a few standard self-defense moves. I want you to pretend you're an attacker coming at me."

She balked. "Me? Attack you? I'm all out of breath-freshener spray."

He shot her a look. "Just lunge at me. Go for a vulnerable spot."

She stood there, motionless.

Okay, so he needed to provide her with a little motivation for attacking him. "I should have known you wouldn't have the spine to take this seriously."

Anger flashed in her eyes, and she made a lunge for him, her knee coming up to make contact with his groin.

He grabbed her leg and flipped her onto her back, and a second later he was on top of her.

"Now, care to take this a little more seriously?"

"Yeah, but could we just get to the point here?"

He peeled himself off of her, careful to keep his mind focused on the task at hand and not on how badly he wanted her body pressed against his. There would be time for that soon enough. He helped Jane to her feet, and she eyed him warily.

"Don't worry. I won't topple you again—at least not for a few more minutes. Right now I want to go over two self-defense moves you can do without being armed. I'm going to pretend to attack you from behind, and then I'll talk you through the moves."

Jane nodded, and Luke approached her quickly and locked one arm around her neck while securing her arms against her body with his other arm.

"Now, what's your first instinct?" he asked.

"Scream for help?"

"Good idea, but I can easily cut off your air supply. Then what?"

"I elbow you in the ribs, kick you, stomp your toes?"

"Yes, try all of those things. First though, if an attacker grabs you like this, try to stay calm. If you can, move your head so that your chin is pointing toward the crook of his arm. That will give you a little more air supply."

Jane did as he'd instructed. "Okay."

"The most vulnerable bones you have access to on your attacker are the bones in the top of his foot, and the bones of his fingers. So I'll teach you a technique for breaking the foot bones with a sharp stomp kick and another for breaking the bones of one or more fingers…."

Luke went over the self-defense techniques with Jane until she seemed confident with the information, and then they practiced a few mock attack scenarios, but by the third one, all the close contact was getting to him—and her too, if he wasn't mistaken.

When he had her pinned to the floor for the second time, his cock went hard, and he could no longer focus on self-defense.

Luke pressed her against the mat with his body, and his erection found its home between her legs. He resisted the urge to grind into her, to simulate what he'd been dreaming of doing every day since she'd declared sex off-limits.

"Now that your attacker has you pinned to the ground, what are you going to do?"

"Kick him for real this time."

"But I've got your legs spread. You're wearing a pair of baggy gym shorts. All I have to do is tug aside some fabric, undo my zipper, and—"

"I could bite you."

"Good idea. But what happens when I shove a piece of your clothes inside your mouth?"

"I guess I'm in trouble."

"You stay on alert. You look for any and every opportunity to fight back and escape. You don't give up until you're out of his control and safe again."

Jane closed her eyes and exhaled. "I think I've got it. You can get off of me now, can't you?"

"I could, yeah."

"But you've got me right where you want me?"

"Mmm-hmm."

He loosened his grip on her wrists a bit, but she didn't try to squirm out of his grasp. Instead, she wrapped her legs around his hips and moistened her lower lip with her tongue.

She wanted to be here as badly as he did, and maybe she was finally ready to give in to that desire again.

"That's what I was afraid of."

"I'll bet. Is that why you just wrapped your legs around my hips?"

"My mind and body aren't exactly in synch where you're concerned. My body has one agenda, and my brain has another."

"Which agenda's going to win out, do you think?" He pressed himself a little harder between her legs then, letting his erection strain against the soft fabric of her shorts.

"I think you know the answer to that better than I do."

Luke kissed her then. Slowly, tentatively. He wanted to see her respond with a little enthusiasm of her own, and she didn't disappoint. She deepened the kiss, tasting him hungrily, all the while grinding her hips against him and pulling him closer with her legs.

"Have I unleashed wild Jungle Jane again?" he asked when they came up for air.

"I'm afraid so," she whispered.

A snippet of something she'd said the first time they'd made love popped into his head. She'd told him she wouldn't mind a little restraint in the bedroom, and he figured now was as good a time as any to find out. It was a pretty safe bet that once he had her tied up, at his mercy, and unable to resist his seduction, she'd be a lot more hard-pressed to change her mind in the middle of things. Changing their minds this time wasn't an option—he needed her too fiercely to stop once they got started.

And so he let go of her wrists and peeled himself off her, then lifted her into his arms and carried her to the bedroom. She rested her head on his shoulder and went along without protest.

"I noticed some scarves in your closet. Mind if I borrow them?"

Jane gave him a strange look as he placed her on the bed. *"Scarves?"*

"We could use handcuffs, but I thought that might be going overboard. I just want to make sure you stay put—not arrest you and take you in for custody."

A look of understanding dawned in her eyes. "You're going to tie me up?"

"That's the best way I know to deal with wild jungle women. They have a tendency to get out of hand, otherwise."

She rose up on one elbow, smiling as though she knew a good secret. "What if I don't let you tie me up?"

"You want to try out your new self-defense skills on me?" Luke had never gotten especially turned on by domination and submission, but the idea of subduing Jane and having her at his mercy for an hour or so had definite appeal.

"What good is a lesson learned without an opportunity to practice the subject taught?"

"You don't stand a chance against me. You've lost the element of surprise."

She tugged off her sweatshirt and unsnapped her bra. Luke stared at her with all the blood in his body racing toward his crotch as she sat on the bed topless, her full round breasts an impossible temptation. "Surprised yet?"

"Yeah."

She stood up from her bed and slipped her shorts and panties down over her hips and legs, then stepped out of them. Luke's gaze fell to the triangle of dark hair at the apex of her legs, and he forgot for a moment why he'd been opening the closet.

Jane walked over to him, her gaze locked on his, then

she brushed past. She reached into the closet herself and pulled out a couple of brightly colored silk scarves.

"Maybe I'll tie *you* up," she said.

Sounded like fun, but he wasn't about to back down now. "Not likely."

"Okay, if you can get the scarves away from me, you can tie me up."

Luke reached out to grab her, but she slipped from his grasp and darted to the other side of the bed.

"You'll have to be faster than that."

He surveyed his options and made a move for the far side of the bed, but Jane started to climb over the bed, so he dove after her and caught her by the waist. She screeched and laughed as he pinned her beneath him and tried to grab the scarves, which she hid behind her back until he began to tickle her.

"Okay, okay!" she squealed, breathless and laughing. "Here!" She thrust the scarves at him and he grabbed them before she had the chance to hide them again.

When he'd gotten her arms pinned above her head, he gave her a warning look. "Behave while I get you tied up. Otherwise I'll make this pure torture."

"Torture?"

"Believe me, I've got methods."

"You wouldn't."

"Dare me. You can either have an afternoon of pleasure, or one of frustration—you choose."

She must have remembered his skill at bringing her just to the edge of orgasm and then pulling back, because she let him tie her to the bedposts without a fight. Once he had her at his mercy, Luke sat back to survey her nude body at his leisure. This was his reward for weeks of desiring what he couldn't have, and he intended to savor every moment.

And he'd make damn sure she'd never be able to resist him again, even if it took all night.

Luke undressed and then climbed back onto the bed, his erection at full mast. Jane watched him with a half-lidded gaze.

"I've never been tied up before," she finally said when he was sitting on his knees only a few inches away.

"How does it feel to have no control?"

She wet her lips. "It's very arousing."

Luke slid his hand across her belly, then down through her pubic hair and between her legs. She was slick and hot. "You've been wanting me these past few weeks, haven't you?"

"Yes."

"Practicing your self-control?"

"Yes."

"So being tied up when we have sex sort of makes it okay, right? Like you're doing it against your will?" He slid one finger inside her as he spoke, and she closed her eyes and sighed.

"Maybe."

"Aren't you glad one of us isn't interested in self-control?" He found her clit with his thumb and began to massage.

She moaned in reply, arching herself toward his touch, and after a few moments, Luke withdrew his hand from between her legs and positioned himself over her.

"Not so fast," he whispered. "There's plenty of time for fun."

He trailed kisses up her belly, on her breasts, over her collarbone to her neck. As he tasted her neck, he cupped her breasts in his hands and let his erection strain at her entrance. Now that he was so close to the prize, he could wow her with his self-control, let her feel a bit of the suffering he'd endured lately.

But when he tried to kiss her on the mouth, she turned her head away.

"You want to do this the hard way, hmm?"

"Maybe," she whispered.

"Would you feel scandalized if I tasted between your legs now?"

"Yes."

"Good." He lingered over her breasts, sucking and teasing her nipples, then moved back down.

When he licked her clit, she gasped and writhed around, but he gripped her hips to still her. He tasted and massaged her with his tongue until he knew she was about to come, and then he withdrew. She emitted a frustrated growl.

"Remember, tonight is a night for punishment, not reward."

Jane's eyes shot open, and she looked at him as if he were the last man on earth. "Please…"

"Doesn't take much to make you beg, does it?"

"You know what I want."

Luke ran his hands along the smooth length of her legs. "I wonder what it would take to make you admit this is a lot more than a sexual fling we're having here."

He hadn't planned to say that. And judging by the sober expression on Jane's face, she hadn't expected it. But he had to admit it—he wasn't just falling for Jane. He was *in* love with her.

Somewhere between having the greatest sex of his life and deciding Jane was his most frustrating client ever, he'd let himself fall in love. It had been as natural as breathing, letting those emotions develop, but the problem was that Jane—he could almost guarantee—didn't feel the same.

At least not yet.

Something kept her from letting herself get close enough to get hurt, probably all the losers she'd fielded questions from in her magazine column over the years. She had no idea how much those guys had skewed her outlook and kept her from having normal, healthy relationships, so much that she didn't have a clue what she really wanted in a man.

Luke intended to show her that he knew what she wanted and what she needed even better than she did. Starting tonight.

"I'll admit," she said, "that the attraction between us is too powerful for me to resist at times. If that equals more than a sexual fling, then okay."

He decided not to comment. Getting into an argument in the middle of foreplay wasn't going to help him win the battle. Instead, he positioned himself between her legs and spread her thighs open wide. She didn't bother to put up a pretend fight, and when he dipped his fingers inside her again, she expelled a sigh of pleasure.

"You want me?"

"Yes, right now."

"You're not in the position to be demanding. Maybe you should try begging a little more."

"Please," she nearly purred.

He pressed his cock against her and rubbed it back and forth on her clit. She was so ready, no way could he wait another minute. So much for a long, drawn-out punishment. He was feeling a little too punished himself. Grabbing a condom from his wallet, he slid it on and covered her with his body, easing into her slowly.

They began to rock together, and Luke cupped the back

of her head in his palm, watching pleasure soften her features as they moved toward climax.

This woman… This woman he made love to, this woman he'd tried to protect, this woman who'd resisted his every attempt to win her heart… She'd captured his, and he knew he was in trouble.

Big, big trouble.

12

I don't know what the hell I'm talking about.
>—Jane Langston,
> a deleted line from her work-in-progress,
> *Sex and Sensibility*

LUKE AWOKE while it was still dark and glanced at the clock. 3:46 a.m. He looked around the room, staring into the darkness, trying to determine what, exactly, had woken him. He was wide awake, and his senses were on alert. It was the feeling he got when danger was near. He sat up in bed and strained to listen for a sound—anything—but all he could hear was Jane's slow, steady breathing as she slept.

He slipped silently out of bed and felt around on the back of a chair for his jeans, then pulled them on. That's when he heard it—a slight rustling outside the window. Luke froze in place and held his breath, wondering if he'd just imagined the sound. And after half a minute had passed without any other noise, he admitted that maybe his mind was playing tricks on him.

He crept over to the window and peered out through a small gap between the curtains and the wall, expecting to see nothing, so his stomach dropped to his feet for a few seconds when he saw a man standing at the window, staring in.

Luke recognized him immediately—Jane's lawn guy.

He felt like kicking himself for not checking the guy out more closely, for just assuming that since his record was clean, he probably wasn't a serious threat.

The creep must have just begun looking in and hadn't seen Luke yet, wasn't aware that he was being watched just as he watched Jane sleep. Luke followed the man's line of vision and saw what he saw—Jane lying in bed with the covers at her waist, her arms up over her head, her lush breasts totally exposed.

He looked back to the guy outside the window and took in all the details he could in the span of a few seconds— memorized everything—and then the guy began fumbling with the front of his pants, and right there in the bushes, he started jacking off.

A wave of anger overtook Luke as he shoved his feet into his boots, grabbed a pair of handcuffs and a gun from his jacket, and crept along the wall to the door, then slipped down the hallway silently. He wasn't sure what he'd do when he got outside, but he damn well wasn't going to let the guy get off while staring at his woman.

His woman.

He had no idea when she'd become that in his mind, but he knew he'd allowed himself to feel a sense of possessiveness for her that was unwarranted.

Luke's fury built with each step. As he carefully unlocked the front door, stepped outside, and crept silently around the side of the house, his anger solidified into the resolve to kick the peeping lawn boy's ass from here to Abilene.

When he was close enough to reach out and grab the jerk by the neck, that's exactly what he did. He had the guy on the ground in a matter of seconds and planted a knee in the middle of his back, then slipped the handcuffs around one of his wrists. Glancing around for a place to secure the scumbag until the police arrived, he spotted a utility pole.

"Get up," he said, tugging the guy off the ground as he spoke.

"Hey man, I didn't mean no harm. I was just—"

"Just doing a little yard work at four in the morning?"

Luke dragged him to the pole and cuffed him to it, then stood back and took in the sight of the guy facing the pole with his fly open and his schlong still hanging out. He let out a disgusted laugh.

"You're not gonna leave me like this, are you? I mean, I got customers around here. They ain't gonna want me doing their yards...."

Luke turned and walked back to the house, resisting the urge to slam the door. With any luck, Jane would have slept through the commotion and he could spare her a little fear by waking her up to explain why the police were coming.

After he'd put in the call to the police, Luke went into the bedroom, where Jane was leaning on one elbow, blinking at the clock.

"What's going on?"

He explained everything to her as she got dressed. She listened silently, her expression grim and her shoulders tense.

"You think he's the one?"

"I don't know. I think we should wait and see what he tells the police before we draw any conclusions. Maybe his fingerprints will match up with the ones they found on the box of porn."

"I didn't think it would be someone I knew," she said, standing in the middle of the room hugging herself.

Luke went to her and took her into his arms. She stiffened for a moment but then melted into him, and he wanted very badly to tell her how he felt, to tell her that she never had to worry about being alone, because he wanted to be there with her for good. But then she pushed away and said she needed coffee, leaving him standing there empty-handed as she disappeared into the kitchen.

After the police had come and picked up the peeping lawn boy, they spent a tense morning in silence, waiting for news. Jane was in her office, and Luke was going back over his files on her case, trying to figure out how he'd missed the lawn-care guy as a culprit, when the phone rang. Luke listened to her conversation, not really getting any information until the end when she said, "Thank you, Officer. It's such a relief to know that creep is caught."

He went to her office and stood in the doorway. When she hung up the phone, he raised his eyebrows in a silent question.

"He confessed to making phone calls, sending a few letters, and trespassing outside my house on at least three occasions."

"What about running you off the road, breaking into your car, sending you a box of porn?"

"He hasn't owned up to any of that yet, but the police are fairly certain they've got their man." She smiled, leaned back in her chair, and expelled a sigh of relief.

"That's great if they do, but I think we should consider the possibility that there's another stalker out there who's responsible for the other acts."

"Isn't that a little extreme? I mean, I know a lot of men hate me, but *two* simultaneous stalkers?"

"Why'd he confess to some of the crimes but not all, and what's his connection to your sisters?"

"Maybe he only confessed to the least serious ones, and I know he has met my sisters at least once when they were here."

"Yeah, he's probably just trying to cover his ass, but it's my job to look at all the possibilities."

Was that it? Was he really just looking out for Jane's best interests, or was he letting his dick do the thinking?

No, he was definitely doing what he would do for any client, so the suspicious look she gave him felt like a blow.

"You just want to keep hanging around here to draw out this sex thing we've got going on."

"No." Yeah, sort of. But not for the reason she thought. "I want to do my job." That part, at least, was true.

"You have, and I can't thank you enough. But I wouldn't be doing you any favors by keeping you away from other paying clients who need your services now. I think your work here is done."

Her words, completely unexpected, hit him in the gut. "You're firing me?"

"No, I'm ending our professional relationship. Feel free to pack your bags and leave whenever you're ready."

AT A RED LIGHT, Jane peered into the visor mirror and inspected her face for major flaws—no mascara smears, no lipstick on her teeth, no hairs sticking out from her head in odd places. She looked presentable, maybe even hot, if such a look was possible for her. Bradley Stone, it's now or never.

Tonight, at the wedding rehearsal dinner, she would ask Bradley out, once and for all. If he said no, she wouldn't be heartbroken, and at the very least, she wouldn't feel like a coward anymore. If he said yes, then maybe she'd be able to get her mind off Luke.

It had been a month—what felt like the longest month of her life—since she'd told him she wouldn't need his services any longer. She realized now that her decision had been a bit rash, based more on her desire to gain some control over her sex life again than any sort of common sense. She still had angry readers, still faced the possibility that someone could do more than just write a letter, but it didn't seem likely.

Ever since the lawn-service guy had been arrested, she'd actually felt safe. She went about her normal life free of fear, and it was wonderful.

Well, except for the gaping hole Luke had left in her personal life. She'd underestimated how much she had come to enjoy his companionship, how much he'd become a part of her life. And then, he was gone. She'd wanted it that way. She'd made it clear that ending their professional relationship also meant ending whatever other connection they had.

So why the hell did it hurt so much that she hadn't heard from him even once? And why did she find herself wondering what he was doing, or letting her mind linger over memories of him?

The traffic light turned green and Jane drove through the intersection and turned into the parking lot of the church where Heather and Michael were having their wedding. Cars she recognized populated the lot, and some members of the wedding party were standing near the church entrance talking.

She spotted Brad right away. He wore a crisp blue button-down shirt with a tie, and he had a sports coat slung over one shoulder, looking for all the world like a catalog model.

Strangely, her heart didn't skip a beat upon seeing him. Instead, she found herself looking away from him, searching the parking lot for Luke's SUV. Then she saw the familiar Land Cruiser, and her stomach clenched. Memories of their last night together flooded her mind—the way he'd tied her up and teased her, the way he'd made love to her, the way he'd looked at her with such emotion in his eyes.

Her stomach tightened into a ball, and she banished the memories from her mind.

Jane parked and got out before a case of nerves could send her speeding from the parking lot. As she walked toward the church, she rehearsed the steps of her Bradley plan in her head. First, she'd wait for a moment when he was alone and no one else was within listening range. Then, she'd casually approach him and...

And what? Her mind was a complete blank.

She smoothed the fabric of her little green dress over her hips as she climbed the steps to the door where Bradley still stood, oblivious to her approach. Now that she was close enough, she could hear that he and two other groomsmen were discussing some clandestine details of the bachelor party. She heard words like *surprise* and *keg* and *G-string,* and she suddenly wasn't sure what bothered her more, the idea of Bradley attending a wild bachelor party—or Luke.

Jane passed the groomsmen, tossing them a cursory smile. Instead of meeting Brad's gaze like the bold and empowered woman she was supposed to be, she let her gaze fall to the ground and stared at his shiny black wing-tips. Without saying a word to him, she entered the church.

Inside, the sanctuary was quiet, except for echoes of the flower girl and the ring bearer playing somewhere nearby. With her parents, her sisters, and the bride and groom nowhere in sight, she allowed herself to relax a bit, let out a pent-up breath, and absorb some of the tranquility of the dimly lit setting.

That is, until she saw Luke sitting in the last row. He stared straight ahead at the altar, seemingly deep in thought.

She was about to turn around and walk back out when he saw her.

"Sorry, I didn't mean to intrude," she said.

"You didn't. I was just daydreaming," he said, his tone neutral and his expression unreadable. He motioned to the empty space beside him. "Have a seat. Your sisters and parents are coming in the same car, and they just called the church to say they were running late."

"No surprise there." She smiled, but the tension in the air between them was nearly palpable.

"No more problems lately, I guess, since I haven't heard from you?"

"I haven't had a single phone call since the arrest, and just a couple of angry letters, but not the crazy, threatening kind."

Luke nodded, studying her. "That's good."

Jane crossed her legs and bobbed one foot nervously up and down. "Yep."

He nodded.

Okay, so she owed him an apology. "I'm sorry for the way things ended. It was rude of me to just pretend you were nothing more than my bodyguard, and—"

Their conversation was interrupted by the commotion of the rest of the wedding party arriving in the church lobby. Before Jane could say another word about her lousy behavior, her family came bustling into the sanctuary along with the rest of the wedding party and the minister.

She endured the rehearsal, the entire time confused over her desire to finish her conversation with Luke versus her preconceived plan to approach Bradley tonight. Strange that when she was in the same room with both men, only one of them drew her attention now. And he was the one she already knew she'd be doomed to failure with.

After the rehearsal, everyone drove the short distance to the restaurant where the rehearsal dinner would be held.

Once inside the dining area, Jane was shocked to see seating assignments, with her name card located right next to Luke's. Of course, everyone would just assume they were still an item. She'd avoided discussing anything about Luke with her family, so they had no idea the sexual frenzy had ended.

Luke, already at his seat, noticed Jane hanging back and narrowed his eyes at her. "Don't worry, I won't bite," he said as he stood up and pulled out a chair for her.

She forced a smile and sat down. "Let's call a truce, okay? I want to enjoy my sister's wedding, and I want you to know that I'm truly sorry."

His expression softened. "Apology accepted."

Waiters brought shrimp cocktails to the table, and as she ate, Jane scanned the room, taking in the crowd of family and friends that had been invited to the dinner. She realized that there was no one she would have rather been sitting next to than Luke, and she looked over and smiled at him again.

"How's the new book coming along?" he asked.

"Not good. I guess certain things that I've done recently have forced me to reexamine my relationship theories. I may have to do some major revisions."

Luke's grin revealed that he knew exactly what she was talking about. "What sort of revisions?"

"Stop looking so pleased with yourself," she warned, but she couldn't help laughing. "I was wrong about a *few* things."

She popped a shrimp into her mouth, just as she saw her mother heading straight toward them from the other side of the room.

"What's the matter?" Luke asked.

"My mother," Jane nodded her head in the direction of Luke's left shoulder, "approaching at eleven o'clock."

Luke glanced over at her mother and smiled.

"And how are you two lovebirds doing?" her mother said as she slipped one arm around Luke's shoulders.

"We're fine, Mom. But Luke is my former bodyguard, not my boyfriend."

Her mother gave her a knowing look. "If that's what you'd like me to believe, fine. I won't meddle any further."

"You look lovely tonight, Mrs. Langston."

"Why, thank you, Luke. I'm surprised I managed to get myself pulled together at all, I'm such a nervous wreck about the wedding tomorrow."

Jane saw her opportunity to escape, while her mother was still focused on her own worries. "If you two will excuse me—"

"Just a minute, dear. It's you I need to talk to, actually." She turned to Luke and flashed her best beauty pageant smile. "If you could just excuse us for a few teeny-tiny moments."

Luke nodded. "I think I'll go find a waiter and get this drink refilled."

When he was out of earshot, Livvy said in hushed tones, "Janie, darling, you really should think about wearing a support undergarment tomorrow."

"A *what?*"

"You know, a girdle."

Jane knew she shouldn't have asked, but she did anyway. "Why, exactly, should I wear a girdle to my sister's wedding?"

"I just noticed tonight, in that dress you're wearing, it's very obvious that you're...jiggling a bit."

An image of strawberry Jell-O popped into Jane's head. Strawberry Jell-O taking a ride on a hay wagon.

"Um..." She was speechless.

"I thought you'd rather I point it out to you than have someone like that hunky boyfr—*ex-bodyguard* of yours notice it, if he hasn't already."

Oh. God.

Jane thought of the way she'd felt totally comfortable with her body around Luke, the way she'd walked around naked in front of him, feeling like a ripe peach, when all the while she'd looked like Jell-O.

"Gee, thanks, Mom. I'll hurry right over to the mall after this and buy myself a nice, sturdy, support undergarment."

"Have you tried that new Hot Zone diet? I've lost three pounds on it in the past week. My dress for the wedding is almost too big!"

Fad diets were all a part of her mother's lifelong quest to remain a size two.

Jane looked around, desperate for an escape. "Excuse me, but I need to use the ladies' room," she said, praying her mother wouldn't decide to join her.

Jane hurried out of the room and down the hallway, passing Michael along the way. He'd just left the men's room, and he smiled and nodded as he passed. Jane went into the women's rest room, then closed the door behind her and leaned against it, savoring the silence. After a moment, a shuffling sound from one of the stalls alerted her to someone else's presence.

She made her way to a stall and closed the door, before

someone else could come out and start talking to her about lipstick or support undergarments or anything else.

Doing the obligatory before-peeing check for toilet paper, she found a full roll, and the rest of the stall looked refreshingly clean too. For the prices at this restaurant, the rest rooms had darn well better be sparkling clean.

Jane was searching for the top of her panty hose when she heard it.

A moan, loud and clear, in the next stall.

She froze and strained her ears to listen, then called out, "Are you okay?"

Whoever it was didn't answer, but she was almost positive she heard someone say "shh."

Bending down, she then saw something she could honestly say she'd never seen before in a women's rest-room stall—two sets of feet, one a man's, and one a woman's, toes facing the same direction.

Black trousers sagged around the ankles of the male feet, which were clad in a very large pair of black wing-tips. Oddly familiar shoes, she realized, because they were identical to the ones she'd noticed Bradley wearing to-night.

But when her attention focused on the woman's feet, Jane's stomach stopped hovering around her knees and dropped straight to the ground. Those were Heather's strappy white heels, the same ones she'd bought with Jane a month ago, and that was undoubtedly Heather's signature ankle bracelet, the tiny gold chain with a heart attached.

What in the hell was going on?

Jane blinked, and blinked again, waiting for her brain to process the incomprehensible. Heather couldn't have been in a stall with Michael, because Jane had passed him heading back into the restaurant on her way in. And she couldn't have been in a stall with Bradley, even if those did look exactly like his shoes…could she?

Her heart racing, she irrationally tried to think of logical reasons why a man and a woman would be in a bathroom stall together, in what looked like a *very* compromising position. Maybe she'd dropped her engagement ring down the toilet and he was helping her find it? With his pants down? Okay, that made no sense, but maybe he'd…lost a contact lens…down his pants, and she was helping him… Helping him do what, exactly, while she was facing away from him and standing nearly between his legs?

Okay, so every explanation except for one made absolutely no sense. Jane swallowed the tight, burning sensation in her throat that came with accepting the horrible truth—that her sister, who was about to get married tomorrow, was in the next stall doing it doggy-style with a man who was not her fiancé.

With a man who was wearing the exact same shoes as the object of Jane's nearly decade-long crush.

A faint shuffling, and the motion of their legs, suggested that they'd continued with their little bathroom tryst in spite of Jane's unwelcome presence. She squeezed her eyes shut tight and sat down hard on the toilet seat.

A few moments later, a muffled grunt—the unmistakable sound of a man coming but trying not to be noisy—came from the stall and Jane felt her shrimp appetizer coming up the wrong way.

She stood and turned to the toilet just in time to lose her shrimp into it, the sound of her sickness echoing throughout the rest room. She grabbed some toilet paper to wipe her mouth as lots of shuffling took place in the next stall, and she turned around just in time to see, through the gap between the stall and the door, a male figure pass by. Tall, blond hair, blue shirt.

Bradley.

She turned back to the toilet and heaved again.

A toilet flushed, and a moment later, Heather's voice asked, "Janie, are you okay?"

Frozen with anger and betrayal, Jane didn't know whether to cry or stick her size nine shoe under the stall and stomp her sister's dainty little foot. Instead, she flung open her door and went to the sink, rinsed her mouth out with water, and stared in the mirror at her tear-streaked face.

How could she have been such a fool? How could she have believed for so many years that Bradley was different, worthy of all her pining and idolizing? And how could her traitorous bitch of a sister be screwing that very same guy the night before her wedding?

Suddenly it all made sense—Heather's prewedding cold feet, her efforts to talk to Jane about her "big problems," Jane finding Heather and Bradley alone at Heather's house early in the morning. Jane realized in a rush of horrible understanding that she knew nothing. She wasn't just a fool, she was naive and misguided, the biggest idiot in the state of Texas.

Heather's stall opened, and Jane swung on her.

"What the hell were you doing in there?"

Her sister blinked her blue saucer eyes slowly, taking in Jane's appearance. "Janie, I've been wanting to tell you—"

"Tell me what? That you're screwing around on your fiancé?"

Heather's face crumpled. "It's not like that…. I mean, it is, but it's not, but…"

"Either you are or you aren't, Heather. I heard what just happened in there."

"Stop! Please, we can't talk about this here. Not right now."

She removed a makeup kit from her purse and began touching up her face with amazing skill. But Jane saw that her hands shook as she dabbed at her eyes and reapplied her lipstick.

"Where then? Tomorrow during the wedding photos? Or maybe right after you say your vows?"

Heather winced, then rolled her eyes toward the ceiling to keep tears from ruining her reapplied makeup. "Janie, I'm ashamed of what I've done, but I need to explain it to you. And I need more time than we have now. Everyone is probably wondering where I am right now."

"Did you know how I felt about Bradley?" Jane heard herself ask through clenched teeth. She didn't want to make this about her, but she couldn't help herself.

"I'm so sorry." Heather looked at her then. "I tried to tell you what was going on, but you didn't want to listen."

Jane thought of her big-sister strike, of all the times in the past few months when she'd been too stressed-out to deal with Heather's problems on top of her own. Little had she known....

"Are you calling off the wedding?"

"No! I love Michael."

"So much that you're screwing one of his groomsmen? What if he finds out?" Jane, for one vengeful moment, imagined telling Michael, not so much for him, but just to get even with Heather and Bradley.

But then she remembered that it was her own cowardliness that had kept her from pursuing her attraction to him, and now that she knew what kind of guy he really was, she was pretty damn happy with her cowardly tendencies.

"Jane, you aren't going to tell him, are you?"

In spite of the perverse impulse to keep Heather wondering, she glared at her sister and said, "No, that's your job."

Before Heather could say anything else, Jane turned and left the rest room, not sure where she would go but dreading having to go back into the reserved dining room and finish having dinner with so many people she didn't want to see.

But where else could she go? It would be too obvious to just disappear from the rehearsal dinner when she was one of the wedding party. She could say she'd gotten sick, which was true, but then someone might insist on driving her home.

Her stomach clenching, she entered the restaurant dining room again and immediately spotted Luke sitting alone, sipping a glass of water. Some small part of her reached out to him, wanted to run into his arms, but she stood still, unsure. Then he turned and read the emotions on her face like the oddly perceptive male that he was, and without hesitation he stood and went to her.

"What's wrong?"

Jane bit her lip, imagining how foolish she would sound if she admitted she'd just discovered the guy she'd been mooning over since college doing the wild thing with her sister. And then the truth of it hit her all over again. She willed herself not to gag.

Luke grasped her shoulders and pulled her to him, then encircled her with his arms. She rested her face against the solid wall of his chest and tried to compose herself enough to make it out of the room without calling attention to herself.

"Let's go outside," she whispered.

He guided her out the door, through the main restaurant, and into the parking lot, led her to his car and helped her into the passenger seat, then went to the driver's side and got in himself.

"I don't guess we could skip out early without invoking everyone's wrath," he said, and Jane laughed in spite of herself.

"Let's just run away and blow off the whole wedding." She found a tissue in her purse and began dabbing at her eyes, hoping to escape looking like a raccoon. "It shouldn't be happening anyway."

"Why not?"

Jane stared out the window for a moment, unsure of how much she could tell him. But she knew Luke, knew he could be trusted, knew that if she were going to tell anyone a secret, he'd be the best person to choose.

"I caught my sister and Bradley in the rest room having sex."

"Your sister? Which one?"

"Heather."

He stared at her hard, as if waiting for her to take back the accusation.

"Seriously. I'm not making this up."

"I didn't think you were. But what about Michael? What about the wedding?"

"I guess it's still going to go on, unless Michael somehow finds out."

"*Somehow?* We have to tell him."

Jane flashed him a look of warning. "No, we don't."

"What the hell are you saying? That you're willing to protect your sister's adultery?"

Jane shook her head, too confused to know anything for sure. "No, it's not about that. I don't think it's our place to say anything. That's something Heather has to tell him herself."

"They're about to get *married* tomorrow!"

"I know, but maybe we should stay out of it. They love each other, they make each other happy—and what if we ruin that? Heather's betrayal is something she has to deal with, and it's something they'll have to work through on their own."

"Is that what you'd tell people in a book or your column?" he asked, sounding more bitter than curious.

"I honestly don't know what I'd say. I'm just too freaked out right now to think clearly. I need a little time."

"Okay, so we've got until tomorrow morning to decide what to do."

She let her head fall back against the headrest and closed her eyes. "Deal."

"I mean it, Jane, we find a solution we're both happy with, or I'll go straight to Michael with this information regardless of what you say."

Jane squeezed her eyes shut tighter. "Okay."

"Are you ready to go back in?"

"No!" Jane said too harshly, then softened her tone. "I just need a few more minutes."

"So, Heather didn't know how you felt about Brad?"

She winced, wishing they could have avoided any talk of Bradley Stone. "She did, I think."

"He's an even bigger jerk-off than I thought he was."

"Go ahead, point out that you were right about him and I was wrong."

"I wasn't going to say that."

"But you were thinking it."

"No, I was thinking that I wish you hadn't gotten hurt."

"Well, you *were* right, and I was wrong. You win."

"Jane, it's not a competition." He reached across the cab and took her hand in his.

But he had known Brad was a jerk, and she hadn't. She'd been a fool—a fool who dished out relationship advice for a living. So that made her a charlatan too.

Jane recalled the night at the wedding shower, when she'd been so sure Bradley had looked at her with interest in his eyes. If there had been any interest, she understood now, it had been purely based on whatever he thought might have gone on between Jane and Luke in the bathroom, not any real attraction to her. Maybe he'd just been wondering if she put out for any guy who wanted some action.

"Thanks for trying to warn me about him, anyway."

"Any time."

It struck Jane then how attentive Luke was, how attuned to her emotions. He'd comforted her without hesitation, in spite of the way she'd treated him, and he'd known just what she needed and when.

She took a deep breath and let it out. "Okay, I'm ready to go back in, but could you do me a favor and stick close by? I don't think I can handle dealing with much small talk tonight."

"No problem. I'll just tell everyone you need to get laid."

"Ha ha."

He was only joking, but Jane realized the truth of it— she could think of nothing she'd rather do than spend one last night with Luke, forgetting all her cares in his arms.

"Will you come home with me tonight after dinner?" she blurted before she could talk herself out of it.

Luke stared at her for a few moments before speaking. "You're inviting me to bed?"

She blushed and stared out the window. Finally she

looked back over at him to find his expression neutral. "Just for tonight, for old times' sake?"

He looked out at the parking lot, and in the silence, Jane's nausea returned. He had every right to say no, but she'd be crushed if he did.

"Okay," he finally said. "I'll come home with you tonight."

13

Sex should be the physical evidence of love that exists between two people, not a pop quiz that determines whether you'll go on a second date with him.
—Jane Langston,
from Chapter Eight of *The Sex Factor*

IT TOOK ALL of Luke's willpower not to tell Michael the truth or escort Brad out of the building and beat him senseless in the parking lot. He held it all in only because he'd told Jane he would do so, at least until morning.

By the time they made it back into the restaurant, Heather had told everyone she'd heard Jane getting sick in the rest room, and that she wasn't feeling well. It turned out to be the perfect lie for the occasion, causing everyone to leave Jane alone, and allowing her to slip out of the rehearsal dinner early. Luke begged off attending the bachelor party, claiming he wanted to follow Jane home and make sure she got settled in okay.

So what if everyone mistook him for the doting boyfriend? Under different circumstances, that's what he might have been. He didn't entertain any more illusions that Jane would ever want a relationship with him, but at least he'd given it his best try. And tonight, for whatever it was worth, had the feel of an ending—a long, drawn-out goodbye. She was inviting him to bed one last time, and he was powerless to turn her down.

As he followed her back to her place, he steeled himself for the inevitable and vowed to put any goodbyes out of his head until tomorrow. He tried not to worry about Jane's physical safety, resistant as she was to any more of his professional help. He'd done as much as he could in the past month, anyway. Regardless of the fact that she'd relieved him of his duties as her bodyguard, he'd still conducted random surveillance of her house, without ever seeing anything suspicious. And he'd checked up on her as discreetly as he could to make sure she was okay.

The past month apart from Jane had been a long, slow form of torture. He'd forced himself not to call or make any kind of direct contact with her. After the way she'd said goodbye to him, as if they had nothing more than a business relationship, he could only wait and see if she came to her senses. Obviously, she hadn't, but he had one last night to show her why they were meant to be together.

Tonight, he wanted to think only about the two of them, and like Pavlov's dogs, his body responded instantly to the pleasures that awaited when he imagined a night in Jane's bed…or on her floor, or in her bathtub.

When they pulled into her driveway, Luke parked behind Jane, and his pulse began to race. By the time they were at her front door, his entire body pulsed with anticipation. Jane said nothing as she let him into the house and closed the door behind them.

They stood in the darkness, and Luke understood by the way she made no move to turn on the lights that she didn't intend to waste any time with small talk. Her face, illuminated by the porch light outside the foyer window, was a calm mask hiding what he suspected was a torrent of emotions.

He had no intention of just doing a wham-bam-thank-you-ma'am. There were things that needed to be said. If she wanted to say goodbye, she needed to understand what she'd be leaving behind—what she'd be missing out on.

"Are you sure you want to do this?" he asked.

"Yes. Are you?"

"I wouldn't be here if I weren't sure."

She lifted up her dress and tugged it over her head, then let it drop to the floor. Luke watched, mesmerized, as she removed her bra, then her heels and panty hose, and finally her panties. She stood before him naked, as tempting as ever.

He reached out to touch her, but she dodged his hand.

"No, no," she chided. "Tonight, I call the shots. You're not my bodyguard anymore, so I don't have to do as you say."

A little smile betrayed her act, but Luke was more than willing to play along.

"Hmm, I do whatever you say?"

"That's right."

"You're not going to tell me to do anything scandalous, are you?"

"I'm afraid so. Will that be a problem?"

Luke pretended to give the question some thought. "I think I can deal with scandalous."

"Good, then come with me to the kitchen."

"The kitchen?"

"I'm hungry. I was too upset to eat at the restaurant."

Following her, he admired the curvy shadow of her figure in the darkness and imagined what they might do once Jane had gotten one of her appetites sated. He had some ideas—him, her, the kitchen table, a few well-placed squirts of whipped cream...

"Babe, you could have done some of this nude snacking while I lived here, you know. I wouldn't have complained."

"I'll bet."

She opened the refrigerator and pulled out a cheesecake. "Want a piece?"

"Mm-hmm, but not of the cheesecake."

When she turned to the counter and the light from the refrigerator illuminated her profile—the sweet curve of her ass, the lush slope of her breasts, the erect nipples that were an invitation to his mouth—he had to grip the table and will himself not to take her on the counter right then and there. He watched as she put a piece of the cake on a plate and then switched on the light over the stove, which cast a soft, warm glow on the kitchen, just enough so that Luke could see the luscious details of her body, the dessert she was making him wait for.

She brought her plate to the table and sat down, but Luke was too mesmerized by the sway of her breasts to be tempted by cheesecake. She cut a bite with her fork and offered it to him.

"No, thanks. I'm saving my appetite."

"There aren't many things I love more than cheesecake," she said, then took a bite, letting the fork slip between her lips on the way out in a motion so slow and seductive it made him think of her mouth on his cock.

That was what she'd intended, of course, and he was playing right into her hands.

"I bet I can name the things you love more than cheesecake."

She raised an eyebrow at him as she took another bite. "Go ahead and try."

Luke hesitated for only a moment, wondering what she'd make of the fact that he knew her so well, that he'd

paid such close attention to her in the two weeks they'd
lived together. "Dark chocolate, the imported stuff. Perfect, ripe peaches. Coffee, which you like to drink with
whole milk. Chicago-style pizza with pepperoni. Key
Lime pie."

"You've done your homework."

"And those are just in the food category. I could keep
going."

"Please do." She smiled, clearly enjoying the game.

"Okay... You love the scent of freshly cut grass. The
feel of humidity on a warm night. Bathwater just short of
scalding hot."

She ate the cheesecake slowly as she listened to him.
What Luke understood about her that he suspected she
didn't understand about herself was that Jane was a pro-
foundly sensual woman.

All her written advice about restraint and the negative
impact of sex were evidence of her denial. She didn't
understand how essential sensual experiences were to her
happiness. And in the past two months, Luke had unlocked that side of her in bed, unleashed the wild lover
inside of her that had needed for years to escape.

No, she may not have understood it, but he hoped that
tonight, if he accomplished nothing else, he could show
Jane her sensual nature.

"And when it comes to more physical pleasures..."

"You have a list of my bedroom preferences?"

"A mental one. There usually isn't time to take notes."

She finished the last bite of her dessert and pushed the
plate aside. "I've always suspected cheesecake is a dish
best eaten naked."

"Is it?"

"Maybe if we'd been sharing it, and you'd been naked,

too." She stood up and came to him, placing her hands on his shoulders.

When she straddled his lap, her breasts were nearly at mouth level, and Luke was reminded of the dessert he'd been longing for all evening. But he'd agreed to play by her rules tonight. That didn't mean he couldn't gain the advantage.

"You love to be kissed, long and slow, and especially on the neck."

Jane smiled. "What else?"

"You love when I bite your nipples. When I run my fingertips along your skin lightly, with a feather touch. When I bring you just to the edge of climax, and then pull back and make you wait a little longer. And you love when I quiet your moans with kisses."

"Is that all?"

"That's just the PG-rated list."

She dipped her head down and kissed him, a slow, exploring kiss—a promise of more to come. "I want to hear the adults-only version."

"I'll need to do some demonstrations for that list."

"Aw, come on, quit with the shy act. You're not afraid to talk dirty to me, are you?"

He grasped her hips and pulled her closer until his rock-hard erection pressed into her crotch. "If I start talking dirty, I'm gonna have to start acting dirty, too."

"Oh yeah?" The wicked smile she flashed made it clear that's exactly what she wanted.

He rocked his hips against her, and she closed her eyes and let out a little gasp.

When he stilled, she shook her finger at him. "No fair, unauthorized hip thrusting."

"See what I mean? My self-control is slipping." He

mentally forced his hands to remain still on her hips, not to explore even more tempting territory.

"Guess I'll have to speed things along a bit then, hmm?"

"I don't need speed so much as I need…stimulation."

Jane loosened his tie, then pulled it off and flung it aside. After she unbuttoned his shirt, she moved to his belt. Then the button and zipper on his pants.

Her fingertips brushed the ridge of his erection, and Luke's heart rate went up.

"How about I tell you what you like."

"Babe, I like it when you breathe in my direction. It doesn't take a rocket scientist to figure out what guys want."

"Maybe not, but it does take a little extra attention to notice what really presses your buttons."

In spite of himself, Luke felt flattered that she'd paid attention, too, that she might know his desires, as well as he knew hers.

"Okay. I'm listening."

"You'll need to take those clothes off."

"To listen?" he asked, but he was already setting her on her feet. Then he was up and tugging off his shirt, kicking off his shoes, stepping out of his pants and briefs.

"I'll be doing a hands-on demonstration, if you must know."

He stood before her completely naked, his cock straining toward her like a racehorse ready to burst from the gate. "I was hoping you'd say that."

"Sit back down."

He did as she commanded, she knelt on the floor, between his legs. Her gaze remained locked with his as she slid her hands up his inner thighs, stopping just before ground zero.

"You love it when I tease you," she said. "When I come this close to touching you where you want to be touched, and then make you wait."

He did love it. And that was exactly what she did. Her fingers lingering on his thighs, she tickled and massaged, dancing around where he really wanted to feel her touch.

Then she moved closer. She slid her fingers through his pubic hair, down along the edge of his scrotum to the base of it, where she began to massage lightly. Luke's breath caught in his throat.

And when she dragged her fingernails lightly over his balls, he moaned deep in his throat, sat back in the chair, settled in for a nice long wait. Judging by her slow, deliberate seduction, she had no intention of rushing things along the way his little head would have tried to do, had he been in charge. Luke closed his eyes and focused all his attention on her touch.

When she finally made contact with his cock, it wasn't with her hands. Luke gasped at the exquisite sensation of her lips and tongue encircling him, taking him into her mouth. But it only lasted a few sweet moments, until she withdrew.

"And you love when I do that, don't you?"

"Of course," he whispered. "Who wouldn't?"

"But you like the teasing more."

Maybe he did. He'd learned over the years that the anticipation was almost always sweeter than the reward—except with Jane. With her, it was impossible to measure or compare the two pleasures. They were equally intoxicating parts of the whole experience of making love to a woman whose sensual side, when unleashed, was wild and insatiable.

Jane took his hand and pulled him up from his seat.

She sat on the kitchen table and brought him between her legs.

"I'll need your, um, cooperation for this part."

"Babe, I don't think you could get anything but co-operation from me now." His body, tensed with desire, was ready to spring into action at the slightest invitation.

She smiled, eyeing his erection. "Point taken."

He felt her hands sliding down his back, grasping his hips, and she urged him forward until his cock rested against her hot, wet opening. Luke clenched his jaw, willing himself not to take control of the situation.

And then she whispered, "You have my permission to move things along as you wish."

That was all the invitation he needed to take her into his arms and kiss her, search her with his tongue. She moaned into his mouth, and he knew it was time.

"Just a second," he said as he bent down to grab his wallet from his pants.

A few moments later, he'd donned the jimmy cap and was back in position, his pulse racing. Bracing his palms against the table, he pressed himself to Jane, and she snaked her arms around his neck to hold on.

"You love the moment just before you enter—the anticipation, the buildup…"

Maybe so, but he'd had enough anticipation to last him the rest of the damn night. So he tugged her hips a bit more toward the edge of the table, and without another second of anticipation, slid into her.

It felt like coming home. She was so slick, so ready, the only resistance was her body's natural tightness, the incredible sensation of her stretching to accommodate him. And then she tightened her muscles around him, and he gasped.

"And you love when I do that."

"There's not a single thing you do to my body that I don't love. Understand?"

He withdrew a little, then thrust his full length into her, again and again, to make sure she understood that he'd had enough talk. He was ready for action. Judging by the way she let her head fall back and her lips part as she expelled little gasps of pleasure, he guessed she felt the same way.

Their bodies, molded together, grew toward a strong, hard climax that shook them when it finally came. Luke felt himself spilling inside of her, incredible sensations racing through his body, when Jane locked her legs tight around him and bucked against the strength of her own orgasm. They held each other through the aftershocks, breathless and kissing as if it might be their last chance, until finally, there was calm again.

Luke buried his face in Jane's hair and savored her scent, let his body relax as they held each other. After a minute, he reluctantly drew away from her to dispose of the condom.

Then he lifted Jane from the table, and with her arms around his neck and her head resting on his shoulder, he carried her down the hallway toward the bedroom. That is, until her reclusive cat Homer darted out of nowhere and tangled himself in Luke's legs. He cursed as he felt himself losing his balance, and he forced himself backward so that he would take the impact instead of Jane.

They landed in a heap on the hallway rug, and the cat calmly padded toward the kitchen, probably in search of a nighttime snack.

"Are you okay?" Jane asked.

"Yeah, I think so. How about you."

She stretched herself out on top of him. "I'm fine. You broke my fall. But you must be hurt somewhere," she insisted as she began kissing his shoulders and neck.

"Mm. You're right. I'm starting to feel aches all over."

"Here?" she asked, as she placed a kiss on his chest.

"Yeah."

"And how about here?" She moved lower, to his navel, where she placed a slow, lingering kiss.

"Oh, yeah."

"And I'll bet you're in terrible pain here," she said, a little breathless, right before she placed a kiss on the head of his cock.

Luke felt himself grow erect. "I think I'll need some extra attention there."

"Mm-hmm," she murmured as she took him into her mouth, picking up where she'd left off in the kitchen earlier.

And as her tongue and lips worked his cock, Luke tangled his fingers in her hair and closed his eyes, allowing himself to pretend that this never had to end.

Of all the times they'd made love, tonight felt the most urgent, the most necessary, the most inevitable. Jane had somehow, in the past two months, become as vital to his existence as air and water, as essential to his happiness as comfort and rest.

He didn't know how it had happened, and he didn't know how to stop feeling the way he did. He only knew one thing—that he had to remember every moment, every touch, and every sensation of this night, because there might not be another night like this. Probably not another night with Jane, ever. She'd made that much clear.

For tonight, he would forget and savor every last moment.

THERE WAS SOMETHING about the light of day that always managed to change Jane's perspective on the previous day's—or night's—events. When she woke up spooned against Luke and heard his slow, heavy breathing, memories of the night before came to her in a mental flood. The kitchen, the hallway, the bed…they'd made love as if it were a matter of life and death, as if their survival depended on it.

But now she remembered why she'd ended their relationship in the first place. Being with Luke made her lose her mind, made her into a bigger and bigger hypocrite every time they fell into bed together. It was best that they make a clean break from each other for good before her career was ruined.

She sat up in bed and squinted at the clock, which told her she had exactly thirty minutes to get herself to the salon where Heather had scheduled herself and all the bridesmaids to have their hair and makeup done before the wedding.

"Damn it!" She nudged Luke, and he groaned and rolled over. "Wake up. I'm going to be late for my hair appointment."

Luke opened one eye and peered at her. "You told me we'd decide what to do about Heather and Michael this morning."

Pretending to ignore him, Jane climbed out of bed and hurried to the bathroom, where she took a quick shower. Heather's two-timing was the last thing she wanted to think about right now. What *was* the right thing to do? She couldn't let loyalty to her sister outweigh basic human decency, but she also didn't want to meddle in a relationship problem that was too intimate for outside intervention.

Then again, considering what an idiot she'd been recently—carrying on a meaningless sexual fling, pining after a guy who'd turned out to be a bigger jerk than she ever could have imagined—Jane wasn't sure she could trust her own judgment at all anymore.

After she finished her shower, she toweled off and went to the closet. As she tugged on a pair of black pants, she finally responded to Luke. "If Heather hasn't told Michael, you think we should, right?"

Luke nodded, his expression sober as he sat on the edge of the bed, gloriously naked.

"Then I will. I'm the one who discovered the affair, so it's my responsibility to talk to him. But first, I'll talk to Heather." Jane's stomach rebelled at the thought, but Luke was an honorable guy. If she couldn't trust her own judgment, maybe she could trust his.

Luke stood up and went to her, but she stepped back before he could take her in his arms. "I can go with you."

"No, that's not necessary." She turned back to the closet and grabbed a stretchy T-shirt, then pulled it on. "I hate to rush you out of here, but I have to go."

His expression darkened. "So this is it?"

"We'll see each other at the wedding later. We can talk then." She smiled at him as she slipped on a pair of wedge sandals, but she felt like she'd just stabbed him in the back.

He deserved a lot more than a brusque goodbye as she rushed out the door, but she just wanted to get away before things got any more complicated between them.

Luke was still getting dressed when she tossed him the extra key and asked him to lock up on his way out and give the key back at the wedding. He answered with a silent glare, and she turned and hurried out the door.

Jane sped across town trying to focus on the freshly brewed coffee the salon would surely offer her when she got there, but her thoughts kept volleying between saying goodbye to Luke and having to deal with Heather and Michael. By the time she arrived at the sleek, upscale salon full of stylists dressed in black, she'd decided she would need at least three cups of coffee to survive the morning.

She spotted Jennifer and Lacey undergoing some kind of facial treatment on the spa side of the salon, and as a platinum-blond buzz-cut receptionist led her back to the waiting area, she looked around for Heather, but her sister was nowhere in sight.

"Has Heather Langston arrived yet?" she asked the receptionist.

"No, but she was scheduled for eight o'clock."

Jane puzzled over her missing sister as she flipped through a *Cosmo* magazine and pretended to look interested in it. What if Heather had decided to run off with Bradley, or she and Michael had gotten into a big fight, or she had decided to call off the wedding but hadn't told anyone yet, or—

"Hi, Janie."

Jane looked up to see Heather standing a few feet away, looking for all the world like a woman who hadn't slept all night. "Heather, we need to talk."

Her sister's expression fell and she nodded as she sat down next to Jane.

"I haven't tried to stop your wedding yet, but I feel dirty knowing about the affair and saying nothing, when Michael is about to commit his life to you."

Heather stared at the ground for several moments. When she turned to Jane, she had tears in her eyes. "I love Michael, and I want him to be my husband."

"You should have realized that before you started screwing his friend."

Her sister shook her head and buried her face in her hands.

Jane put down the magazine and steeled herself to tell Heather that she was going to talk to Michael unless she did it herself.

But then Heather looked up, tears streaming down her cheeks, and said, "I told Michael about the affair last night, after the rehearsal dinner."

"How did he react?"

"He's furious, of course. At first he wanted to break up, but we had a really long talk. Now he's not sure if he wants to go through with..." Her chin began to quiver and her voice broke. "....the wedding."

Jane blinked at the news. Heather had just demonstrated a surprising amount of backbone—unless she'd told Michael the truth to ease her own guilty conscience, as was the case with most confessions.

A stylist appeared for one of them, but before she could speak, she spotted Heather's teary-eyed state, and Jane held up a finger, silently asking for a few more minutes. The stylist nodded and left.

"Michael deserves a lot better than the way you've treated him."

"I know. I've ruined everything!" Heather expelled a bitter laugh. "He broke up with me once in college, and he slept with three other people. I never did."

"That's not an excuse for betraying him."

"No, it isn't. I've been a fool, Janie. I was terrified of only making love to one man in my whole life, so I thought I needed to go out and get some experience before I got married."

"And Bradley was such a good friend, he couldn't help but oblige you."

She sighed. "I actually thought I loved him, for a short

time. Then I realized last night, after the way he reacted when I told him I was going through with the wedding, he was only using me.''

Jane crossed her arms over her chest, unwilling to feel sorry for Heather's soap-opera romance problems.

"He laughed. He said he'd never expected me to do otherwise, that he thought we were just having a little pre-wedding fling.''

"Weren't you?''

"I guess so, yeah. But I was such a fool I couldn't keep my heart out of it. Now I realize how stupid I was for wanting to sleep with another man. I could have had something pure and sweet with Michael....''

She looked so miserable then, Jane couldn't help but throw her a rope. "You still can. You can have a devoted marriage, starting right now on your wedding day. That's more than a lot of people can say.''

Heather looked up at her then and wiped her cheeks with the back of her hand. "If Michael forgives me, that is. Janie, can you forgive me?''

Could she? Jane sat silent, her gaze focused on a framed poster of a woman with a really bizarre hairdo on the wall.

Heather continued. "I guess I knew about your crush on Bradley, but I thought it was nothing serious, since you'd never pursued him. Or maybe I just told myself I didn't know, but if I'd been honest, I could have figured out, from the way you looked at him...''

"Stop.'' Jane fought to keep her voice even. "I was just as big an idiot as you when it came to Bradley. I was naive enough to believe that pining after a guy for my entire adult life was the same thing as having a relation-ship with him. I was a coward, and I wasted a lot of energy wanting a guy who wasn't even worth my attention."

"You can do so much better than him."

"I know that now."

"I'm sorry, Janie. I'm really, really sorry." Heather scooted over on the couch until she'd closed the distance between them. She encircled Jane in her arms and held her close until Jane finally gave in and hugged her back.

"I forgive you," Jane whispered. "And I hope today is your wedding day."

14

How do you know if it's love and not just lust? Does your soul wake up when she comes into the room? Do you look into her eyes and see the future? Does being in her presence make you want to be a better man?

—Jane Langston,
in the May issue of *Excess* magazine

JANE REMINDED HERSELF to suck in her gut. It was her turn to walk down the aisle. In spite of Heather's betrayal, Michael had demonstrated a stunning amount of forgiveness in deciding to go forward with the wedding. There was one groomsman conspicuously missing from the wedding party, and rumor had it he'd paid a visit to the emergency room late last night after Michael had knocked out a couple of his teeth.

As she walked slowly down the aisle to Pachelbel's "Canon in D," Jane forced herself to smile and look straight ahead, as if she weren't painfully aware of one particular set of eyes that were watching her from the altar. She met the gazes of family members in the pews, but it wasn't until she'd made it to the altar and taken her place that she allowed herself to look at Luke.

Just as she'd suspected, his gaze was locked on her. Her palms began to sweat on the bouquet of spring flowers she was clutching, and she forced herself to look away from Luke again. She turned to the back of the church as the bridal march began and Heather started walking down the aisle.

Jane had never paid much attention to weddings. Sure, she'd heard the vows a hundred times, and she knew all the conventions, but all those times she'd played "wedding" with her sisters when they were kids, she'd never really tried to imagine herself getting married. She realized now that even as an adult, she'd never visualized herself walking down the aisle, standing before a minister with a man, exchanging vows.

And why not? She had no idea. Maybe she'd been too busy trying to succeed, trying to prove to herself and the world that she deserved recognition…trying to keep anyone who might hurt her at arm's length.

"Do you, Heather, take this man as your lawfully wedded husband, to have and to hold, to love and to cherish, in sickness and in health…"

Jane forced herself to focus on the wedding vows, to pay close attention to the words, and it felt as if a big, gaping hole opened up in her chest. She'd never allowed herself to love anyone enough to say those words. She'd never been so close to a man that she wanted to keep him as her partner for life. And for the first time ever, she realized she was missing out.

Blinking back an unwelcome dampness in her eyes, she watched the rest of the ceremony. When the minister introduced Mr. and Mrs. Michael Bell to the world, Jane saw something she hadn't expected to see, unabashed happiness on Heather and Michael's faces, and she was humbled by the truth that two people could love each other enough to put aside something as awful as what had happened last night and still commit their lives to one another. That was a love deeper than she'd ever felt, and she knew in an instant that she wanted to find it.

She'd been paired up with Luke to do the walk back down the aisle. When he offered her his arm, she hesitated for a moment, all too aware that touching Luke inevitably caused sparks. But slipping her arm in his and exiting the church with him felt oddly comfortable, so much so that she allowed herself to put aside all her worries and just enjoy the festivity.

They endured the inevitable wedding photo session, and then Luke invited her to ride with him to the reception hotel. In the passenger seat of his Land Cruiser, Jane settled back and took in the side view of Luke in his tux, his hair pulled back into a sleek ponytail. He looked delicious.

"You clean up pretty well," she said as he pulled out of the parking lot.

"You don't look too bad yourself." It was a friendly enough comment, but Jane knew by the flatness of his voice that he wasn't happy with her.

"I'm sorry we didn't get to say a proper goodbye this morning."

"It doesn't matter."

"You're angry with me."

Silence.

Jane squirmed in her seat. "This is why I never wanted us to have a sexual fling in the first place. I knew we couldn't end up happier people for it."

His gaze remained focused on the road, and for several long minutes, he said nothing. When he finally spoke, the sound was jarring. "Just so you'll know, I have to leave the reception a little early to catch a flight to Puerto Rico. I wouldn't want you thinking I've gone off to lick my wounds over your rejection."

She ignored his sarcasm. "What's in Puerto Rico?"

"A client. He vacations there and occasionally has me fly down."

"Oh. Well, have fun." She swallowed the dryness in her mouth and puzzled at the prickly feeling behind her eyes. It shouldn't have upset her to hear that Luke was leaving on a business trip. Rather, she should have felt relieved, right?

So why didn't she?

They rode in silence the rest of the way to the hotel and still managed not to speak as they made their way into the reception, where the party was already going strong. Luke disappeared from Jane's side when her aunt Claudia stopped her to ask where Heather was, and for the rest of the night he wouldn't make eye contact with her whenever they were near.

Jane ate dinner at the wedding party table that faced out toward the rest of the reception hall. As she watched people laughing and having a great time, she resolved to do the same, and when dinner was over and Heather and Michael danced their first dance, Jane felt a real sense of happiness settle in her belly. She smiled at the obviously happy couple, a little amazed herself for not having a single jaded thought about their troubles the night before.

Jennifer came back to their table and sat down beside Jane.

"I just want to thank you for telling me to give up on Eli. I don't know what I was thinking, letting him come between Lacey and I."

Jane looked at her sister and for once didn't feel a single resentful big sisterly feeling. "So everything's okay now?"

"Yep, we both agreed to give him the cold shoulder,

which pissed him off, I think, but he'll get over it. Lacey even let me wear her leather skirt last weekend.''

Well, then. What could be more harmonious than a shared leather skirt? Jane managed to even feel satisfied that she'd helped her sisters out of a conflict. Maybe she wasn't totally incompetent after all. Maybe she did occasionally have useful advice to give.

When Jennifer left, Jane's gaze fell on her parents, sitting at a table next to the dance floor, smiling and holding hands as they watched Heather and Michael dance. Her parents were clearly as in love now as they had always been, and it struck Jane that she'd never even bothered to be thankful for having two parents who loved each other before. On a whim, full of the wedding spirit in the air, she stood up and went to their table to sit with them.

''You two are looking awfully googly-eyed.'' She leaned over and gave her dad a kiss on the cheek.

Her mother sighed. ''Weddings always remind us of our own wedding. We were so sweet on each other we could hardly make it through the reception without slipping away for a little hanky-panky.''

Jane winced at the reference to her parents' sex life, and her mother caught her look.

''Oh, there's nothing shameful about two people not being able to keep their hands off each other. That's the same passion that's kept our marriage strong for thirty-three years now.''

Her father grinned at her then. ''We want to see you girls as happy as we've been.'' He took her hand in his then and kissed it, the same gesture he'd always made when Jane was a little girl and he'd called her his princess. ''I try not to meddle in you girls' lives, but I'm going to just this once, okay?''

"Okay, Daddy," Jane heard herself say. She hadn't called her father Daddy since her Barbie-doll days.

"Don't waste your whole life writing books about relationships, princess. Go out and find your own true love."

Jane felt her eyes well up with tears. Maybe her dad wasn't such an airhead after all.

JANE DANCED with her father, then fast-danced with her sisters until she had blisters on both of her little toes, but she hadn't seen Luke anywhere in the crowd of merrymakers on the dance floor.

As the reception wound down, she wandered around the reception hall and out into the hotel lobby, not realizing until she spotted the front doors of the hotel that she was looking for Luke, hoping he hadn't left yet. Her father's words replayed themselves again and again in her head, along with the comment her mother had made about their passionate marriage.

When she tried to picture herself having that kind of passionate, long-lasting love, only one image came to mind—one of herself and Luke. Why had she been so sure that their relationship couldn't grow into something deeper?

Maybe she hadn't thought she was good enough, maybe she had been too afraid of getting hurt, maybe she'd been terrified of being wrong about relationships…there were lots of maybes. But only one thing she knew for sure.

She wanted Luke. Not just in her bed, but in her life. She wanted to give them a chance, to see if maybe they could have what her parents had. To see if the stirring she felt deep down in her soul whenever she thought of a future with Luke really was true love.

Someone placed a hand on the small of her back, and

she jumped. Jane turned to see that it was Eli, the former object of Jennifer and Lacey's affection. She had to admit, he did look handsome in his black tux, but his attractiveness was marred by his eternal arrogant smirk. He had the air of a guy who was used to getting what he wanted with women.

"I've got a surprise for the bride and groom. I was hoping you could help me with it."

"Um, sure. What do you need?"

"Could you help me carry it down and present it to Heather and Michael before they leave? It's in my hotel room on the second floor—it was a little too big to keep concealed, so I had to hide it up there."

Jane frowned. "Sure. You've got my curiosity piqued."

He smiled. "Follow me. You're gonna die when you see it."

She followed Eli to the elevator, which they stood waiting for in awkward silence. Once inside it, Jane flashed a strained smile at him.

"So," she said, "great wedding, huh?"

"Yeah, I can't believe Michael finally tied the knot."

The elevator stopped and they got out. As she followed Eli down the hallway to his room, Jane got the feeling something wasn't quite right, but she decided it was probably just her awkwardness at being alone with the same guy she'd urged her sisters to get rid of.

Eli stopped at a doorway and inserted a key card. He opened the door and stepped aside for her to enter.

Jane stepped into the darkened room and flipped a light switch on the wall. "So where's the big surprise?" she asked as she went farther into the room.

She heard the lock on the door click. A strange, hollow feeling filled her gut.

Eli turned from the door to face her, and his friendly expression was gone, replaced by a menacing glare.

"I'm the surprise, you stupid bitch."

Jane's breath caught in her throat. Eli's voice had dropped several octaves. She recognized it as the voice from the late-night phone calls and the creepy answering machine messages.

"What do you want?"

"I want you to stop giving out your idiotic advice to all the stupid women in the world. You ruined my chances with Lacey and Jennifer and just about every other dumb bitch I've met lately."

Her mouth went dry. She took a few steps backward, but that only got her closer to a king-size bed and Eli's suitcase resting on top of it.

"I'm sorry you're having a bad-luck streak, but women make their own decisions. I don't decide for them who they should date."

"Do you realize how close I came to nailing your sisters? You owe me big time."

Looking around for a weapon, Jane spotted a bottle of cologne on the nightstand, along with a lamp and an alarm clock. Great, she could perfume Eli to death. She decided to go for the lamp if he made a move toward her, figuring she could at least get away if she swung hard enough at his head with the base of it.

He dove toward her, and before she could react, she found herself pinned to the bed, Eli's large body pressed against her, his hands holding hers at her sides.

"Did you like the little gift I left for you in your car?"

"What gift?"

"The book, you stupid bitch. I thought you might like my customized copy."

She tried to force the tears from her voice as she spoke.

"Listen, this isn't necessary. I could talk to Jennifer and Lacey for you, convince them that I was wrong about you before. I'm sure they'd give you another chance."

"I'll get my chance. If I can't have them, I'll have you."

Jane found herself wondering if her bridesmaid dress would survive this ordeal, and she realized with a start that she was practicing avoidance thinking, ignoring the fact that the real question was whether *she* would survive.

All Luke's self-defense lessons got rolled up in a jumble of nonsense in her head, until she recalled his most frequent words, to stay calm and to always fight back.

She drew back her head and then thrust it forward as hard as she could, making contact with Eli's mouth. He grunted, then spit on her, and after he'd trapped one of her hands between their bodies, he grabbed a roll of duct tape from the open suitcase beside them.

"Nice try. Did your hired ape teach you how to do that, or was he too busy sticking it to you to teach you any self-defense?"

Jane felt the rage that had been gathering inside her come to a head, and she used all her strength to buck against him as he tried to bite off a piece of the duct tape. In the scuffle, his ear ended up next to her mouth, and she bit down hard until he got his hands around her throat.

Gasping for air, she realized her own hands were free now, and she reached for his little finger, just as Luke had taught her, and once she'd gotten her hand around it, she gave it a sharp tug down, until she heard and felt the sickening sound of cracking bone.

Eli cried out at the pain and fell to the side, giving Jane her freedom to climb off the bed.

"You bitch, you broke my finger!"

She remembered one more lesson Luke had taught

her—not to stick around and see if her attacker was going
to get up. She ran for the door, unlocked it, and ran down
the hallway yelling for help as loud as she could.

HAVING GIVEN her statement to the police, explained everything to her family, wished the newlyweds a happy
honeymoon, and shrugged off all suggestions of a trip to
the emergency room, Jane went back out to the hotel
lobby and asked the man at the concierge desk to call her
a cab, then wandered through the dwindling crowd. With
each step she took, her path became more clear, her resolve more determined. She wasn't sure if she had time—
maybe his flight was already on its way to Puerto Rico—
but she had to try. What she wanted to say to Luke
couldn't wait.

When the cab arrived, she let the driver know she was
in a big hurry, and they sped to the airport, with Jane
praying the whole way that she could somehow catch
Luke.

Once inside the terminal, Jane ran. She took off the
midnight-blue satin heels that had been dyed to match the
bridesmaid dress she was still wearing, and she ran as fast
as she could through the airport. If the mere fact of running through an airport in her bridesmaid dress wasn't
enough to convince Luke that she loved him, then nothing
would.

She halted in front of a monitor with a scrolling list of
departing flights. San Antonio, San Francisco, *San
Juan*...Gate B-17, departing on time at 8:30 p.m....in
thirty minutes. She had time to find him, but she had no
idea how she'd get past airport security.

Unless she was a ticketed passenger on the flight.

Did she really want to fly to San Juan, Puerto Rico in
a bridesmaid dress, with nothing but her dainty little

bridesmaid purse and an uncomfortable pair of satin shoes as baggage? And then she thought of Luke, of what he'd done for her, of what empty her life would be without him, and she knew the answer without a doubt.

If it hadn't been for Luke, she wouldn't have been able to fight off Eli, and more importantly, if it hadn't been for Luke, Jane would still be a lonely, repressed thirty-year-old woman without a clue what she wanted out of life.

She picked up her skirt again and took off, following the signs to the airport check-in area. Luckily, there weren't any hordes of people flying on a Saturday evening, so ten minutes later she had an unbelievably overpriced ticket in hand and she was running for the departure gate.

By the time she made it through the security checkpoint and to the gate, her hair had fallen all the way out of its sophisticated French twist, her stockings had an undetermined number of runs, and she was sweating like a woman who'd just run a marathon. She'd given up feeling embarrassed about all the people who'd stopped to stare at her along the way. The security guards at the gate eyed her warily but waved her through, by some miracle.

When Jane stepped onto the plane, a flight attendant at the entrance gave her a once-over and produced a strained smile. "I can't wait to hear your story," she said, then took Jane's boarding pass and looked at it. "You can use the left aisle to get to 23C."

Jane stopped to catch her breath and then offered up a silent prayer that Luke would forgive her hardheadedness, that he'd be able to overlook all her stupid assumptions and all the times she'd taken him for granted. Most importantly, she prayed for him to take her, flaws and all.

She made her way down the aisle, looking for his face

in the anonymous crowd of passengers. It didn't take long to spot him. He was sitting in an aisle seat near the middle of the plane, his head reclined against the headrest, his eyes closed. The window seat next to him was empty.

Jane stopped next to him. "Excuse me, I just need to get into my seat."

Luke's eyes opened and he gazed up at her, completely perplexed. "Jane."

She tried hard not to smile. "Didn't I tell you I was on this flight, too?"

"What are you doing—"

Holding up her hand to silence him, she said, "Do you mind if I sit first? I'm looking a little conspicuous here."

He seemed to take in her marathon-running-bridesmaid appearance for the first time and raised an eyebrow. But mercifully, he stood up and let her get into the window seat.

When they were seated side-by-side, Jane turned to Luke. "Could we just back up a little, pretend a few things didn't happen, maybe sort of…start over?"

He shrugged, rightfully unwilling to forget the way she'd behaved. A shrug was a start.

Jane took a deep breath. "So, what takes you to San Juan?"

"Business," he said, tossing her a strange look.

"Ah, what sort of business are you in?"

He looked at her again, pausing for a long moment before he answered, probably deciding if he was willing to play along. "Security."

She continued in her airplane chit-chat voice, "That sounds interesting. I recently had to hire a personal security specialist, myself."

Luke was silent. A flight attendant began announcing

safety procedures on the intercom as the plane taxied down the runway.

"You see, I'm an author. Maybe you've heard of my book, *The Sex Factor?* I've made quite a few men angry with it, and I had to hire someone to help protect me from them.

"But I made a huge mistake. I didn't learn everything he tried to teach me, and I let him go when I shouldn't have."

"Sounds like you've got problems." He pulled an inflight magazine out of the seat pocket in front of him and began flipping through the pages.

"I was misguided. I wrote a book that gave some bad advice, and he tried to make me understand that I'd missed the mark. He was right."

Luke looked at her then, his dark eyes inscrutable. "Could you say that first part again?"

"I was misguided?"

"Yeah, that." He revealed a half smile then, and Jane's pent-up emotions released by a tiny degree.

"I just don't know how to tell him what I really feel."

"Why don't you try out what you have in mind on me. I'll tell you if it sounds good."

The roar of the plane engines grew louder, and the aircraft slowed to a stop, then accelerated. As they lifted off the runway, Jane looked out and saw Dallas just beginning to light up. To the west, the sun had splashed streaks of orange and pink across the sky as it set.

She turned back to Luke and took his large hand in hers. Where his was cool, hers were hot and shaking. "I'm sorry, Luke. I never should have let you walk out of my life, even for an hour. When I was listening to those wedding vows today, I realized they were words I'd heard countless times before, without really thinking about their meaning...."

Jane took a deep breath. Could she really say the next part? Could she really bare it all? Yes, if she was going to be known as a relationship guru, she had to take a chance on true love. She had to give it all if she wanted to have a great romance, a love that would endure.

Luke watched her silently.

"Thanks to you, I finally understand what it means to have a love so strong that two lives can be bound into one because of it. I understand that sex and love and intimacy are all intricately intertwined, and that removing one from the mix damages the other parts. You showed me that."

"What are you saying?"

"That I've fallen in love with you, and I want us to be more than just lovers or friends or business associates."

Luke closed his eyes, and for the first time, Jane saw his vulnerability. She'd always thought of him as invincible, which she realized now she'd used as an excuse for treating him badly. An indescribable mix of emotions played across his face.

"Jane, I don't want you as any of those things, either."

His words, spoken slowly and with deliberation, hit her low in the belly. Maybe she'd wreaked irreparable damage, and maybe her chance with Luke was lost.

He opened his eyes and penetrated her with his dark, sensual gaze. "I love you. I want you in my life permanently."

Jane blinked again and again, stunned to silence. Before she realized she was crying, she felt Luke's fingertips on her cheek, wiping away the dampness.

"Do you mean—"

"Shh," he said, putting a fingertip to her lips. "Let's do this right."

Ignoring the seat-belt signs lit up in the cabin, Luke unbuckled his, and Jane followed suit as he tugged on her hand. When he had her standing in the aisle, he knelt on one knee, and people all over the cabin began straining their necks to see what was going on with the man and the crazy bridesmaid chick.

Holding both her hands in his, he looked into her eyes, oblivious to the stares. "You are the most amazing, exciting woman I've ever known. Will you marry me, Jane Langston?"

"Yes," Jane whispered, her voice suddenly failing her.

Applause burst out in the cabin, and nearby passengers congratulated them as Luke stood up and took her into his arms. When he kissed her, Jane knew she'd finally figured out the difference between the wants of a girl and the needs of a real, grown-up woman.

Epilogue

"When in doubt, follow your heart. The answers are more often found there than in the pages of a self-help book.

—Jane Langston,
from her newly titled work-in-progress,
Sex and Sensuality

St. Thomas, Virgin Islands, one week later

"No, Mom, I do not want little girls dressed up as fairies sprinkling fairy dust down the aisle before I walk out." Jane looked over at Luke, reclined on the bed wearing nothing but a lazy smile, and rolled her eyes.

He patted the empty space on the bed beside him and gave her a meaningful look.

But Jane knew she wasn't going to get off the phone that easily with her mother, not after just having told her about their marriage. They'd decided to elope privately on the beach in Puerto Rico, but they both were in agreement on doing a "real" wedding for the family later, once they'd enjoyed a lengthy honeymoon in the Virgin Islands.

"Honey, don't you worry, we'll get all the details settled when you get home. I just want you to know, we're proud of you, very, very proud."

Jane found herself gripping the phone a little too tightly, straining to be sure she'd heard her mother clearly.

"You're proud of me for eloping?"

"Of course not. Don't get me wrong, Luke seems like a fine man, but I mean I'm proud of *you*. Not just all you've accomplished with your book, and not just the way you defended yourself against that awful man at the wedding, but you—the lovely woman you've grown into."

Jane leaned against the door frame, stunned to silence.

"Maybe I forget to say it, and I know I've been pre-occupied with Heather's wedding…"

"Thanks, Mom."

"Well, I'll let you two lovebirds get back to your honeymoon."

When Jane hung up the phone, she gave Luke a stunned look. "That was weird."

"You can tell me all about it later. Right now I have plans for us, and they don't involve talking about your mother."

Jane untied her white silk robe and shrugged it off her shoulders, letting it fall in a puddle at her feet. "Those sound like my kind of plans."

"Come here, woman." He pulled her onto the bed on top of him, encircling her in his arms.

Ever since she'd told Luke about what happened at the wedding reception with Eli, he'd been even more protective of her than usual, always wanting her within the safe haven of his arms.

Jane ran her hands up his bare chest and neck, then buried them in the dark curtain of his hair. "So what are these plans, anyway?"

He nudged her legs open with his knees, and she felt his erection pressing against her, where she was already wet and ready for him. He slid inside, and Jane expelled what she had come to recognize as the sigh of a well-pleasured woman.

"I was just thinking about your next book," he said.

"Hmm?" Jane became less and less interested in conversation with each delicious thrust.

"Now that you have a more balanced view of men thanks to me, maybe you could write a little letter of appreciation to me at the beginning."

She smiled. "Oh, believe me, I've got a letter of appreciation for you."

"Good, then you're already thinking about what you should say."

"Mmm-hmm. 'To my dear husband Luke, thank you for always remembering when to shut up and make love to me.'"

"That's not quite the message I had in mind," he said, then paused to give her a long, slow kiss. "But I get the point. We'll continue this conversation later."

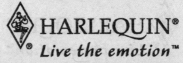

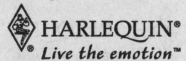

HARLEQUIN®
Temptation

THE WRONG BED

What happens when a girl finds herself in the
wrong bed...with the *right* guy?

Find out in:

#866 NAUGHTY BY NATURE by Jule McBride
February 2002

#870 SOMETHING WILD by Toni Blake
March 2002

#874 CARRIED AWAY by Donna Kauffman
April 2002

#878 HER PERFECT STRANGER by Jill Shalvis
May 2002

#882 BARELY MISTAKEN by Jennifer LaBrecque
June 2002

#886 TWO TO TANGLE by Leslie Kelly
July 2002

Midnight mix-ups have never been so much fun!

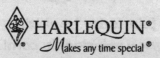

HARLEQUIN®
Makes any time special ®

eHARLEQUIN.com

The eHarlequin.com online community is *the* place to share opinions, thoughts and feelings!

- Joining the community is easy, fun and **FREE!**

- Connect with **other romance fans** on our message boards.

- Meet your **favorite authors** without leaving home!

- **Share opinions** on books, movies, celebrities...and *more!*

Here's what our members say:

"I love the friendly and helpful atmosphere filled with support and humor."
—Texanna (eHarlequin.com member)

"Is this the place for me, or what? There is nothing I love more than 'talking' books, especially with fellow readers who are reading the same ones I am."
—Jo Ann (eHarlequin.com member)

Join today by visiting
www.eHarlequin.com!

If you enjoyed what you just read,
then we've got an offer you can't resist!

Take 2 bestselling love stories FREE!

Plus get a FREE surprise gift!

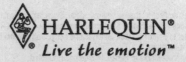